# OSMOSIS JONES™

## A BLOOD-AND-GUTS ADVENTURE.... SET INSIDE THE HUMAN BODY!

### Adapted by James Patrick

**SCHOLASTIC INC.**
New York   Toronto   London   Auckland   Sydney
Mexico City   New Delhi   Hong Kong

No part of this publication may be reproduced in whole or in part, or stored in a retrieval system, or transmitted in any form or by any means, electronic, mechanical, photocopying, recording, or otherwise, without written permission of the publisher. For information regarding permission, write to Scholastic Inc., Attention: Permissions Department, 555 Broadway, New York, NY 10012.

ISBN 0-439-26090-6

Copyright © 2001 by Warner Bros.

OSMOSIS JONES, characters, names, and all related indicia are trademarks of Warner Bros. © 2001.

SCHOLASTIC and associated logos are trademarks and/or registered trademarks of Scholastic Inc.

12 11 10 9 8 7 6 5 4 3 2 1          1 2 3 4 5 6/0

Printed in the U.S.A.
First Scholastic printing, July 2001
Book Design: Michael Malone

# TABLE OF CONTENTS

# PROLOGUE

Burping and grunting like an ape, Frank Ditello pushes around a mop and bucket at the Providence Zoo. He's a janitor. That means Frank cleans up animal slop for a living. It isn't a pretty job. But then again, Frank isn't a pretty guy.

Today he's dressed in flip-flops and a tank top. Looking at Frank in that shirt, three words spring to mind: Too...much...flesh. *Yuck*. No one wants to see that disaster area he calls a body. The fact is, the only push-ups Frank has ever experienced are the ones he bought from the ice cream man.

But that's the outside of Frank. This story is about the inside of Frank. *Way, waaay, waaaaay* inside. But first, let's meet Frank's daughter, Shane. At age ten, she is everything that Frank is not. Shane is young, bright, and energetic—while her father is overweight, dim as dusk, and out of shape. Still, Shane adores her father. And she knows he loves her.

Shane likes visiting Frank at the zoo. What daughter wouldn't? She enjoys it all, even the peculiar smells, the endless scratching and snorting, the repulsive facial expressions, and the big, slobbering lips. (And after hanging out with her dad, Shane likes looking at the animals, too!)

Frank joins Shane on a bench near the monkey cage. He sits with a weary *ooomph*. Sweaty and exhausted, Frank complains, "Y'know, Shane, I don't belong here. I mean, look at these animals." He eyes a monkey munching on a banana. The monkey scratches itself and meets Frank's gaze.

"Disgusting," observes Frank.

"You know, Pop," Shane says, "primates are our first cousins, genetically speaking. In fact, some scientists say that monkey diets are much more evolved than our own."

"Oh no, here we go again with the diet," Frank sighs, rolling his eyes. He takes a hard-boiled egg out of his lunch bag and squeezes a thick ribbon of mayonnaise onto it.

"It wouldn't hurt you to eat more fruits and vegetables like monkeys do," Shane suggests.

Frank's heard it all before. Shane is always on him about his eating habits. He replies, "Honey, the only reason monkeys eat fruits and vegetables is because they don't know how to butcher a cow. Trust me, you give one of those hairy little midgets a meat cleaver and a barbecue, he's gonna make cheeseburgers."

Frank smiles. That simple word, *cheeseburgers,* brings back a happy memory. He nudges Shane. "Hey, remember the time your mother, God bless her soul, ate those three double-deckers at the ball game?"

The death of her mother still upsets Shane. "Yeah, I remember," Shane answers, staring sadly at the ground.

Frank puts his arm around Shane. "Okay, baby, I'm sorry," Frank apologizes. "I'll try to take better care of myself."

Shane asks hopefully, "Does that mean you'll go on the school hike with me?"

Frank hands her a package of Twinkies, hoping to change the subject. "We'll talk about that...after lunch."

Suddenly a hairy arm reaches through the bars of the monkey cage. It snatches the egg out of Frank's hand! The monkey licks the egg with a long, slow, disgusting slurp.

Frank is furious. No monkey is going to make a monkey out of him. He wants that egg back—now! In an instant, Frank and the monkey wrestle, reaching through the bars of the cage. The egg drops to the floor and rolls, *phlppt, phlppt, phlppt,* across monkey filth, zoo grime, and dead bugs. Frank lunges and grabs the egg.

He triumphantly pops the egg into the air and catches it with his mouth. *Snaaarff.*

"Ugghhh! Dad, that's filthy!" Shane protests.

Frank chews happily. He explains, "Honey, ten-second rule. It hits the ground, you pick it up in ten seconds, you can eat it."

Ugh.

And now, brave reader, buckle your seat belt. Place your seat in the upright position. And keep your barf bag on your lap, for here our story takes a wild turn, through the lips, past the teeth, and over the gums.

Look out, Frank.

*Heeereee we come!*

# CHAPTER 1
## MULTIPLE BOGIES

Inside Frank's mouth, the great, lolling tongue sits like an island amid a sea of saliva. Bits of egg wash up and down the gumline. Beams of sunlight slice through the gaps between Frank's front teeth.

Suddenly a microscopic helicopter whirls into view. It's the Spit Patrol, the body's first line of defense against germs. Two uniformed officers search the sludge with a spotlight.

The older pilot speaks first. "When I was a rookie cell," he recalls, "this place was clean. Look at it now. What a disgrace."

The younger officer, Osmosis Jones, barely listens. Instead, he flips through the pages of a magazine.

"See anything, kid?" the pilot asks.

Osmosis doesn't bother to look up.

"JONES!" the pilot roars. "I wish you'd take this job a bit more seriously."

Osmosis Jones throws down his magazine. He snaps back, "Yo! You see this badge?! You see this gun?!!"

The older pilot sighs. "Here we go again."

Ozzy continues, "Well, you're dealing with a white blood cell here. I should be out in the veins fighting disease—not here in the mouth on spit duty!"

"You're lucky you ain't in a scab," the pilot replies. He spots movement below. "Uh-oh," he says, pointing. "Looks like something came in on that egg."

Osmosis Jones feels a tremor of excitement. He's always up for a little action. Getting bad guys (correction: bad *germs*), that's what Osmosis Jones is all about. "Mmmm, baby," he purrs. "It's Ozzy time."

They watch as a bizarre bunch of little creatures—germs, actually—jump off the egg. Tiny, miserable hosts of disease and decay, the germs attempt to invade Frank's body.

"Halt!" the pilot orders through a megaphone. "You have entered the city of Frank. Put your hands up and surrender for digestion."

The chase is on as the germs scatter. The chopper darts and whirls sharply in hot pursuit. The pilot calls after the germs: "This is a private organism. There's no use running."

Ozzy snatches away the megaphone. He bellows, "You don't want to get me mad, 'cause I *will* turn into a germicidal maniac!"

The germs, frantic to escape, steal a Spit Patrol dune buggy. They grab guns and start firing upon the chopper.

"Uh-oh," Ozzy says, "you gone done it now."

It's almost a sad sight. One by one Ozzy picks off the germs like fish in a barrel, covering them in big sticky mucus sacks with each shot.

Suddenly a fierce tug jerks the chopper sideways. "Oh my God!" the pilot exclaims. "He's about to yawn!"

A cyclone of air rushes through Frank's mouth. The germs catch the current—and sail down into the throat like kites in the wind.

With the pilot struggling to keep the chopper from crashing, Ozzy calls into the radio, "Osmosis Jones to Dispatch! We got multiple bogies, I repeat, multiple bogies coming down the windpipe. Request permission to pursue!"

# CHAPTER 2
# OFFICER DOWN!

In the Immunity Division Headquarters, the veteran police chief peers over the radar operator's shoulder. The chief rubs the back of his neck. He's seen it all before, thousands of times, but it still puts his stomach in knots.

"Chief, listen to this," the radio dispatcher says.

Frowning, the chief listens to Ozzy's request. He barks in reply, "Jones, if you want to keep your job, stay where you are and wait for backup."

"But I can get 'em," Ozzy pleads.

"I said stay put," the chief commands.

Now here's the thing with Osmosis Jones: He's got a little problem with orders. He doesn't like 'em. And he doesn't always follow 'em, either. That's what got him demoted to spit duty in the first place.

Ozzy stands by the chopper doorway, peering below.

"You heard the chief," the pilot warns Ozzy. "They're out of our jurisdiction now. Jones! What are you doing?!"

Ozzy whispers to himself, "Chief, you're gonna thank me for this later."

And then he jumps.

Ozzy falls through the air, gliding like a hawk. Incredibly, he grabs the back of the dune buggy with his outstretched fingertips. The dune buggy races ahead, dragging Ozzy behind. He can't hold on for long, and he tumbles backward, head over heels.

Rough stuff, sure. But that isn't going to stop Osmosis Jones. He grimaces, shakes his head, and takes off in a sprint. The buggy makes a sharp left turn. Ozzy slows to a stop, huffing and puffing. He notices a narrow crevice between two brick-like cells.

A short cut!

"You want Osmosis," he mutters, "you got Osmosis."

Thinking fast and acting faster, Ozzy sprints toward the crevice. He dives into the small opening and squeezes his body through. Liquid Osmosis!

He can slip through semisolid surfaces like a ribbon of toothpaste. In seconds, Liquid Ozzy changes shape again. He's back to his ordinary form, ready to take on the germs.

Ozzy looks up, only to see the dune buggy race past. The driver gleefully laughs, "Bye-bye, cop. Ha ha!"

The germs are getting away. Ozzy has to do something drastic. He looks up and down. Massive power lines crisscross the area: the nerve complex. It's going to be dangerous, but a cell's gotta do what a cell's gotta do. Ozzy pulls out his gun. He aims at the dune buggy. And fires. *Ka-boom!*

He misses by a mile.

The shell explodes off the base of the nerve complex, causing Frank's body to contract in a painful cramp.

("YEOOOOW!!!" screams Frank from the outside world.)

Ozzy ducks and covers his head. It's like getting caught in the middle of an earthquake. Two buildings tumble, pinning Ozzy under the rubble.

"Ahhh!" screams Osmosis Jones. "Officer down!"

## CHAPTER 3

# THRAX

Meanwhile, back in the mouth, it's time for the morning cleanup. A garbage barge drifts through. Two sewage worker cells fish out parasites with suction packs. It's a dull, dirty job—but it sure beats living on a dead maggot.

The first sewage worker, Artie, climbs off the barge and wades through the filthy water. He aims the hose from his pack, vacuuming little bacteria off the gumline.

"Man, would you look at all that gunk?" Artie complains.

His partner in grime merely chuckles.

"Seriously," Artie says. "What does this guy do? Roll his food around on the ground before he eats it? We need to send a letter to the mayor about washing our hands before we eat."

A little rat-sized bacterium scampers to safety, eluding the sewage workers. Artie continues working, poking through the filthy water. He turns his back on a large chunk of egg.

It's the last mistake Artie ever makes, because behind him a glow burns hot from the last remaining bit of egg. In a moment, after a stifled cry, Artie is dead.

"Artie?" his alarmed co-worker calls. "What's going on over there?" He finds Artie—gruesomely sucked into his own containment pack. Thrax emerges from behind the egg. He's an evil, poisonous organism, built to kill. He wears a bracelet of multicolored beads on one wrist. Instead of a hand, Thrax has a claw with fingers like samurai swords.

Thrax whispers menacingly, "Careful. I'm contagious." And with a ferocious slash, he kills Artie's partner. Then Thrax plummets into the dark cave of the throat, leaving shock waves of infection in his wake.

One unseen witness remains. The tiny, terrified rat cell cowers in fear. And why not? He's just seen the grim face of death.

...............................................................................................

**Laying on a sofa, Frank coughs.**

**"Are you okay?" asks Shane.**

**Frank takes a bite from a drumstick. It hurts when he swallows.**

**"This chicken ain't going down so easy," he complains to Shane.**

**And so it begins. With a little cough. Some mild irritation in the throat.**

**No biggie, really.**

**Just a common cold. . . .**

# CHAPTER 4
## THE BRAIN

Every city needs a mayor, even when the "city" is, in fact, a walking, talking, belching slob named Frank Ditello.

Because to every creature who survives and thrives inside Frank—every cell and enzyme, every germ and parasite—Frank is The World. They call it the city of Frank. And who calls the shots? That would be Mayor Phlegmming, a fat-cat brain cell with one thing on his mind: reelection. More than anything, he wants to stay in power for a good long while.

No matter what it takes.

The mayor steps out of a long, slick limousine outside his office in City Hall. A crowd of reporters surrounds him, shouting out questions.

"Mister Mayor!" yells one reporter. "Do you have a plan to deal with the fat cell housing shortage?"

The politician offers a practiced smile to the cameras. He slickly promises, "We're beginning construction on a third chin."

Another reporter pushes forward. He says, "Your opponent, Tom Colonic, has accused you of using vitamin money to buy Skittles. How do you respond?"

The mayor isn't happy to hear the name of his political rival. "People, people, you worry too much," he says. "The body is in perfect shape. No more questions. Thank you."

Grumbling, the mayor slams the door behind him. The mayor's bright assistant, Leah Estrogen, looks up from her computer. Leah smiles. "Mr. Mayor, I've got a copy of Tom Colonic's new campaign ad."

Leah slips the videotape into the television. The mayor watches, teeth gnashing, as Colonic's advertisement appears on the screen. He sees Tom Colonic walk through an old, rotting slum. Colonic speaks to the camera.

"The bowels," Colonic begins, shaking his head sadly. "They didn't always smell this way. No, there was a time when eating right and exercise kept this whole area a vital center of activity. But during Mayor Phlegmming's term we've seen rot and stagnation paralyze this neighborhood.

"Well, I think it's time we get things moving again. I'm Tom Colonic. As mayor I would set long-term goals that include ordering salads and eating bran. Mayor Phlegmming may think that things are fine just the way they are. But I think if we pull together and put in a little hard work, a new Frank could be right around the corner."

Red with anger, the mayor rages, "Can you believe those lies?!"

"Sir, he's got a point," Leah contends. "When I first came to work for you, you promised you would concentrate more on health issues."

"Leah, I *want* Frank to be healthy," the mayor replies. "But think of the sacrifices. The hard work. The lack of potato chips. That's not what the voters want."

Leah asks pointedly, "Then why are you behind in the polls?"

"Don't you worry about the polls," he answers darkly. "I have a plan that's going to flush Colonic down the toilet."

A screeching alarm interrupts their conversation. They turn to view a large map of Frank's body. The throat flashes red.

"Sir, turn on the optical feed," Leah advises.

The mayor switches on a monitor beside his desk. It offers an amazing sight of the outside world, as seen through Frank's eyes.

Frank coughs.

The mayor watches intently, looking through Frank's eyes into Shane's worried face....

---

**"Definitely red," Shane says. She moves toward the phone.**

**Frank asks, "What are you doing?"**

**"Making an appointment," Shane answers. "I'm taking you to the doctor."**

**Frank, enjoying Shane's tender care, rubs his sore throat. He agrees, "Maybe that's a good idea. I'm starting to feel sick."**

---

"Sick!" exclaims the mayor, turning to Leah in a panic. "We're NOT getting sick. We have far too much planned." He knows how to handle this kind of situation. It's time to send a message to Frank. The mayor's eyes slide to a red phone on his desk, protected under a glass cover. Ignoring Leah's warnings, the mayor flicks up the glass cover, turns a key, and lifts the receiver. "Voice manual control on," he says.

"That's only for emergencies!" Leah protests.

The mayor snarls, "Leah, this is an emergency!" At the turn of the key, something strange happens inside Frank. He goes into a sort of trance. Somehow, the mayor has taken control of Frank's brain.

The mayor speaks into the phone: "On second thought…"

········································································································

"…on second thought," repeats Frank, echoing the mayor, "I think I'll just take one of those cold pills."

Frank walks into the bathroom. He opens the medicine cabinet and reaches for a box labeled DRIXENOL. After all, who needs to go to a doctor for a common cold? An everyday cold pill should do the trick. Frank pops a yellow-and-red capsule into his mouth.

# CHAPTER 5
# THE GERMINATOR

The Third Police Precinct swarms with uniformed officers of the Immunity Force. Amid the jostle and push of rough cops and tough criminals, Osmosis Jones tries to sneak in unnoticed.

But one officer spots Ozzy. He shouts out teasingly, "Hey, hey, it's the Germinator!"

All the cops laugh at Osmosis Jones. They high-five each other and roar like bullies.

"Okay, guys. You got me there," Ozzy says, trying to cut short the laughter. "Let's save a little for the criminals, aw-right."

"Jones, when's the last time you caught anything?" a cop asks mockingly.

"Hey, hey," Ozzy protests. "You should have seen this thing. This ain't any ordinary household germ. This thing is bigger than all of us. This ain't even from Frank's body. This is like an Al Roker germ, a Heavy-D germ."

Two cops step forward. They have a germ from the chase in handcuffs. He's small and puny. "Looking for this?" one cop, Kurtz, asks.

Everyone in the room howls with laughter.

Everyone except Osmosis Jones. But what do you expect? The joke's on him.

Kurtz sneers, "We're getting pretty sick of cleaning up your messes, Jones." He pushes the tiny germ toward Ozzy, who cuffs the germ to a chair.

A familiar voice booms from down the hall. "JONES! IN MY OFFICE!" shouts the chief.

Osmosis is glad to escape the ridicule of his fellow cops. He makes himself at home in the chief's office. Ozzy eases himself into a chair and puts his feet on the desk.

"Chiefy-weefy," Ozzy says with exaggerated cool. "Whassup?"

The chief growls and throws down a newspaper. The headline blares, CRAMPS DEVASTATE DOWNTOWN. "Don't Chiefy-weefy me!" he bellows. "Have you seen the headlines?! The papers are calling it the most powerful cramp since Shane made us try the Tai-Bo workout video!"

Ozzy tries to object. "Hold on a second…"

"I told you to stay put!" the chief interrupts. "I told you to wait for backup. But once again, you had to do it your own way."

"Man, I was right there," Ozzy explains. "I could have done it."

"When are you gonna learn you can't do it, Jones," the chief replies.

And with that one simple statement—"you can't do it"—all the casual cool masquerading as self-con-

fidence seems to seep out of Osmosis, the way air
leaks from a balloon. He's failed. Again. And there's
nothing he can say to make it otherwise.

The phone rings. The chief turns from Ozzy and
answers it. "Chief here," he says. "Uh-huh. Oh, yes
sir, Mr. Mayor. What?! You're kidding. But...
well...yes, sir! You have my vote, sir."

Ozzy watches with interest as the chief slams
down the phone. The chief mutters, "Stupid political
decisions." He turns to Ozzy. "Now, where was I?"

Osmosis smoothly replies, "Ah, you were just
starting to say how you were giving me a promotion
to head of brain security, I believe. Yep."

"You know what, Jones? You're right. Maybe it is time I give you a case. We have a situation in the throat and I'm putting you on it."

Ozzy's thrilled. "Thank you, Chief! You won't regret this. You're a good man. You're a fine man."

The chief pays no attention to Ozzy's gibberish. "Now our pill is getting swallowed as we speak," the chief tells Ozzy. "So I suggest you get your nucleus down to the stomach, pronto."

"Pill? What pill!?" Ozzy asks.

"You didn't think I was gonna trust you to take care of a sore throat by yourself, did you?" the chief answers.

Ozzy's not happy. He doesn't want a partner, no way, no how. "Chief," he argues, "you can't let some pill screw this up. Let me do it on my own."

" 'Let me do it on my own,' " echoes the chief in a high-pitched voice. "Yeah, right. Seventy-eight trillion cells in the body, all working together, and you're the only one who thinks he can do it alone." He stares hard into Ozzy's eyes. "You ever think that might be your problem, Jones?"

## CHAPTER 6
# DRIX ARRIVES

*Boom, boom, da-BOOM.* Rap music blasts from the speakers inside Ozzy's patrol car. He pulls the car to a stop, cuts the radio, and heads inside the bus terminal.

We're inside the stomach, a hustling, bustling area for arrivals and departures. Hundreds of travelers crowd the area. Gobs of food are being directed into a dark tunnel marked SOLIDS.

An announcement comes over the loudspeaker: "Peanuts now boarding for the intestinal tract and the liver with direct service to the colon. Now boarding. Attention, all fat cells. Proceed directly to the love handles. Thank you."

Ozzy spies Leah waiting by the arrival gate. She speaks into a phone while impatiently checking the big overhead board. She reads from three columns: BREAKFAST, LUNCH, and DINNER. The new cold pill should be arriving soon, right after Frank washes down a few Ding-Dongs with a glass of milk.

"Well, well, well! What do we have here?" Ozzy flirts. "Somebody's been working out. Leah, you're looking fine, girl! Mighty fine."

Leah grimaces. "Ahh, Jones. Did they *have* to assign you to this?" The frost in her voice says it all: Shoo fly, don't bother me.

Ozzy shrugs, eyes twinkling. "Wasn't my idea. But now I'm starting to like it." Leah's cold reaction doesn't stop Ozzy from laying on the full-court press. "Baby, when are you and me gonna hook up? I know this little spot right behind the eye that has a perfect view—perfect for a little rendezvous between me and you. You know what I'm saying? Do you *know* what I'm saying?"

Leah is *sooo* not impressed. "Jones, what in the world makes you think I would ever go out with you?"

"Whatcha talking about?" Ozzy says, enjoying the back and forth. "I'm a legend, girl."

A new announcement interrupts them. "Now arriving with some milk, drixobenzomethapherdramine, with a pleasant fruity flavor."

A sudden flurry of activity comes from the stomach gates. A heaping gob of brown mush rumbles to a stop. As workers spray the mush with stomach acid, a gleaming yellow-and-red pill emerges. The capsule's shell starts to fizz and gurgle. The hull drips away with a crackle while thousands of tiny pellets spill out.

Drix stands revealed. He's quite a sight. Large and in charge, a laboratory-produced, cherry-flavored Robocop, his shoulders are huge. He's made of hard gelatin. And, get this, Drix has a cannon for a right arm.

But Osmosis Jones isn't impressed. He's seen this type before. Sure, Drix is big and strong. But there's something stiff about Drix. Unnatural. Just another Boy Scout who always goes by the book. He'll never follow a hunch. Never break a rule.

What a snooze.

Drix steps forward. In a stiff, mechanical voice, he introduces himself. "Drixenol, the brand that eases your coughs and sneezes. Warning: Do not exceed recommended dosage. If symptoms persist consult a physician. May cause drowsiness. Do not attempt to operate heavy machinery. Pregnant women should not handle broken tablets."

Ozzy stifles a yawn. "Wow, I'm feeling better already."

"You can call me Drix," suggests the cold capsule.

Leah extends her hand, beaming. "Welcome to the city of Frank."

"I'd like to examine your irritated areas," Drix informs her.

"Never on the first date, Drips!" jokes Ozzy.

The feeling between Drix and Ozzy is mutual: Instant dislike. Leah pulls Ozzy aside. "Jones, this ain't working out. I'm going to call the chief and ask him to assign someone else."

"Wait, hold up now," Ozzy says. He looks plead-

ingly into Leah's eyes. "I need this job, Leah. C'mon, just gimme a shot."

Leah hesitates. Everything in her says that this is a bad match. But there's something in Ozzy's pleading eyes. He really wants to do this right. "All right," she relents. "But no screwups. You dig?"

Ozzy beams. "Baby, I promise everything is gonna be fine." He pauses, then adds, "Not as fine as you, but fine."

Ozzy leads Drix to the patrol car. Suddenly Ozzy smells something, and it's not home cooking. He fans the air, pinches his nose, and points to Drix's fizzing trail of gastric antacids. "Man, whatchu been eating?" he asks.

"That's my effervescent propulsion," Drix proudly explains.

"Aw-right. It's cool, but we're driving with the windows open," Ozzy remarks. "I don't want none of those fruity bubbles stinking up my ride!"

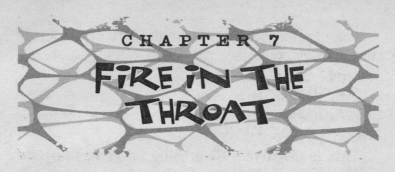

# CHAPTER 7
# FIRE IN THE THROAT

It's hard to imagine two more different, er, *people* than Osmosis Jones and Drix.

Ozzy is cool and loose, a white blood cell who knows every inch of Frank's body—the scabs, the cysts, the long, twisted length of Frank's hardened arteries.

Drix? Well, let's just say he's not exactly gettin' jiggy with it. While Ozzy cruises, bobbing his head to the beat that blasts from the car radio, Drix stares straight ahead, unblinking. He looks about as comfortable as an elephant on a tricycle.

Ozzy tries to start up some conversation. "So, where you from, tough stuff?"

"I was developed at the University of Chicago, where I graduated Phi Beta Capsule," Drix answers flatly, still staring straight ahead.

"Great. Got me a college boy," Ozzy groans.

Drix recites his credentials. "I received my FDA certification in cold and flu studies, as well as a master's in multisymptom relief. Where did you study?"

"Study?" Ozzy echoes. "When you grow up on the wrong side of the digestive track, you don't got no money for no fancy schools. I'm not kidding, man," Ozzy continues. "My high school was crack central."

"Oh, drugs?" Drix asks.

"No. It was *in* the crack," Ozzy says. "Right in the stanky, puckered center."

Drix is disgusted. Clearly, he never met anyone quite like Ozzy back in the lab. He doesn't know how to react to Ozzy's wiseguy, street-smart motor mouth.

But Ozzy keeps jabbering away, inwardly delighted at shocking mild-mannered Drix. Ozzy says, "We were so poor we lived on peanut butter and dingleberry sandwiches. You ever try and blow dry your hair with a fart, man?"

"Okay, I get it," Drix says, cutting Ozzy short. "You were poor."

"You bet I was," Ozzy enthuses. "You ever try to make a snowman out of toilet-paper cling-ons? Now *that's* poor!"

"Okay, please," Drix pleads. "You're going to make me vomit."

"Vomit?! We couldn't afford no vomit. That's for rich folks!"

Ozzy screeches the squad car to an abrupt halt. There's a raging fire inside the throat. Firemen hose down the flames.

"Okay, y'all are new, so follow my lead," Ozzy advises, acting the big shot. He unlatches his seat

belt and turns…but the passenger seat is empty.
Drix has already left the car!

Drix strides purposefully toward a fireman. He
rips right through the yellow CRIME SCENE tape.
Ozzy calls after him, annoyed, "Yo, yo, wait up!
Didn't they teach you no manners in that Ivy League
petri dish?!"

Drix gets right to work. He opens his medicine
chest and tears off the tamper-proof plastic. Inside,
there's a large supply of drug cartridges. Drix
selects one and loads it into his cannon-arm. He performs a system check on his firing nuzzle. Then he
begins to spray down the hot walls with a soothing
jet of blue crystal frost.

Meanwhile, a fireman explains to Ozzy that it's

just a routine sore throat. No big deal. He adds, "Looks like a saliva boat went haywire and crashed."

"Saliva boat?" Ozzy repeats. "That's unusual."

Ozzy takes a look around. The walls of the throat are red hot. Searching deeper into the throat's cavern, Ozzy discovers one of the sewage worker's vacuum packs. "Whoa," he gasps. "What the dilly?"

Osmosis stands amid the wreckage from the trash barge, which is splintered and burnt. A nasty scratch on the wall gets his attention. He knows it's an important clue. What kind of germ could leave such a deep gash? Not any cold that Ozzy's ever seen.

Ozzy pulls out his gun when he hears a whimpering sound nearby. *Whap!* Out of nowhere, the little cell leaps on Ozzy's face. After a brief struggle, Ozzy frees himself from the panicked germ.

Stuttering uncontrollably, the frightened eyewitness tries to speak. "*La M-m-m-muerte*, man. *Está aquí. Por favor*, please, man, don't shoot!"

"Slow down," Ozzy says. "Talk English, man."

"*La Muerte Roja* is coming, man," cries the terrified cell. "I saw him!"

But before the cell can utter another word, Drix's jet spray blasts the whole area. It showers Osmosis and the cell.

Ozzy shakes off the frozen spray. He glances down at the cell, who's now frozen solid. Osmosis storms over to Drix. "Excuse me, what do you think you're doing?!"

**Osmosis Jones** and Drix are protection from outside infection!

An inside view of the city of Frank!

He's a **white blood cell** born and raised on the tough streets, er, *veins*, inside the body of Frank Detorri, a sloppy guy who **doesn't** take good care of himself. **From** sweating armpit to ugly scab, from bubbling burp to hardened artery, Ozzy has a tough job keeping Frank **healthy!**

**Now arriving** with some milk, Drixobenzomethapherdramine — you can call him "Drix" — a cherry-flavored cold capsule on a strict time-release program.

ARRIVALS

BREAKFAST  LUNCH

Coffee
Corn Flakes
Toast
Waffles

Pancakes
Chili-Fries
Banana Shake
Kebob

Peanut
Sandwich

**Meet the cast** (from left to right): The power-hungry Mayor; Thrax, a deadly virus; Chief, head of Frank's Immunity Force; Drix; Osmosis Jones; and Leah, a white blood cell who works for the Mayor.

Thrax is a **killer virus**, out to **destroy** the city of Frank. Can Ozzy **stop him** before it's too late? **Yo**, like you've got to ask?!

Drix answers matter-of-factly, "I am soothing the irritation."

Ozzy can't believe this guy. "You just soothed my witness into a germsicle!"

Drix notices the frozen cell. He taps on its head. Yup, he's iced. "Oh, gosh. Hmmm, well, don't worry," Drix concludes. "He'll be back to normal in a few days."

"A few days is too late!" Ozzy erupts. "He might have some important information 'bout what went down here!"

Drix can't understand why Ozzy is so worked up. A frozen cell, big whoop. "Officer, nothing went down here. This is just a common sore throat," he tells Ozzy.

"No," Ozzy answers. "This is a crime scene."

# CHAPTER 8
# MEET THE NEW BOSS

A gang of dangerous characters, hardened criminals all, relax shirtless in the hot sauna of Frank's steaming armpit. In the center sits Scabies, the leader of the gang. Behind them, a tall, shadowy figure moves unseen.

They talk idly of petty crime until suddenly Thrax appears. He towers above them. "So this is where the scum of Frank comes to fester," Thrax observes.

A tough germ speaks up. "Hey, you lost, pal? This is a private sweat gland. Now beat it."

Thrax pays him no heed. "I'm looking for volunteers. Some nasty germs who want in on a big score."

Scabies can't believe the ectoplasm of this guy. Doesn't he know that Scabies runs things? "Yo, Red," Scabies threatens, "we run the rackets around here. Take your little hustle someplace else."

Thrax grins, all sinister menace. "Baby, this ain't about no hustle," he purrs. "This is about the baddest illness any of you all have ever seen."

Scabies laughs. "Look who thinks he's the Ebola virus."

"Ebola?" Thrax repeats, insulted, the anger burn-

ing hot inside him. He leans in close. "Let me tell you something about Ebola, baby. Ebola is a case of dandruff compared to me!"

"All right, pal. You're out of here," Scabies angrily fires back. He turns to Bruiser, his right-hand germ. "Take this punk up to the face and bury him in a blackhead."

Thrax calmly eyes Bruiser. "Sounds like a gas, baby." Thrax grins. "Bring it on."

The germs look at each other, confused. What's with this guy? Does he enjoy pain? Bruiser shrugs like a big lug and throws a punch. Thrax catches Bruiser's fist and squeezes. Bruiser falls to his knees, howling in pain.

A tremor of fear creeps into Scabies's voice. "What's he doing? What's he *doing*?!"

Without warning, Thrax slashes Scabies across the chest. He's a goner. The gathered germs watch in horror, and newfound respect, as Thrax wipes the slime from his claw. Finally, Bruiser speaks up. He says to Thrax, "So, uh, what kind of sickness do you have in mind...boss?"

Thrax answers, "Deadly."

---

Frank and his brother, Uncle Bob, who also works as a janitor at the zoo, are busy cleaning out the camel pen. Sweat pours from Frank's armpits.

Shane appears by the fence. "Hey, Dad. Hey, Uncle Bob," she greets them. "So. Dad, I stopped by the camping store and got us some trail mix for the father-daughter hike."

Frank closes his eyes. "Right, er, about this hike," he says. "Is your teacher gonna be there?"

"Yeah, my whole class is. Why?"

"I don't know," Frank answers. "Maybe I should take a rain check."

Shane immediately understands. Her father is still embarrassed about "the thing" that happened at the science fair. "Dad," she says. "Mrs. Boyd isn't still mad at you."

"Hey, can't we come up with something else to do?" Frank asks. "I get enough hiking during the week. I mean just yesterday, I hiked all the way from the convenience store to that warehouse where I get those cheap cigarettes. Then I hoofed it over to Taco Bell. I would have walked all the way home, but I ran into Bob at the Dairy Queen."

"But you said . . ."

"I said I'd *think* about it," Frank interrupts. He pauses, sensing Shane's disappointment. Frank smiles warmly at his daughter. "Look, we are going to have a great weekend. I mean, it's being together that's important, right?"

"I guess," Shane answers glumly, not quite convinced.

"Now, don't you worry," Frank reassures Shane. "I've got something really special up my sleeve."

# CHAPTER 9
# SEE WORLD

The biggest tourist attraction in the city of Frank is, without a doubt, an amusement park called See World. It's located in the area directly behind Frank's eyeballs. Like any amusement park, See World pulses with noise and activity. There are carnival games and rides, roller coasters and prizes, all jammed with happy visitors.

"What are we doing here?" Drix asks Ozzy. "Do I have to remind you that I'm on a strict twelve-hour time-release program? First the throat, then the nose, then the aches and pains."

"Yeah, I got it. Real important stuff," Ozzy replies, his voice dripping with sarcasm. "Now get your butt out of my car."

"I don't have a butt," Drix protests.

Drix reluctantly follows Osmosis through the park. He complains, "Officer, if I don't get to the sinuses my entire relief mission could be jeopardized."

Ozzy gestures upward, to the world beyond Frank's eyes. "Yo. It's time to take a look at the big picture. See?" Together, they stare through Frank's eyes into the world outside. At this very moment, Frank checks his reflection in a jeep's sideview mirror. "That's what this is all about," Ozzy explains to Drix. "The big F. He's the one we're here to protect and serve. I mean, just look at him," Ozzy says with admiration. "Doesn't he make you want to be a better cell?"

Drix pauses, briefly touched by Ozzy's heartfelt emotion. He looks up to see Frank accidentally dribble saliva from his mouth.

"Eeew!" Drix says, revolted. "I see why you feel such a strong connection."

"Hey, show the man some res demands. "He's the reason all of us are

"Just take me to the nose," Drix state ly storms away.

Ozzy shouts after him, "Dude, just wa I got police work to do." He orders donuts from a refreshment stand.

Then Ozzy flips open his cell phon answers: "Brain memory library. Can I h

"You got any information on somethin Mory Rojo?" Ozzy asks, struggling to the Spanish phrase.

Ozzy's still troubled by the rat cell's in the throat. He had told Ozzy, "*La Mu* coming." One thing was for sure, that r scared out of his cytoplasm. Ozzy knew important clue. Too bad Drix iced th before he could explain more. Maybe th could provide some answers.

"*La Muerte Roja*," the librarian corr using a perfect Spanish accent. "That's means 'the red death.'"

"The red death?" Ozzy repeats. "W some kind of taco sauce?"

eyes into the world outside. At this very moment, Frank checks his reflection in a jeep's sideview mirror. "That's what this is all about," Ozzy explains to Drix. "The big F. He's the one we're here to protect and serve. I mean, just look at him," Ozzy says with admiration. "Doesn't he make you want to be a better cell?"

Drix pauses, briefly touched by Ozzy's heartfelt emotion. He looks up to see Frank accidentally dribble saliva from his mouth.

"Eeew!" Drix says, revolted. "I see why you feel such a strong connection."

"Hey, show the man some respect," Ozzy demands. "He's the reason all of us are here."

"Just take me to the nose," Drix states. He angrily storms away.

Ozzy shouts after him, "Dude, just wait in the car. I got police work to do." He orders a couple of donuts from a refreshment stand.

Then Ozzy flips open his cell phone. A voice answers: "Brain memory library. Can I help you?"

"You got any information on something called El Mory Rojo?" Ozzy asks, struggling to pronounce the Spanish phrase.

Ozzy's still troubled by the rat cell's words back in the throat. He had told Ozzy, "*La Muerte Roja* is coming." One thing was for sure, that rat cell was scared out of his cytoplasm. Ozzy knew it was an important clue. Too bad Drix iced the witness before he could explain more. Maybe the librarian could provide some answers.

"*La Muerte Roja*," the librarian corrects Ozzy, using a perfect Spanish accent. "That's Spanish. It means 'the red death.'"

"The red death?" Ozzy repeats. "What's that, some kind of taco sauce?"

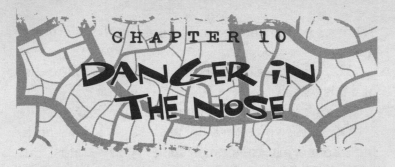

# CHAPTER 10
# DANGER IN THE NOSE

Inside the nasal cavity, all appears normal. When particles of dust float in through Frank's nose, guards shoot down each speck with expertly aimed mucus shots. At the push of a button, the guards eject the newly formed booger from the sinuses. It's vitally important to keep the sinuses clear of germs.

Unseen by the guards, Thrax enters the fortress of Nasal Command. He leads a small gang of dangerous-looking germs. Thrax commands his crew, "Now get to work!"

Down below, Ozzy and Drix pull up in the shadow of the grand, crusty booger dam. "We're here," Ozzy tells Drix. "You happy?"

Suddenly machine-gun fire fills the air.

"You hear that?" Drix exclaims, alarmed by the gunshots. "Quick, Jones, the dam is under attack!"

Ozzy steps lazily out of the car. "Chill, pill," he calmly says. "It's just snot guns booger-coating some dust."

Drix and Ozzy see a yellow, snowflake-shaped crystal float by. Drix reaches for it. But Ozzy quickly grabs it away. "Yo, yo, be careful!" Ozzy warns.

"That's a pollen pod, man. Frank is totally allergic to this stuff."

Ozzy squeezes the pollen crystal down to the size of a basketball.

"I didn't know we had allergies," Drix says.

"Of course you didn't. No useless pill knows nothing about what goes on in here," Ozzy states. But while he's distracted, the pollen crystal slips out of Ozzy's hands—"Whoops!"

Drix watches as the crystal sails into the nasal passage. A rumbling sound soon follows.

"GET DOWN!" warns Ozzy.

*Ah...ah...ah-choo!*

Frank sneezes.

It rattles the nasal cavity like a dynamite blast. Drix and Oz are blown across the dam. Once the dust settles, Drix stands and brushes himself off. "You nitwit!" he fumes. "You could have damaged the dam."

"Relax, this baby was built to last," Ozzy replies, tapping the dam wall. "Solid cartilage. I guarantee you, there ain't nothing wrong with this dam."

Drix has little faith in Ozzy's cool assurances. "Oh, you're an engineer now," Drix scoffs. "Excuse me, I need to test the mucus viscosity."

Drix begins to gather samples in test tubes. Meanwhile, in Nasal Command, Thrax's henchmen push buttons and throw switches. Warning sirens blare. And the dam begins to shake and crumble.

"The membrane is cracking!" Drix warns. He aims his cannon-arm and desperately sprays goo at the cracks. But it's not working. In spurts and gobs, green fluid begins to pour out. The dam could blow!

While Drix labors, something catches Ozzy's eye. It's Thrax's henchmen, fleeing Nasal Command. Ozzy draws his gun. "Stop! Immunity!"

The germs climb into a car and race away. Ozzy looks up to see a dark, ominous figure high in the command building, staring out the window. Not an ordinary germ, no. This is something far more dangerous to Frank. Ozzy knows at once that he's staring into the face of a killer virus.

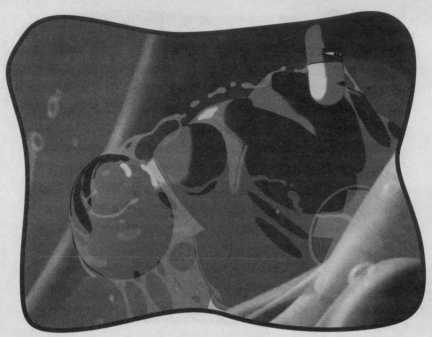

Thrax stares back at Ozzy, pure hatred in his eyes. Thrax grins, then laughs like a madman.

But before Ozzy can make a move, Thrax pulls a lever and the dam begins breaking up all around him. The mucous-filled dam won't hold, despite Drix's valiant efforts. It suddenly bursts.

Drix looks up, momentarily confused. A tidal wave of yellow-green gunk roars toward him. He turns and runs for his life. Raging waves of sickly green liquid roll behind him, gaining ground.

In moments, both Drix and Ozzy are washed into the vast sea of raging goo (which is, of course, another word for...*snot!*). A bright light looms before them as they are whooshed along with the thick green tide. They are headed toward the hole in Frank's nose…and the world outside the city of Frank.

There's nowhere to run.

The light grows brighter and brighter.

To the sound of helpless screams, our heroes are whisked out of the body into the perilous world beyond.

# CHAPTER 11
# SAVED BY A SNORT

Claw as they might, Drix and Ozzy remain trapped in the giant, slobbering goober as it leaks from Frank's nose. They can barely move in the thick sludge. The light from the outside world is unbearably bright.

"Well, this is a fine mess you've gotten us into," Drix snaps at Osmosis.

"Me?! What are you talking about?" Ozzy barks back. "You got a lot of nerve."

"Oh, don't act so innocent!" Drix angrily answers. "When I first entered this body, I knew things would be difficult. But I never imagined I'd have to put up with…"

"Uh, Drix," Ozzy says, interrupting. "Look behind you! We're about to be wiped under a table!"

Drix turns and sees a giant finger coming straight at him. He tries to crawl through the gunk. But it's too thick. There's no escape.

Frank is about to pick his nose!

Ozzy acrobatically latches onto a nose hair. With great effort, he pulls himself to safety. Then, risking his own life, he reaches out to save his partner.

"Gimme your hand!" he cries out.

Ozzy pulls Drix up. Together, they cling for life on a strand of nose hair. They try to climb higher and higher.

The finger comes closer.

And closer.

"We're going to die!" Drix screams.

Suddenly Frank gives a huge, rippling snort— and sucks the snot back into his nose.

*Waaaaaaaaarrrgghh!*

At the sound of Frank's seismic snarf, Drix and Ozzy are sucked back into the nostril. They cling together while a torrent of green goop whips over them like a flash flood.

Finally, silence. They've survived!

Drix looks at Ozzy. He notices for the first time that Ozzy's arms are wrapped around him.

"*Ptwew!*" Drix spits. "If it wasn't for you none of this would have ever happened. Now, if you'll excuse me, I have a nose to dry."

Separately, one after the other, the two partners begin the long climb back up the nostril.

No words of thanks are uttered.

# CHAPTER 12
# PARTNERS QUARREL

Mayor Phlegmming sits behind his desk at City Hall. A television camera focuses on his face. The mayor smiles; the camera light turns on.

"Good evening, citizens of Frank," the mayor states. "In the past few weeks of the campaign my opponent has thrown around a lot of fancy words to try to confuse the issues. Words like exercise, low fat, and diet. Words designed to scare us into changing what has worked for so many years. Well, I say, let's stay the course. Remember, a fat Frank is a happy Frank."

Leah Estrogen stands to the side, listening carefully. Something's wrong. "What?" Leah says to herself. "That's not what I wrote."

The mayor continues, "I propose something that every organism in this city will enjoy."

The lights dim. A movie screen unrolls behind him. A slide flickers on the screen. It's a shot of a vacation brochure—held in Frank's own hands!

The mayor proudly announces, "I give you ...Buffalo! Winter oasis, entertainment capital of upstate New York!"

While various slides of this dubious vacation paradise appear behind him, the mayor paints a sunny picture with words. A new image appears: A photo of the International Buffalo Wings Festival.

The mayor enthuses, "Ninety-nine different kinds of chicken wings. A hundred twenty-eight dipping sauces. Do the math. The possibilities are endless."

The mayor concludes, "Final plans have been made. And *nothing is* going to stand in our way!" Everyone in the room applauds while upbeat music pours from the stereo speakers.

Leah angrily confronts the mayor. "Sir, that wasn't the speech we agreed on. I thought you were going to talk about…"

The mayor couldn't be less interested. He smiles falsely for the cameras, then slides over to Ozzy and Drix. "Congratulations, boys. Excellent work in the nose today!" he says. "Come over here and let's get some pictures."

"Mister Mayor, excuse me, sir," Ozzy says. "But we have a problem."

"What are you talking about, Jones?" the mayor whispers, still grinning for the cameras.

"I think whatever it was in the sinuses is a lot more than a common cold," Ozzy tells him.

"Sir, don't listen to Jones," Drix advises the mayor.

Ozzy's shocked. So that's the thanks he gets for

saving Drix's life?! Ozzy grumbles at Drix, "You're the little cherry aspirin who iced a key witness to a viral attack!"

"That was an accident!" Drix retorts.

"Yeah, the kind of accident only a time-release dipstick like yourself would have," Ozzy says.

"That's it!" Drix snaps. "I can't work with him."

"Officers, please," Leah steps in, trying to make peace. "Jones, what is this virus that you're talking about?"

"The virus that torched the throat!" Ozzy exclaims. "The virus that caused those half-inch snot crests I was just surfing!"

"Those snot crests were caused by the sneeze," Drix reasons. "And the sneeze was caused by *you*."

"Oh, yeah?" Ozzy argues. "Then how come I saw that viral-looking mother fleeing the scene of the crime?! Tell me!"

This shuts Drix up, and fast. Ozzy hadn't told him

about seeing Thrax at Nasal Command. It's news to him.

Leah hears Ozzy's warnings. If a virus is on the loose, then precautions must be taken. She advises the mayor, "Sir, maybe we should put the city on full alert, you know, liquids, bed rest, just to be safe."

But the mayor refuses to listen. "We will do no such thing," he sharply rebukes. "I'm not going to postpone our trip just because the white blood cell with the worst record in Frank *thought* he saw something."

The mayor turns to Ozzy, glaring fiercely. "Listen," he threatens, "from now on keep those opinions in that mushy little head of yours—or you're gonna find yourself in our next nosebleed."

The mayor turns to Drix. His mood instantly changes. Now he's all sweetness and light, like a kindly uncle. He apologizes to Drix, "Now, why don't we find you another, more capable officer to work with?"

Drix pauses, thinking it over. Maybe Ozzy did see something back at Nasal Command. Maybe there was something to Ozzy's talk of a virus.

Maybe—could it be possible?—Ozzy is right.

Drix tells the mayor, "If it's all the same to you, sir, I think I'll stay with Jones."

# CHAPTER 13
## OZZY'S BiG MiSTAKE

With the squad car snarled in traffic, inching along a clogged artery, Drix voices the question that's been troubling him since the mayor's office. "Hey, Jones," Drix asks, "what did the mayor mean when he said you had a record?"

"Dips, sometimes being too careful is all it takes," Ozzy mutters. Ozzy thinks back to the memory, fixing on it in his mind. His voice trails off…and he tells Drix the whole sad story.

"It was the annual B. F. Norton Elementary School science fair," Ozzy recalls. "Everyone was excited because the winner was gonna get their picture on the front page of the local paper."

Shane, Ozzy explains, was thrilled. She'd made a volcano and was awfully proud. But even prouder was her father, Frank. In his eyes, Shane is the greatest kid on earth.

But being Frank, he also had his eyes open for food, as usual. Especially free food. So he wandered away from Shane. He quickly spotted a boy with a display labeled: MOLLUSKS…OUR SELF-CLEANING FRIENDS.

Frank eagerly picked up an oyster and sucked it down. Despite the timid boy's warnings, Frank grabbed another. And another. *Slurp, slurp, gobble, swallow.*

Yum!

Ozzy continues his story. "I was working the kidneys when I heard about the incoming shellfish. I headed to the stomach, just to be safe. The weather in the stomach was terrible that night," he tells Drix, who sits transfixed, listening intently. "I had a feeling that something bad was about to go down," Ozzy confesses. "So I got prepared."

Ozzy remembers the howling winds and thunder. The stomach was in complete turmoil. And no wonder—Frank kept snarfing down oyster after oyster. "Then I saw him," Ozzy remembers with a shudder. It was a bacteria ninja, a nasty germ who hitched a ride on one of Frank's half-chewed oysters. Once inside, the ninja started destroying everything in sight.

Frank's stomach was doing topsy-turvys within seconds. Frank clutched his stomach. He felt queasy. A shivery tremor rippled through him.

Uh-oh. Frank burped uncomfortably.

Back inside the stomach, Ozzy chased after the ninja germ. But it was too fast, too agile. The germ was headed into the bloodstream. If it got into the bloodstream, the germ could infect Frank's entire body.

Ozzy had no choice.

He slammed his hand onto a button: PUKE.

Suddenly, with incredible force, the germ and everything inside the stomach were expelled back up the esophagus.

(Yes, dear reader: Frank threw up...all over Shane's teacher, Mrs. Boyd. And she wasn't exactly happy-happy about it. Even worse, a newspaper photographer was there to record the blessed event!)

Ozzy turns to Drix. He needs for his partner to understand it all, every word of it. "It was a split-second decision and I did what I had to do," Ozzy explains. "But you can probably guess which photo made the front page of the papers the next day.

"Overnight, Frank became the town laughing-stock," Ozzy says. "Frank got fired from his job at the pea soup factory. Lucky for us, our old friend Bob hooked Frank up with a job at the zoo. Needless to say, none of this helped Shane."

Ozzy sighs, takes a deep breath. "And as for me, well, I took all the heat here on the inside. They said I used unnecessary force and they demoted me to Spit Patrol. Since then, not a day's gone by that I haven't wondered if I did the right thing."

Drix sits in pensive silence. For the first time, perhaps, he feels something. He cares...about Ozzy. "You know, Jones," he finally admits, "in this particular instance, I'd have to disagree."

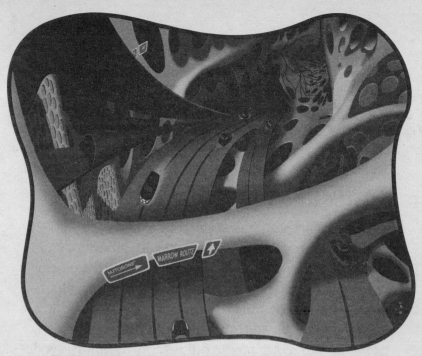

"Excuse me?"

Drix explains, "From your description, it sounds like you were justified in your actions. Oysters are a breeding ground for dangerous bacteria."

Ozzy smiles to himself. Ahead, the traffic starts to move. Ozzy shifts the car into gear, punches the gas, and away they go.

There's a bad guy to catch.

# CHAPTER 14
# A TIP FROM CHILL

Ozzy pulls into a rough, broken-down neighborhood. It's the Liver. And let's face facts, ladies and germs: This organ has seen better days.

Drix, manufactured in a sterile laboratory, is uncomfortable to find himself in such a seedy neighborhood. The veins are filled with tough-looking, mean-talking characters. But to Ozzy, well, it's no big thing. He was born in these veins; they were home to him. Ozzy points out a scrawny, shifty-eyed character. "See that dude?" Ozzy asks.

"That's a virus!" Drix exclaims. "We should arrest him."

"No, man. That *used* to be a virus. Now he's on our side," Ozzy informs his partner. "That's Chill. He's a flu shot. Why don't you just stay here and watch the maestro work."

Ozzy wants information. And Chill is just the type of guy who can give it. Ozzy crosses the street, waving his badge for everyone to see. "Yo, Chill!"

At the sight of Ozzy's badge, the sleazy crowd flees the scene.

"Hey, where you all going?" Chill wonders. He

frowns when he sees Ozzy. The cop scared away all
his pals.

Ozzy, in his best tough-guy voice, threatens,
"Tell me what you know about the sinuses."

Chill doesn't flinch. He answers, "Hey, I was
injected into this body to rat on influenza only. And
this don't sound like influenza to me. Now, beat it."

Ozzy grabs Chill by the collar. But Chill just
shrugs him off. He's in the virus protection program. He ain't afraid of no Osmosis Jones.

Drix suddenly steps in. He jams the muzzle of his
cannon-arm in Chill's face. *Click*. It's fully loaded.
"Yo, virus," Drix says. "I believe children's strength
ought to take care of you."

Ozzy likes what he sees. Maybe there's hope for
Drix yet. Ozzy plays along. "Uh-oh. You gone done
it now, Chill," Ozzy says, shaking his head sadly.
"This guy's a psycho cop. You had a chance to spill

it, but it's too late. This guy's cuckoo for Cocoa Puffs!"

Now they've got Chill's attention, big-time. He goes from nervous to scared to needing a diaper. With Drix's gun aimed at his ugly gob of a face, Chill is ready to talk.

"The guy's big time," Chill begins. "He goes by the name of Thrax. You can find him hanging out at the new place, The Zit. There's a big meeting there tonight. But you didn't hear that from me."

Chill can't get out of there fast enough. Down the sewer he slithers. Ozzy loves it! Drix was really cool right there, acting all mean and nasty with Chill. It worked like a charm. "Woo-hoo!" Ozzy whoops. "Next time, I'll be the bad cop," he tells Drix.

Drix smirks. "You *are* a bad cop." But Drix says it with a smile. Like a partner. Like a friend. At last, Ozzy and Drix have a lead. But now they've got to follow it together—into the most dangerous part of the city.

# CHAPTER 15

# COLD CAPSULES CAN'T DANCE

The police car eases to the curb across from a nightclub named The Zit. A neon sign flickers above the door, casting a strangely forbidding light. Ozzy and Drix watch the door for a few moments. A crowd of dirtbags files inside.

Drix steps out of the car.

"Wait, wait, wait!" Ozzy calls after him. "Where do you think *you're* going?"

"To get our cootie," Drix replies.

"Looking like that!?" Ozzy shrieks. "They'll tear you apart. You better get spiffy."

Drix is mystified. "Spiffy?"

Ozzy just shakes his head. Poor Drix has got to get down with the lingo. One thing's for sure: They can't walk into The Zit looking like a pair of cops; they'd get clobbered. So Ozzy decides to go under-cover. He's got just the body type for it, too. A push here, a poke there, and Ozzy's liquid form takes new shape. He pushes his eyes together to form one large cyclops eye in the center of his face. He stretches and gnarls his fingers and toes into grue-some tentacles. Yup, he'll fit right in with this crowd.

Satisfied with his disguise, Ozzy says to Drix, "Peep this."

Drix examines Oz with new admiration. "Hmm, pliable cellular dynamics," Drix notes. "What an ingenious defense mechanism. Let me try."

Drix tries to squeeze his nose into a new shape. *Crack*. It breaks. He looks to Ozzy hopefully. "What do you think?"

"I think you should guard the car," Ozzy advises.

"Oh, no," Drix counters. "This is my case, too. I insist on going in with you."

"All right," Ozzy relents. "But we gotta get you something to wear." They slap together a little disguise for Drix and head inside.

Dark and cavernous, the nightclub throbs with pulsating dance music. Laser lights slice through the steamy air. Ozzy looks at Drix, who seems hopelessly out of place. "Try to relax," Ozzy suggests. He gestures to the dancers all around the club. "Shake a tail cell or something."

"I don't dance," Drix admits. "I have no left feet."

Ozzy's shocked. "You don't dance!? Come on, don't tell me you ain't never gotten jiggy with it?"

Drix ponders the question. "No," he replies. "I don't believe I have."

Ozzy gives Drix a quick dance lesson, but Drix isn't exactly the fastest student on no feet. "You stay here and practice," Ozzy tells him. "If I'm not back here in five, you come looking, okay?"

Drix nods, dancing happily—although quite poorly.

Ozzy slides over to the bar. He orders a drink— "extra disgusting," just the way he likes it. *Yuck! Phh-tooey!* Ozzy drifts away from the bar when he notices several suspicious germs entering a back room. Ozzy follows them inside. He immediately sees Thrax standing before a conference table. A crowd of some of the dirtiest, foulest characters imaginable is seated around it. These guys thrive on sickness and disease. They're bad news for Frank.

Thrax points to a map of Frank and speaks. "The plan is simple," he tells the gathered hoodlums. "Three teams will move through the cranial artery and one through the nasal passage. We are going to the brain, baby. And we are gonna steal us one of these." Thrax holds up a bead from his bracelet. He explains, "This little sucker comes from a place called the hypothalamus gland."

"The hippowhosamus?" Ozzy yelps, throwing his voice, then ducking behind a germ.

"The *hypothalamus*," Thrax corrects the unseen questioner. "It controls the temperature for the entire body. We are gonna march right in there and we are gonna take the prize. Then Frank's gonna heat up like a sidewalk on a summer day."

All the germs cheer happily. Sickness and disease: Hooray!

"This is going down tonight," Thrax tells them. "I want everyone to be prepared."

Once again Ozzy throws his voice: "Tonight?! Ah, can't we do it next week? Me and Mad Cow got tickets to Wrestlemania."

Thrax fondles his bracelet. Once again, he answers the unseen voice. "Let me tell you something, baby," Thrax says impatiently. "This here DNA bead comes from a little girl in Riverside, California, didn't like to wash her hands. Took me three whole weeks." He fingers another bead on his bracelet of DNA beads. "And this one, nice lady in Detroit, six days flat."

Thrax proudly points out another bead. It soon becomes clear that each bead on his bracelet represents a life destroyed by Thrax. "Then there's this old guy in Philly," Thrax tells the admiring crowd. "I did him in seventy-two hours. Yeah, I'm gettin' better as I go along, baby. But the problem is, I never set a record."

Thrax drags his claw across the table for full effect, leaving a trail of fire. "Until my man Frank, that is. I'm gonna take him down in forty-eight hours, get my own chapter in the medical books."

Ozzy steps forward. "Ah, I got one more question here. Is there anything that, say, a white blood cell could do to stop this evil plan? You know, hypothetically speaking?"

Thrax coldly assesses the one-eyed stranger. "And *who* are you?"

"Who am I? Who am I?" Ozzy stammers nervously. "Ah, Bad... booty... shakin' pickle... nosis! Yeah, that's who I am!"

"Never heard of you."

"Oh, er, that's 'cause you just got here," Ozzy says, trying to talk his way out of this mess. "But when it comes to illin', Badbootyshakin'picklenosis stands above all the rest."

It seems as if Ozzy's disguise has worked. He's been accepted by the gang. But then a germ slaps Oz on the back, causing his eyes to pop apart. All of Ozzy's features fall back into place.

Oops.

A germ shouts, "That ain't no germ! That's a cop!"

The gang moves in to seize Ozzy. They hold him down for Thrax, who steps closer, and closer. Thrax jabs a dagger-like finger under Ozzy's chin. A sick, twisted smile crosses his face.

Thrax murmurs, "Somebody lay down a towel. This is gonna be messy."

# CHAPTER 16
## DRIX SPELLS R-E-L-i-E-F

A deep, commanding voice silences the gang. "Attention, germs. You are surrounded."

All eyes turn to see Drix, who has just crashed through the wall. His cannon-arm is cocked and fully loaded. He warns, "Release my partner at once."

Seeing his chance, Ozzy kicks a germ and escapes. He stands at Drix's side. Ozzy whispers to Drix, "If you get us out of this I will never bad-mouth the surgeon general again."

"No problem," Drix answers, supremely confident. He pulls a grenade out of his chest and reads the label: "ONLY FOR USE AGAINST THE MOST STUBBORN COLD SYMPTOMS."

"Get him!" Thrax orders.

................................................................

**Back in the world outside Frank's body, at this exact moment, Frank Ditello enters Shane's elementary school. He finds Mrs. Boyd's classroom and knocks on the glass door.**

**Mrs. Boyd looks up and gasps. Not him, not now, not again. She waves Frank away, but he won't budge. He taps on the door again, loud-**

er. Angry, Mrs. Boyd comes to the door. She can't help but stare at the enormous pimple in the center of Frank's forehead.

"What a zit!" Mrs. Boyd exclaims. Then, catching her mistake, she stammers, "I mean, what is zit? I mean, what are you doing here?!"

"I need to talk to you," Frank says.

Mrs. Boyd looks back to her classroom, sighs, and reluctantly steps into the hallway. She's not happy to see Frank. "You want me to call the police?" she hisses. "Maybe Shane would like to know about the two-hundred-yard restraining order that's still in effect."

"No, please. We wouldn't want that," Frank quickly says. "She's been humiliated enough."

"You wanna talk about humiliation, Mister Ditello?" Mrs. Boyd comments, the anger rising within her. "You turned me into a walking airsickness bag. I was humiliated. My family was humiliated. Do you have any idea of the teasing my little sons, Ralph and Chuck, have had to endure? Thank God their father, Barf, I mean, BART, is around to comfort them."

Frank lowers his head. He seems genuinely ashamed. "I know, I'm sorry. I heard about your daughter, Hurley—SHIRLEY—having to transfer schools. But we need to put water under the bridge and move past it...for Shane's sake."

Mrs. Boyd glares. "Shane has nothing to do with this."

Frank keeps plodding forward, hoping against hope. He pleads, "Look, all I'm asking is that you lift the restraining order for one weekend so I can go on this father-daughter trip."

Mrs. Boyd looks at Frank. She pauses. He seems so sincere...

---

The germs quickly move in on Drix and Ozzy.

But Drix proves to be an amazing fighter. He kicks nucleus up and down the room. Ozzy tries to imitate the kung fu moves of his partner. He easily flattens a germ. Together, fighting side by side, they bust bacterial butt. Ozzy and Drix high-five. It's the first time they've truly worked as a team. And, well, it's fun.

That is, until a germ smacks Ozzy upside the head. *Ouch.* That hurt. Ozzy falls. A bunch of germs

fall upon him. It's not looking good for the Oz-man.

Meanwhile, Drix struggles with the childproof cap. He can't fire the grenade until he gets past the tricky packaging.

"Drix, I could use a little help here!" Ozzy says, still pinned to a table. Finally, Ozzy snatches the grenade from Drix. He rips off the cap with his teeth, then tosses the live grenade at the germs.

KA-BOOM!

---

**"The answer is no," Mrs. Boyd tells Frank. She refuses to let him go on the hike with Shane.**

**"Please?" Frank begs. He looks at her with pathetic puppy-dog eyes. "Think about it overnight. It would make a little girl very happy."**

**Mrs. Boyd softens, truly touched by Frank's pleas. "Okay," she agrees. "I'll think about it."**

**Frank smiles, relieved. Unfortunately, it's at that exact moment when his enormous pimple, that throbbing pile of pulsating, purplish puss on his forehead, pops—all over Mrs. Boyd's face!**

**"Get out!" she screams. "OUT! The answer is NO! Absolutely NOT!"**

---

Back at The Zit, well, there's not a whole lot left of The Zit. It's been pretty much blown to smithereens. After the massive explosion, every germ has been rocketed through the roof.

Including Thrax.

Ozzy is overjoyed. He celebrates deliriously, grinning happily. "Thanks," he high-fives Drix. "You saved my cytoplasm in there. Now let's call in for a scab and get back to the precinct."

They smile triumphantly, then turn and leave. But...wait. A clawed hand clings to the outside of the huge crater.

Thrax lives.

# FIRED!

"Jones!" the chief hollers from his office.

"Must be about my promotion," Ozzy whispers to Drix as they enter the Third Police Precinct.

But when Ozzy struts confidently into the chief's office, he finds the chief wearing a miserable expression. Leah stands beside him.

"What are you doing here?" Ozzy asks.

A high-backed chair swivels around. In it sits the mayor. "You really did it now, Jones!" the mayor screams at him, launching into an angry tirade. "Disregarding orders, destruction of public flesh, popping a pimple without a permit. What were you doing up there?"

"What was I doing?" Ozzy asks, rising to his defense. "I was promoting good health, sir!"

"Oh, is that what you call it?" the mayor snidely remarks.

Drix offers, "Sir, he was a lethal virus. If we had-n't stopped him…"

"…we'd be eatin' fried eggs off Frank's dead butt," Ozzy says, finishing the sentence.

"Watch your mouth, kid," scolds the mayor. "Talk

like that could cause a panic."

Ozzy smirks. Politicians, they're all the same. They don't know jack about life in the veins. Ozzy answers, "At least that would start people thinking about what's going on in this body, instead of some stupid trip!"

"Okay, Jones, you want us to start thinking? Well, here's a thought. You're fired!" shouts the mayor.

Drix and Leah try to speak in Ozzy's defense. But the mayor silences them with a wave of his hand. He glares at Osmosis. "I'll need your badge, mister."

Ozzy slowly takes off his badge and gun. He lays them on the desk. Ozzy is heartbroken, devastated. He walks out of the room, feet dragging. Gone is his bouncy, confident strut.

"Osmosis," Leah calls after him.

Drix looks from the mayor to the chief. He pleads, "Please, without Jones, Frank could have been in mortal danger."

"Son, do me a favor and read what it says on your arm," Mayor Phlegmming tells him.

Drix reads his sticker: "For the temporary relief of symptoms associated with…"

"Exactly!" the mayor barks. "Temporary. You're nothing but a wannabe—a marked down, over-the-counter, useless TicTac. Now get out of my body. If we had wanted real medicine, we would have gone to the doctor!"

## CHAPTER 18

# FROM BAD TO WORSE

How much worse can things get? Ozzy's kicked off the force. Drix is on his way out of Frank's body forever. And Thrax is back—with a plan to destroy Frank within the next forty-eight hours.

And that's only the inside of Frank's body. The outside isn't faring much better.

Frank stands in his living room, packing for the big trip to Buffalo, New York. He gushes to Shane, "Man, I'm excited. Buffalo's gonna be a ball, baby."

"I'm not going," Shane announces.

"What?"

"I'm going camping with my friends," Shane tells him. Then she says hopefully, "You're welcome to join us."

Frank thinks about it. He still hasn't gotten permission from Mrs. Boyd—that exploding zit didn't help his case any. He can't tell Shane the truth; it's too embarrassing. Frank forces a smile. "Ah, you don't need your old dad huffing and puffing and dragging you down. If you really want to go camping, you go and I'll get Bob to come with me to Buffalo."

It's not what Shane wanted to hear. "Don't you ever think about anyone other than yourself?" she asks, tears beginning to well up in her eyes. "It's not fair. I go where you want to go. I eat what you want to eat."

"Baby, c'mon," Frank soothes. "I'm always thinking about you."

"Thinking about me?" Shane scoffs. "How come the healthiest thing I've ever found in my lunch bag was a fried Slim Jim sandwich?" Shane runs out of the room and slams her bedroom door.

# CHAPTER 19

# THE HEIST

In his despair, Osmosis Jones spends the long, lonely night walking the veins of Frank. Through the tall, swaying hairs of the ear; atop a plaque-covered molar in Frank's mouth; staring out of the cornea of Frank's eye, like a great window to the outside world. He buys a ticket to an all-night dream theater. Maybe it will take his mind off his troubles. Ozzy finds an empty seat and watches as Frank's dreams roll across the movie screen.

Meanwhile, Thrax is back—badder than ever. He's been stopped by Osmosis Jones once. But this time, Ozzy can't stop him. He's been kicked off the Immunity Force. No one believes him!

Tonight, Thrax works alone. Up the spinal cord, through the darkened halls of the brain, Thrax moves silently. Finally, he comes to a door marked: HYPOTHALAMUS—CENTRAL THERMOSTAT CONTROL. AUTHORIZED PERSONNEL ONLY.

He slips in unseen.

The hypothalamus gland regulates body temperature. Normally, it's heavily protected with armed, uniformed guards. But these are not normal times.

All the guards are needed elsewhere, on orders from the mayor. He's too interested in Frank's trip to worry about a little detail like brain security.

Thrax breaks through a series of locked doors and finds himself, at long last, inside the innermost room of the hypothalamus. Before him stand two twisting, twirling, intertwined strands of DNA, the famed double helix, the nuts and bolts of life itself. Like a master jewel thief, Thrax goes to work.

He plucks off one tiny DNA bead, leaving a space in the chain. The twisting helix shakes and hums. It can't function if it's incomplete. And if it can't function, Frank can't survive. The temperature in Frank's body instantly increases. Alarms sound. A security guard's voice comes over the loudspeakers. "All units be advised: We have a break-in."

The DNA bead clutched in his hand, Thrax eludes the guards through the dimly lit corridors of Frank's brain. He sneaks through one door, then another. To escape, he moves stealthily through the unconscious part of Frank's brain. Thrax moves, in fact, through Frank's very dreams....

Half-awake in his theater seat, wallowing in self-pity, Ozzy notices a familiar image flicker past. Hold on—was that? Could it have been? "Thrax!" Ozzy exclaims, jolted fully awake. "He's alive and in the brain!"

Ozzy checks Frank's body temperature. It's heating up. His worst fears are coming true.

"Drix," Ozzy says to himself.

Then he runs out of the room. And run Osmosis must, because time is running out.

# CHAPTER 20
# THRAX TAKES A HOSTAGE

Mayor Phlegmming has other, er, far less important things on his mind. He's on the phone, still planning Frank's trip.

Leah interrupts the mayor with some important news. "Sir," she says urgently, "something freaky is going on with the weather."

The mayor's face tightens. But he refuses to yield an inch. "We're probably drinking some hot coffee," the mayor lamely offers.

"Look at the map!" Leah insists. "What if Jones is right?"

"Jones!?" the mayor says dismissively. "Ha, ha, ha. Funny." He turns his back to her.

Leah finally understands it all. She forcibly spins the mayor's chair around. Leaning close to his face, she accuses him, "You care more about your stupid reelection than you care about our lives!"

The Mayor laughs nervously, but says nothing.

Leah turns away in disgust. She heads out the door. Something strange is going on in the hypothalamus. It's time she checked it out for herself.

When she arrives in the brain, Leah bumps into a

terrifying stranger—Thrax.

Thrax seizes her. "Hi, baby," he purrs.

But it's a stand-off, for an armed SWAT team of white blood cells suddenly surrounds them. They aim their guns at Thrax, who uses Leah as a shield. The guards are forced to hold their fire.

Thrax threatens, "Follow me, she dies."

Thrax grips Leah tightly and together they crash through a cellular wall. They fall to the street below. Acting quickly, with the SWAT team in pursuit, Thrax reaches into a passing car. He yanks out the driver and throws Leah into the passenger seat. He slides in behind the steering wheel. In an instant, he transforms the ordinary vehicle into a red-hot blistermobile. Thrax stomps on the gas—the tires burn—and he races away.

Meanwhile, Ozzy tries to find Drix before it's too late. He heads for the bladder. A long line of creatures waits for the next ship out of Frank, the S.S.

*Kidney Stone*. Drix is among them. A steward cries out, "Now boarding the nine thirty-seven, with non-stop service to the toilet bowl."

Drix looks down to check his ticket. When he looks up, Ozzy is standing before him.

"Jones?" Drix says, surprised to see his partner.

"Get your time-release butt off this boat. Thrax is alive. C'mon, let's go," Ozzy urges.

Drix hesitates. "I'm sorry, Osmosis. I can't help you," he says. "I wasn't designed to combat a virus. Read my label."

Ozzy looks into his friend's eyes. "You got to learn to think outside the pillbox, man," he says. "I've known sugar pills who've cured cancer just because they *believed* they could."

Ozzy's words don't make Drix feel any better. Ashamed, he tells Ozzy, "Look at me. I'm...cherry-flavored." Head bowed, shoulders slumped, Drix steps toward the boat.

"Fine," Ozzy shouts angrily after him. "Flush your life down the toilet."

Ozzy leaves Drix behind. He climbs into his patrol car. There's a tap on his shoulder. It's Drix. "You really know a sugar pill who cured cancer?" Drix asks.

"Nah," Ozzy confesses, smiling. "But it makes for a good pep talk, don't it?"

Drix climbs into the car, a look of determination on his face. He tells Ozzy, "Let's go catch a cold."

# CHAPTER 21
# HEATING UP

Frank's entire body is in an uproar. Fires rage; cells swelter and swoon in the heat. Part by part, systems are breaking down. And traffic crawls to a standstill.

"This city's burning up," Drix observes from the passenger seat of the squad car.

"Just as long as it don't hit a hundred and eight degrees," Ozzy grimly notes. "Or Frank's daughter is an orphan."

The police car radio crackles to life: "All units, all units! We have a hostage situation involving the mayor's aide."

"Oh no," Ozzy says. "Leah!"

The radio continues, "Suspect is headed toward the uvula. Repeat, toward the uvula."

"What is the uvula?" Ozzy asks.

Drix explains, "It's that little dangly thing that hangs down in Frank's —"

"—*boxer shorts!*" Ozzy concludes. "Okay, here we go!"

"NOT that little dangly thing!" Drix corrects. "The one in the throat."

Unfortunately, it's a great distance away. How can Ozzy and Drix make it there in time? Suddenly the stomach heaves and rumbles. It gives Ozzy an idea. "Frank's eatin' again," Ozzy says, excited. "C'mon, I know a shortcut."

"I don't like the sound of that," Drix frets.

Oz drives to the edge of a great precipice. Below lies a bottomless pit of gurgling acid. Drix nervously reads a roadside sign. "That's pure stomach acid!" Drix says with alarm. "We'll be killed."

Ozzy asks, "You got a better way?"

A rumble begins to build from deep in the pit. Frank is about to burp. It's now or never. Ozzy and Drix share a look. And it's decided. Ozzy steps on the gas. The patrol car busts through a ROAD CLOSED barrier...just as Frank lets out a thunderous belch.

A huge fireball geyser blows, hurling the car upward as it rides the crest of Frank's fiery stomach gases. The car hits solid ground with a violent crash. Ozzy's and Drix's clothes are scorched from the scalding burp.

But they've survived. And now they are closing in on Thrax.

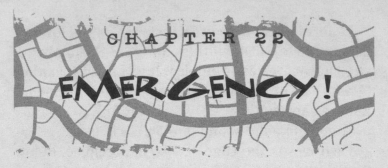

# CHAPTER 22
# EMERGENCY!

Frank and Bob drive to the airport. They're on their way to Buffalo. A madcap weekend of gastronomic gluttony awaits them.

But Frank seems far from happy at the prospect. In fact, he's miserable. He confides to Bob, "She doesn't love me. Why should she, though? I mean, look at me. I'm a fat pig, right?"

Bob can't disagree. He looks over at his friend. Hmmm. Frank doesn't look so good. "Are you okay?" Bob asks. "You look terrible."

From his office, Mayor Phlegmming watches the scene unfold on his monitor with increasing concern. He's tense and worried. Nothing, he tells himself, can get in the way of this vacation.

Nothing.

Once again, the mayor switches to voice override. In a deep voice, he speaks into the microphone. "I feel fine," he tells Frank.

But Frank can't repeat the mayor's instructions. He's too sick. Sweat pours off Frank in buckets. Dizzy, eyes blurred, Frank passes out—and the car swerves off the road.

"Frank? Frank?!" Bob shouts. "That's it. The trip is off. We're going to the hospital!"

Cruising along the very same road, Shane sits glumly on a school bus. The bus is packed with girls and their fathers.

Shane stares out the window unhappily.

Soon a few girls try to cheer Shane up. They play "makeup" with her. Shane puts on eye shadow and lipstick. She adds a pair of false eyelashes. All the makeup makes her look older somehow, like a picture of her mother.

Shane opens her lunchbox. The first thing she sees is a package of Twinkies. Shane frowns. Her father will never change. But wait, what's this? Shane pulls out a sandwich wrapped in wax paper. She unwraps it—and finds a sprout sandwich on wheat bread!

A huge, happy smile fills Shane's face.

He cares after all!

Just then, a girl beside Shane points out the bus window. "Shane, isn't that your dad?"

An ambulance sits parked beside a car. The emergency rescue workers lift a stretcher into the ambulance. It's Shane's father.

Shane runs down the aisle to Mrs. Boyd. "Stop the bus," she says. "Let me off."

Mrs. Boyd hesitates. "Shane, dear…"

"I said do it!" demands Shane.

# CHAPTER 23

# OSMOSIS TIME

Like some crazed King Kong, Thrax carries Leah up to the top of the uvula. The fog is thick and menacing. The uvula stands like the top of the Empire State Building. Teeth appear in the distance like far-off mountain peaks. A river of saliva burbles below.

"Let me go," Leah screams.

Thrax stops suddenly. He smells something. He wonders aloud, "What is that nasty smell?"

"Cherry," a strong voice answers. "Wild cherry." Drix emerges from the fog. He aims his cannon-arm at Thrax. "Now let her go."

"Why? So you can ice me again?" asks Thrax.

"No!" Ozzy calls from above. "So I can!" Ozzy leaps for Leah and snatches her from Thrax. They tumble to safety.

"Say good night," Drix says, about to fire upon Thrax.

Amazingly, Thrax dives out of the way. The frozen goo from Drix's cannon just misses Thrax. But part of his claw and arm get iced.

Leah looks at Ozzy, her savior. "Jones, thank God," she murmurs in relief.

Ozzy grins. "Aw, look at you, girl. You were really jonesing for some Osmosis, weren't ya?"

This is no time for Ozzy's big-man-on-campus routine. "Just get the DNA bead," Leah tells him.

Ozzy calls out, "Hey, Drips! Did you get him?"

"I think I nicked him," Drix tells his partner. Together, they pick their way through the thick fog, searching for Thrax. "Come out, come out, wherever you are," Ozzy calls.

A wall of flesh suddenly rips open. It's Thrax.

At the same instant, spit choppers begin to swarm above, circling the area with searchlights. An officer shouts down through a megaphone: "This is Saliva Patrol. We have you surrounded. Surrender at once."

"Give it up," Ozzy tells Thrax. "You're busted."

"Hand over the bracelet," Drix demands.

Thrax merely laughs. "Y'all are making this too easy," he smirks, pleased with himself. Thrax pulls out a pollen crystal from beneath his coat. He throws the pollen up toward the churning chopper blades.

"Oh, nooo!" Ozzy screams.

The pollen crystal hits the blades and bursts, scattering over Frank's mouth and throat. It's more than his allergy can handle. A violent rolling thunder begins. A powerful sneeze begins to swell. Thrax stands on the railing. Gruesome bat wings sprout from his shoulders. He spreads the dark wings wide.

"Enjoy the funeral, boys!" Thrax calls out. He tests the wind with a finger, ready to escape from Frank forever. The sneeze explodes and a strong gust of wind lifts Thrax out of Frank's mouth...and into the world beyond.

"We're dead," Leah whimpers.

Ozzy takes a few steps back from the ledge. He rolls his head, shakes out his arms. He locks eyes with Drix, then glances down at Drix's cannon-arm. "How's your aim?" Ozzy asks.

"Jones?" Leah asks, fretting. "What do you think you're doing?"

Ozzy gives her a kiss. "Saving Frank," he answers. Then he quickly turns to Drix. "Let's do it."

Osmosis Jones, now in liquid form, fearlessly leaps into Drix's cannon-arm. Drix raises his arm, aiming at Thrax through a narrow opening between the teeth. It won't be an easy shot.

"You want Osmosis?" Ozzy says.

"You got Osmosis!" Drix fires.

# CHAPTER 24
# THE BATTLE RAGES

In the hospital emergency room, frantic doctors try to save Frank's life. His body temperature is 106.2 degrees and rising. Nothing seems to be working.

Shane clings to the stretcher, crying.

Bleary-eyed, Frank looks at Shane, who still wears the heavy makeup from the bus. In his delirious state, Frank can't trust his sight. "Maggie?!" he asks in wonderment, voicing the name of deceased wife.

"No, Dad. It's me, Shane."

---

*Whap!* Ozzy collides with Thrax in midair. Together they tumble, end over end, hurtling through empty space, screaming.

And then something small and microscopic, insignificant, really, to the human world, splashes down in shallow water. Just a white blood cell named Osmosis Jones.

Ozzy hits hard. Stunned, he looks around. Where is he? Slowly, it dawns on him. He's standing in a tear duct—on Shane!

Ozzy stands and faces Thrax.

"You just don't know when to quit. Do you, Jones?" Thrax comments, almost with a touch of respect.

Enough small talk. Ozzy charges at Thrax. They fight hand to hand—punching, kicking, clawing. The raging battle carries them out of the tear duct and out onto one of Shane's eyelashes. It's a long, long way down to her lip.

The fighting is intense. But gradually, Thrax takes control. Ozzy takes a fierce beating, but keeps coming back for more. He won't surrender. Thrax grabs Ozzy by the throat and lifts him high in the air. "You want this bracelet so bad?" he snarls. "Well, Thrax is going to give it to you!"

Thrax wraps the bracelet around Ozzy's neck, strangling him. "Looks good on you, Jones," Thrax snarls. "It's a shame you had to come this far from home just to die."

Not a moment too late, a rolling tear from Shane's eye crashes over them. Ozzy, freed from Thrax's stranglehold, washes onto one of Shane's false eyelashes. Amazingly, the DNA bracelet is still wrapped around his neck! "Hah, who's the Germinator now!" Ozzy taunts, clutching the beads.

More furious than ever, Thrax swings up onto the eyelash. Striking swiftly, he drives his claw right through Ozzy's stomach.

"Oh, look at the time," Ozzy deadpans. "I've got to split."

Liquid Ozzy strikes again! His body separates around Thrax's claw, which remains stuck fast to the eyelash. A cracking noise fills the air. The eyelash—it's breaking up all around Thrax! Sensing danger, Ozzy runs back toward the eye. Thrax can't move. He's trapped, unable to free his claw from the false eyelash.

Helplessly trapped, Thrax falls through the air, tumbling, tumbling through the void. He lands in a bottle of rubbing alcohol.

*Fzzzzzst.*

And dissolves without a trace.

---

**But Frank is dying.**

**"Daddy, no!" Shane cries. "I don't want to lose you!"**

**A doctor, working feverishly, commands the nurse: "Get her out of here!"**

**"No. Wait. That's my dad!" Shane screams, clutching her father.**

**The nurse pulls Shane away, toward the doors. She whispers softly to Shane, "There is nothing you can do in there."**

**Ozzy watches it all like a bad nightmare. He stands in Shane's tear duct, the DNA beads in his hand, watching as his world—the city of Frank—lies dying. With each step Shane takes, Ozzy's world moves farther and farther away. It all looks helpless.**

# CHAPTER 25

# ONE LAST BLAST

Mayor Phlegmming sits in his chair, like the captain of a sinking ship, as the inevitable comes to pass. Frank's temperature keeps rising. Cells all over Frank's sad-sack body weep and moan, hugging loved ones good-bye. They know, like the mayor, that this is the end of Frank. They bravely face their impending doom.

Inside the mouth, Leah stands beside Drix and the chief. "He's not coming back," a heartbroken Leah says. "He's not going to make it."

"He'll make it," Drix answers. He refuses to give up on Ozzy. If anyone can save them now, it's Osmosis Jones. He has to make it back—somehow, someway.

The temperature display reaches 107.9. Death is inches away, just one-tenth of one degree. The doctors wearily step away from Frank. They've lost the fight. "That's it," one doctor says. "There's nothing else we can do."

These words are more than Shane can bear. She tears herself away from the arms of the nurse. Shane rushes to her father's side. "Dad, I'm sorry I said those things to you," Shane cries through bitter tears. "You are the greatest dad in the whole world.

"I love you. I love you!"

At this, a tear rolls from her eye toward Frank's open mouth. Ozzy sees his chance. He leaps...and catches the wave...all the way back into the city of Frank!

Osmosis rolls and comes to a stop at Leah's and Drix's feet. But Osmosis looks half-dead himself. In silence, a crowd gathers around his fallen body. Slowly, with great effort, Osmosis opens one eye. He sees the chief looming above.

"Hey, chiefy-weefy," Ozzy mumbles. "What's up?"

"Did you get the bead?" the chief urgently asks.

Ozzy struggles to raise an arm. There it is, laced in his fingers: Thrax's bracelet! "Get these to the hypowhipowholamus," Ozzy says. "You know what I'm talking about."

There's no time to lose.

In the hospital, Frank's heart stops beating. And for that one moment, he's gone to the other side. To darkness and death and whatever world awaits him there. Yet at the exact moment when the DNA bead is replaced in the twirling double helix, Frank's pulse gives a little flicker of life.

"Wait a minute!" a nurse calls out. Shane and the doctors turn around in shock.

"Dad?" Shane whispers.

Frank coughs.

He looks up and sees his daughter. Frank smiles faintly. "Your mom says hi," he tells Shane.

A doctor checks Frank's body temperature. "It's coming down," he says with amazement.

Frank reaches out, finds Shane's hand, and squeezes.

He's going to make it.

........................................................................................................

Inside Frank, thousands of cells jostle on the ridges of his teeth, cheering with joy. It's a wonderful, rapturous celebration, like New Year's Eve in Times Square. And all over the city of Frank, from toes to nose, every living organism toasts a new hero.

To Osmosis Jones!

The immunity cop who saved them all.

Later, with Frank's temperature returned to normal, the chief happily hands Ozzy back his badge. "Can I count on you to keep Frank in shape?" the chief asks.

Ozzy looks at Drix, who stands nearby. He winks, then tells the chief, "You gonna have to talk to my new partner. If he feels like hanging around a little while."

Drix smiles. He'll be happy to stick around.

Her eyes sparkling with love, Leah pulls Ozzy

close. "Come here, baby," she coos. "I'm still jonesing for a little more Osmosis."

They kiss, long and slow.

And, well, that's the end, folks. Ozzy and Leah are in love. Drix is going to stay inside Frank, working with Oz to help keep Frank healthy and safe.

And Mayor Phleggming?

Well, Frank himself gets the last, er, *word*, on that.

You see, Frank finally did take a hike with Shane. Up they climbed to a mountain view—one with, admittedly, a nearby parking lot.

Frank and Shane sit together.

They are as happy as they've ever been.

Because they know, deep down, that everything's going to be okay.

"I'm so proud of you, Dad," Shane tells her father.

"Why, thank you, honey," Frank says.

And with a single fart, Frank blows the mayor out of his life.

Ain't life a gas?

Teach ® Yourself

# Find Peace with Tai Chi

Robert Parry

For UK order enquiries: please contact Bookpoint Ltd, 130 Milton Park, Abingdon, Oxon OX14 4SB. *Telephone:* +44 (0) 1235 827720. *Fax:* +44 (0) 1235 400454. Lines are open 09.00–17.00, Monday to Saturday, with a 24-hour message answering service. Details about our titles and how to order are available at www.teachyourself.com

For USA order enquiries: please contact McGraw-Hill Customer Services, PO Box 545, Blacklick, OH 43004-0545, USA. *Telephone:* 1-800-722-4726. *Fax:* 1-614-755-5645.

For Canada order enquiries: please contact McGraw-Hill Ryerson Ltd, 300 Water St, Whitby, Ontario L1N 9B6, Canada. *Telephone:* 905 430 5000. *Fax:* 905 430 5020.

Long renowned as the authoritative source for self-guided learning – with more than 50 million copies sold worldwide – the **Teach Yourself** series includes over 500 titles in the fields of languages, crafts, hobbies, business, computing and education.

*British Library Cataloguing in Publication Data:* a catalogue record for this title is available from the British Library.

*Library of Congress Catalog Card Number:* on file.

First published in UK 1994 by Hodder Education, part of Hachette UK, 338 Euston Road, London NW1 3BH.

First published in US 1994 by The McGraw-Hill Companies, Inc.

This edition published 2010.

Previously published as *Teach Yourself Tai Chi.*

The **Teach Yourself** name is a registered trademark of Hodder Headline.

Typeset by Macmillan Publishing Solutions.

Printed in Great Britain for Hodder Education, an Hachette UK Company, 338 Euston Road, London NW1 3BH, by CPI Cox & Wyman, Reading, Berkshire RG1 8EX.

The publisher has used its best endeavours to ensure that the URLs for external websites referred to in this book are correct and active at the time of going to press. However, the publisher and the author have no responsibility for the websites and can make no guarantee that a site will remain live or that the content will remain relevant, decent or appropriate.

Hachette UK's policy is to use papers that are natural, renewable and recyclable products and made from wood grown in sustainable forests. The logging and manufacturing processes are expected to conform to the environmental regulations of the country of origin.

Impression number    10 9 8 7 6 5 4 3 2 1

Year    2014 2013 2012 2011 2010

# Contents

# Meet the author

**Welcome to *Find Peace with Tai Chi*!**

When, over 400 years ago, the geographers and visionaries of
Elizabethan England urged their seafarers to locate a north-west
passage across the top of the American continent to China,
it was not only to establish a new trade route to the East with
all its valuable silks and spices, but it was also to seek
something far more profound. Based on the journeys and
reports of Marco Polo and others, they believed that the
cultures of the East had preserved a very special understanding
of the natural order of things and that the philosophers
and physicians of China were, in particular, the custodians of
much of the hidden knowledge of antiquity – scientific,
cultural and spiritual. This was a good call: ever since then we
in the West have continued to seek knowledge and wisdom
through our associations with the great civilizations of China,
whose philosophy, medicine, martial arts and exercises of
self-cultivation have never ceased to fascinate us right up
to the present day.

As a practitioner of oriental medicine living in the West,
and as a long-time student of subjects such as tai chi and
yoga, I have to confess to being no exception to this irresistible
draw towards a culture that is not my own and that presents,
therefore, all the challenges and difficulties one would expect
when trying to comprehend a way of life that can seem
so very different and strange. Maybe you feel the same.
Maybe, for example, you would like to give tai chi a try,
but are uncertain of how to begin. If so, then this book
will help you get started, to explore the movements for
yourself and see if they interest you. Later on, you might
want to go on to attend classes – to get a feel for the kind of
pace and mood that has to be evoked for tai chi practice.

In tai chi there are many different paths to follow. It can be immensely powerful in the hands of some, while incredibly gentle in the hands of others. The book you are reading now is concerned with the latter, the gentle art of tai chi for the purposes of health and relaxation.

I began teaching tai chi way back in the 1980s, mostly in adult learning centres, because I wanted to help people relax and deal with stress. I could see that stress was implicated in many of our most serious health issues such as heart disease, rheumatoid arthritis, migraine, asthma and much more. If tai chi could make only a small impact on some of these terrible illnesses through combating stress, I thought, it had to be worth pursuing. This was also the inspiration behind this book, which came a few years later and which is intended for anyone wanting an easy introduction to one of the great modern treasures of the East: the Short Yang Form of tai chi. And although it is true that you cannot learn tai chi entirely from a book, it is a good way to start – and a book can provide that all-important quality of inspiration at any time.

This book contains step-by-step instructions for the whole of the tai chi form. But you want to know right now if it is going to be of interest to you, right? That's reasonable enough. After all, it takes many weeks, if not months to learn the whole of the tai chi form all the way through, and probably a lifetime to master it. That's rather a long journey to contemplate without at least a 'taster' of what's to come. This is what these early pages are all about – to give you a one-minute, a five-minute and a whopping great ten-minute practical introduction to the subject. That way you get to know if it's right for you.

As the great classic of Chinese literature the *Tao Te Ching* tells us, 'A journey of a thousand miles begins with a first step'. So why not start on your own voyage of discovery right now? Teach yourself some tai chi. This book has been written with you in mind, and will set you on your way.

# *Only got a minute?*

Tai chi is all about reconciling opposites – the Yang and the Yin of life. I want you to think of your body in a different way for the next minute. Stand upright as shown in Figure 0.1. Think about opposites. Be aware, firstly, of the polarity of front and back. Now shift your attention to the left and right of your body.

*Figure 0.1 Posture.*

Next be aware of the top and bottom of your body. The top should feel as if it is connected to the sky, like being suspended on a golden thread, as the tai chi classic texts tell us. The feet, meanwhile, are like roots connected deep into the earth, supporting and sustaining us, as if drawing up energy.

Finally, think of the inside and the outside of the body. Just keep thinking of all these opposites and try to bring them all together for one minute. That is the start of the tai chi experience.

# 5 Only got five minutes?

In the next five minutes, we are going to try to experience the ch'i – the vital energy of the body.

Stand with your feet a little apart and bend your knees – bouncy, like being on springs. Roll your shoulders a couple of times and loosen up. Then give your hands a rub. Rub your palms together. Keep on doing it. Then rub the back of each of your hands with the opposite palm. Again, keep on doing it. Then curl your fingers and make fists a couple of times, open up and then tighten again. Then shake your hands vigorously. Shake, shake those hands – great!

Now relax. Place your palms out in front of you at about the height of your tummy as if you are holding a large ball between your palms (see Figure 0.2). Breathe in and imagine the ball is inflating, getting bigger.

Then as you breathe out, squeeze the ball gently – squeeze, but with no muscular tension, please. Do it again. Breathe in again; the ball gets a little bigger again, pushing your hands apart as it expands.

Then, as the next natural outbreath comes along, squeeze the ball again without pressure and just 'think' the squeeze. Let the natural rhythm of your breathing guide the movements of your hands – *never* the other way around. Keep repeating this simple movement until you can almost sense the whole of your body partaking in it – the knees bend a little on the outbreath, the shoulders open just a little on the inbreath. Relax. Don't force anything. Don't expect sparks to fly; they won't. But, for most of us, there is a sort of tingling, energetic presence to be felt between the palms. Some might say that it's just the increased

*Figure 0.2 Raise arms to hold ball.*

circulation – but actually there is more to it than that. We all have a certain subtle electrical kind of energy that sustains us – and that is the ch'i (or *qi* as it is also written, pronounced something like 'chee'). That's what you feel when you do tai chi. Interested? If yes, then why not have a go at the next section, the ten-minute taster!

# 10 Only got ten minutes?

A great way to spend the next ten minutes of your life would be to try out the opening movements of the tai chi form itself. I can remember when I first did this. The feeling can be quite extraordinary – learning to move the body with the breath in a very special, focused kind of way that I had never done before. Don't worry about thumbing through the pages to find these movements. Here they are – presented as a separate exercise. Go through the instructions carefully. Don't worry about adding the breathing directions until towards the end of your ten minutes – and then only if you feel confident with the movements themselves. Never force your breathing into any pattern that feels uncomfortable to you. Be patient, and the breath will then guide the movements naturally.

---

## Step-by-step instructions

### OPENING

1. Stand upright, feet together, toes pointing out and the heels not quite touching. Take a moment to experience how the body feels. Tuck in the base of the spine and relax the shoulders and fingers. Make space under your arms, as if you have a small balloon under each armpit. Breathe in gently and begin.

*Note*: Make sure your spine is vertical, as if suspended from above, as illustrated in Figure 0.3.

*Figure 0.3 Posture.*

*Figure 0.4 1 Opening inbreath.*

2. Sink onto the right foot. Raise the left foot and place it down to the left, shoulder width from your right, the toes pointing forward. Adjust your right foot so that it also points forward. The feet are parallel, and the weight evenly distributed. The foot diagram here shows the new rectangle on which you should be standing (solid line) as well as the location of the previous rectangle (dotted line). This technique will be adopted occasionally in these pages to enable you to see major changes in position more clearly.

50%

*Figure 0.5 2 Outbreath.*

3. With wrists relaxed and fingers pointing slightly downwards, allow your arms to rise to about chest height, the forearms parallel with the ground. Let the arms 'float' upwards – though only as far as you can comfortably go. The shoulders should remain still when the arms rise – one of the ways in which tai chi teaches us to relax and, in time, to eliminate tension from that area altogether. The neck and shoulders are, of course, a common place for tension and pain to gather. Keep them relaxed!

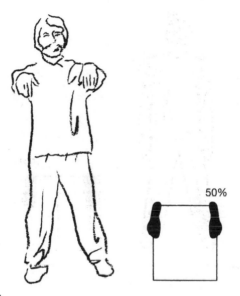

50%

*Figure 0.6 3 Inbreath.*

4. As you breathe out, very slowly raise and straighten your fingers so that the tips are pointing forward. Think, also, of the wrists dropping as well as the fingers straightening. Do this without tension. Monitor the stiffness or otherwise of your finger joints during this exercise. How slowly can you move them without them trembling or tightening up? The more relaxed you can make your hands, the better will be the blood supply to the joints.

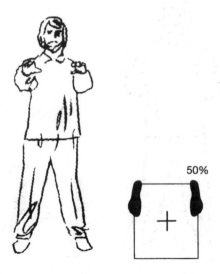

*Figure 0.7 4 Outbreath.*

50%

5. Draw the elbows back. Try to keep your arms away from your sides. Look at the illustration closely. See how much space there is between the elbows and the sides. Be aware, also, of the space behind, between your shoulder blades. Make sure that, in drawing the elbows back, you do not create tension in this place. Bring the elbows back only as far as is comfortable.

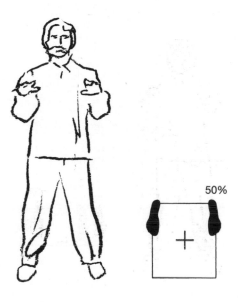

50%

Figure 0.8 Inbreath.

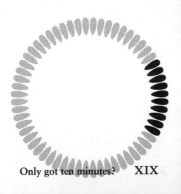

6. Lower your arms slowly to your sides and let your weight sink. Try to imagine roots going down into the ground from your feet. Relax the shoulders, relax the fingers and let the knees bend a little too. Try to feel a connection with the ground beneath you, but at the same time continue to imagine your body suspended – traditionally described as a 'golden thread' attached to the top of the head and going right up into the sky.

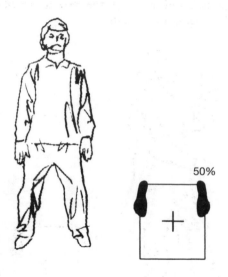

50%

*Figure 0.9 6 Outbreath.*

## TURN RIGHT

1. Sink onto the left foot and turn your waist slowly clockwise by pivoting on your right heel. Do not lift the right heel – this is not a step, just a turn. Simultaneously, raise the right arm to a near vertical position but with the wrist loose, palm down. The left hand, meanwhile, rises as well – palm up – to 'cup' the right elbow. The term 'cupping the elbow' should not be taken too literally. There is plenty of space between your upturned palm and the elbow, and the palm is also not directly beneath it. Think of holding a large ball and try to get the movements of the waist and the arms to flow smoothly together.

90%

*Figure 0.10 1 Inbreath.*

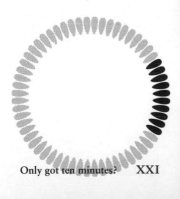

2. Allow the right foot to go flat down and shift your weight onto it, so that the knee goes just over the tip of your toes as you look down. Your right hand is at about chin height, your eyes looking over it towards an imaginary distant horizon. Try to feel the ball, the ch'i connection, between your palms. Keep the back straight.

*Note:* At first, as you learn this movement, you will need to concentrate on the hands and feet separately, but it does not take long before the whole thing starts to flow. Keep trying, until all of the body feels co-ordinated.

*Figure o.11 2 Outbreath.*

Feels good, doesn't it! These are, of course, pretty basic movements here right at the start – and the tai chi form gets a whole lot more complicated later on. But if you enjoyed that, then you will probably do well with what's to come. Remember, nature does not surrender her secrets lightly, and tai chi is an activity that is very much rooted in the natural world. The rewards for perseverance and patience are great indeed with this kind of work. The more you put in, the greater your gain. With these short taster sessions, you have had a good look at the way ahead. Now for the start of the journey itself ...

# 1

# Background

Tai chi is many things to different people. The beautiful, controlled and yet freely flowing movements have for centuries inspired men and women from all walks of life, people of all ages and all levels of fitness. Vitality, relaxation, tranquillity, enhanced personal creativity and a sense of purpose – these are just some of tai chi's enduring gifts to the world.

In my work, I often meet people seeking a means of relaxation or of managing stress. Sadly, it soon becomes apparent that many have never known what it feels like to be relaxed in any meaningful way. This interference through tension and stress with the body's natural healing process is perhaps one of the greatest misfortunes of our times and it is in a bid to help combat this situation – in no matter how small a way – that this book has been written.

In these pages we will be looking exclusively at the health and relaxation aspects of this ancient and yet thoroughly modern art, with step-by-step instructions on how to learn and perform the basic sequence of the Short Yang Form of tai chi. Don't worry if you have only limited leisure time. Your study can easily be integrated into a normal lifestyle. All it takes is ten minutes each day to get results. And it really is worth it. In the East, exercise systems like tai chi are very popular; they are undertaken in a spirit of moderation and realism and this book urges you to do likewise. Simply do what you can, with the time available – then go ahead and enjoy it!

Tai chi is much more than just a physical exercise, and to a great extent many of its inner qualities can be 'self-taught' through continuous practice and observation. It is hoped that this book will help you in this endeavour – making, therefore, a useful companion to any practical work you might undertake in classes or with teachers. Allowing the magic of tai chi to enter your life means being open to the currents and forces of nature, within yourself and within the world around you. And if it is true that tai chi is a journey of a kind, then there has to be a beginning somewhere. Why not here?

In this chapter you will learn:
- *the nature of ch'i*
- *the origins of tai chi*
- *the energy pathways of the body.*

## What does 'tai chi' mean?

When talking about tai chi today, we usually refer to a system of gentle physical exercise (the subject of this book) or to the martial art of that name – more properly termed 'Tai Chi Ch'uan'. However, the term 'tai chi' appears to pre-date both these activities by many centuries and has its roots in ancient Chinese culture and philosophy. 'Tai' in translation into English means 'great' or 'supreme', while the word 'chi' (also written as *Ji*) means something like 'ultimate'. So tai chi is often referred to as 'the supreme ultimate'. It was, in a sense, the goal of the early Taoist philosophers – the state of oneness and inner peace that could be reached through contemplation of nature and by working in harmony with its energies.

### Insight

There are two ways of transcribing Chinese characters into Western writing: one is called the Wade–Giles method (e.g. the capital city of China is written as Peking) and another more recent method is called Pinyin (e.g. the capital city of China is written as Beijing). This is why you see different renderings of tai chi – sometimes written as tai ji, for instance, or as t'ai chi.
In this book, we stick to the popular Western rendering of tai chi.

Nevertheless, it is important at this stage to understand that the word 'ch'i' – which is used to describe the concept of vital energy, and is found in all manner of diverse areas of Chinese culture such as medicine, feng shui, calligraphy or martial arts – is a different word (different Chinese character) from the 'chi' in tai chi. This is an important distinction.

In classical Chinese literature such as the *I Ching*, sections of which can be dated back confidently to at least the eighth century BC, we are told of a special state of harmony that exists in all of nature, and this is called the *Tai Chi* – the Supreme Ultimate. It is also often pictured as a symbol called the 'Tai Chi T'u' (see Figure 1.1).

Sometimes also called the 'double-fish diagram' because it looks a little like two fishes chasing each other's tails, what we have here is clearly a circle divided equally into a light and a dark sector. These are called the 'Yang' and the 'Yin' respectively. You will have noticed that the division between Yang and Yin is not just a straight line, it is a graceful curve, suggesting movement and the interplay of opposites. Light (or Yang) changes into darkness (Yin) and then changes back to light again. Note, also, the eye or seed of each opposite located deep within each sector, indicating still further the possibilities of change and transformation.

You can probably think of other examples of Yang and Yin in the world around you: day and night; summer and winter; hot and

*Figure 1.1 The Tai Chi T'u symbol.*

cold; the positive and negative force of electricity; advancing and retreating armies; or the rise and fall of empires, both personal and global. All this is the tai chi in action. The philosophy that underlies it, therefore, views life as a kind of dance, an energetic interplay of opposites. When these opposites are brought together in a state of harmony, the goal of the ancient philosophers is achieved. In a similar way, in the field of oriental medicine, for example, a state of health and internal balance can also be reached through harmonizing the energies of the Yang and Yin of the body. When this state of harmony is reflected in physical movement, the result is the exercise system known as tai chi.

### Insight

The Yang and Yin within the tai chi are not only opposite in nature, they are also supportive of one another, interdependent in character and can also transform from one into the other. The one, therefore, cannot exist without the other and they are rarely in conflict. It is above all a relationship of harmony.

## The tai chi form

The special arrangement of movements that you will find in these pages is collectively called a 'form'. The form is made up of lots of separate movements that are eventually strung together to produce one continuous sequence lasting several minutes. The form has a beginning and an end, and the movements within it are always done in the same order, like the components of a specially choreographed dance. The idea is that you go through this sequence daily. This, in turn, can not only strengthen your health, but can also keep you free of stress and perhaps even ward off some of the ravages of time. All this just by keeping to a daily routine of gentle exercise.

The emphasis on daily practice is crucial here. The health benefits of tai chi show through only if regular practice is maintained. This is why tai chi is usually regarded as an ongoing preventive strategy for improving and maintaining health rather than as a 'cure-all' for illnesses. Just keep on doing it! That's the simple message of tai chi.

The rest, especially once you have learned the form itself, is really very simple. There is no expensive equipment or clothing to buy, and you don't have to belong to any special club or association (unless you really want to, of course). In fact you will soon discover that tai chi is in many ways very different, refreshingly so, from most other forms of exercise or recreation, not least because it is un-competitive. You don't have to win or 'beat' anybody at this game. In fact, rather than making yet more unwelcome demands upon your time and energy, tai chi becomes something that you actually *want* to do each day, something that you really enjoy, not just something that you feel you ought to be doing because it's good for you.

Moreover, because tai chi practice places such emphasis on developing a sense of inner peace, and on seeking external qualities such as fresh air and tranquillity for practice, it places you in harmony with your environment in a way that is quite unique. Tai chi is rooted in nature and consequently it helps you become closer to nature, as well. This is something that becomes apparent when you start to learn, and is a very good feeling. Perhaps this is because each of the movements has a Yang and a Yin aspect to it. So when you do tai chi you are also participating in the interplay of opposites: harmonizing yourself over and over again with the cyclical forces of nature. The individual 'tao' then becomes connected to the greater, universal Tao. Tai chi is a celebration of nature and of your place within it.

---

## Origins of tai chi

There have been, and still are, many different kinds of tai chi, the origins going back very far indeed and, inevitably, cloaked in their fair share of mystery and legend. For example, Huang Ti, the

Figure 1.2 The Crane and the snake.

legendary Yellow Emperor of China, was said to have practised special exercises for maintaining health, based on the observation of animals, as long ago as 2700 BC. This is the earliest reference we have to anything like tai chi. But, as with acupuncture and the many other branches of medicine and self-culture developed by the Chinese, activities of this kind probably have their origin in the days before recorded history. Incidentally, Huang Ti was said to have reigned for a hundred years and to have had over a hundred wives, so he must have been doing something right!

Around the thirteenth century, these exercises seem to have joined forces with the martial arts, or were at least developed by them to great effect. The martial arts in China were already at that time being practised to a very high standard by the Ch'an (Zen) Buddhist monks. And although no one really knows for sure how the process took place, the combination of all these diverse strands of thought and action eventually gave birth to the practice of T'ai Chi Ch'uan (the great way or system of tai chi) as we know it today.

All the historical confusion surrounding the subject has not in any way discouraged the spread of numerous stories concerning the origin of tai chi. One of the most interesting of these relates to the illusive 'founder' of the art, Chang San-feng, a Taoist priest, who most probably lived around the time of the Sung dynasty – thirteenth century or earlier.

The legend has it that one evening he had a particularly vivid dream in which he saw a great bird – a crane – and a snake engaged in combat over a morsel of food. Neither creature seemed to be able to overcome the other. Each time the snake attempted to sink his fangs into the crane, the bird would gracefully side-step and enfold the creature in its powerful wing and sweep it away. Each time the crane tried to crush the snake or pierce it with its sharp beak, the snake would recoil and twist, often launching a counter-attack of its own. The beauty and grace of this contest impressed Chang greatly. The next night he had the same dream. Once more, the crane would come down from the heavens and the snake up from the earth and the contest would begin again.

The Yang and Yin imagery here is very powerful and symbolic of an eternal contest, the eternal state of dynamic balance in nature, exemplified in the Tai Chi T'u.

It is probably because of stories of this kind, and the alliance with the fighting monks of medieval China, that tai chi often appears somewhat martial in character when compared with the numerous comparatively passive ch'i-generating exercises from which it originally sprang. Indeed, tai chi is still practised very much as a martial art, and a very effective one, too! Many of its greatest living exponents are martial artists of a very high calibre indeed. There is a common energy pattern used both for health and for martial skills, and what is good for one is invariably good for the other. Thus, these two often quite disparate applications of tai chi in the modern world still exist quite happily side by side.

The kind of tai chi we will be devoting ourselves to in this book is a somewhat more recent variation on this great tradition, called the Yang style. Although itself a development based on a long tradition of tai chi technique, this Yang style emerged as recently as the nineteenth century. Its founder was Yang Lu Chuan who lived from 1799 to 1872. His grandson, Yang Cheng-fu, taught tai chi into the twentieth century and it was one of his pupils, Cheng Man-ch'ing, who most helped to spread tai chi in the West – basically by shortening the form into a concise eight-minute sequence. This is called, naturally enough, the 'Short Yang Form' and is the form featured in this book.

> ### Insight
> Don't worry if you encounter different renderings of some of these names. For instance, Yang Cheng-fu can also appear as Cheng-fu Yang. Cheng Man-ch'ing can also appear as Cheng Man Ching.

Cheng Man-ch'ing (1900–1975) was a remarkable individual, not only a superb exponent of tai chi, but also a professor of literature, an expert in the use of Chinese medicinal herbs, a calligrapher and a painter. He studied tai chi originally as a means of keeping at bay a serious illness, tuberculosis. He found that whenever he stopped doing his tai chi, he became ill again. This was possibly one of the reasons he believed so passionately in teaching tai chi for health purposes as well as for martial applications. This is also undoubtedly why his condensed version of the form has become so popular. It is clearly designed for relaxation and for strengthening the body's own healing energy. There has, of course, also been a huge resurgence of interest in the original principles of energy flow that underlie tai chi in recent times, as more and more people, drawn by tai chi's inherent grace and beauty, are once again setting out to explore its healing and inspirational qualities for themselves and to make it part of their daily lives. So much of this is due to the work of Cheng Man-ch'ing.

---

## How long does it take to learn?

I once heard a fellow student ask the question in a tai chi class, 'How long does it take?' The reply was, 'Well, how long have you got?' – implying that, in a sense, you never really reach the end of the learning process. Nevertheless, it was a reasonable question and if it could possibly be modified to something like, 'How long will it take before I can do the form all the way through and gain some benefits from it?', the answer would probably be less ambiguous. But it still depends on how much you are prepared to work at it. There are no short cuts or fast results with tai chi. It takes around six months to learn the form adequately and a lifetime to master it. As you learn, it is essential to practise every day for around ten minutes, adding newly learned movements each time. Then, once you have learned the form, you still keep on working at it every day. Ultimately, you will be spending at least 15–20 minutes daily on your tai chi studies, since these might eventually also include some reading, meditation or breathing exercises.

The best time to do tai chi is in the morning or evening, when the forces of Yang and Yin are most harmonized (sunrise and sunset).

Outdoors is best, for there you will find an abundance of natural energy. Traditionally, tai chi is done beneath trees or near water, but any time and anywhere is better than never.

The time spent practising will never be wasted. It will repay you over and over again in terms of health and well-being. The rate at which you progress is entirely up to you, therefore. The more you work at it, the quicker you will learn – simple as that.

## What are the benefits?

Numerous independent scientific studies, both in the West and in China and Japan, have proved beyond any shadow of a doubt the enormous benefits that tai chi and its related disciplines of ch'i kung (additional breathing techniques that we will be looking at later) can bring in terms of good health, recovery from illness and the strengthening of the immune system.

Of course, we all know that exercise helps us to keep fit and therefore to stay well. This is because exercise helps to maintain the heart and lungs and so improve the circulation. Tai chi, however, goes far beyond this, since it enhances the health and performance of all the organs and systems of the body. Tai chi also works on a deep emotional level. It puts us in touch with our body's needs, strengthening the mind, calming the emotions and releasing considerable personal creativity in the process. It helps us to cope with stress and to find solutions to problems more easily.

All this takes time to cultivate, of course. But here are some of the benefits that should come to you fairly soon, providing you really do practise every day. You will start to notice an overall improvement in balance after just a few weeks so that you feel stronger and firmer on your feet. You will become more relaxed, especially after doing the form; more aware and content. Your circulation will improve, your joints become more mobile and, as long as you take care of yourself and avoid the obvious drawbacks of junk food, cigarettes and other stimulants, your overall state of health will strengthen.

**Insight**

'My husband deeply felt that Tai Chi Ch'uan could benefit everyone, and he was anxious to spread this art to all. He followed the proverb, "The good doctor cures people before they become ill."' Madam Cheng in her introduction to Master Cheng Man-ch'ing's *Thirteen treatises on T'ai Chi Ch'uan.*

## The nature of ch'i

Tai chi makes great use of the body's internal energy – 'ch'i', or '*qi*' as it is alternatively rendered in translation. The former variant (ch'i) is the more commonly encountered spelling in the West, however; and in this book, we will stick to this version. Translations into English of 'ch'i' are many and varied. The nearest we have for it in our own language is probably 'life force' or 'vital energy'. Those already practising yoga might also be familiar with this concept as 'prana'.

We store ch'i in our bodies. Ch'i is to be found in the lines of force, or 'meridians' as they are called, which circulate through the body and which are used in oriental medicine to balance the internal energies and so maintain health. This is why a doctor specializing in acupuncture or shiatsu can improve, say, the state of a patient's lungs by stimulating the surface of the inner arm with small needles or finger pressure. When we practise tai chi, we are not only absorbing this vital energy through our breathing but are also setting the ch'i in motion around our bodies.

The body is a wonderful self-regulating system. It uses the vital energy where and when it needs it. You simply set the ch'i in motion; the body takes care of the rest. Figure 1.3 gives a representation of

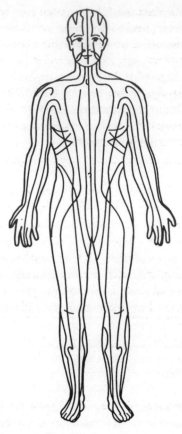

*Figure 1.3 The energy channels.*

the superficial energetic pattern of the body, collectively termed the jing lou. There are many deeper channels supporting these.

Recent scientific investigation has located the distribution of ch'i in the human body and has found this to correspond closely to the old medical charts of the Chinese acupuncture system – mapped out all those centuries ago by the brilliant doctors and physicians of those times. It has been found that each acu-point has a lower electrical resistance than the surrounding tissues; and so also with the acupuncture channels, along which these points are ranged.

For centuries in the East, such knowledge had been in broad circulation, of course, and today, those of us working in the field of oriental medicine need no proof of the existence of the body's subtle energetic system, since we can feel it for ourselves during treatment. But it is good to know that anybody embarking on a course of tai chi study, or any related system of energetic body work, can do so today confident that they are dealing with very real forces that work deep within the human body, sustaining it and nourishing it throughout its life.

## Insight

Within our bodies, the ch'i (*qi*) is created through a combination of the food that we eat and the air that we breathe – rather like the combination of fuel and air in an internal combustion engine. The spark that makes it 'ignite' comes from a special finite substance within each of us called the jing, a kind of inherited essence – a little bit like our modern concept of genetic inheritance. When these three work together, we have strong energy and a vital constitution.

## Atmospheric ch'i

Ch'i is not simply something we have inside us, by the way. Outside the body, science has also located something akin to ch'i in the electrical field of the atmosphere. There are certain electrically charged particles in the atmosphere, positive and negative ions in the air we breathe. The positive ions are associated with dust and pollution and are to be found mostly in cities, while the negative ions are in abundance in clean, moist air, in sunlight or by the sea. Thus, as we all know, housework and traffic jams are debilitating, but fresh air and trips to the seaside are invigorating. This is why tai chi places such emphasis on the breath and on practising outdoors wherever possible.

Traditionally, as well, ch'i has always been considered as something that flows through the natural landscape. This belief lies at the heart of the ancient study of feng shui, a special art of placement that has always been used in China and the Far East but which is gaining great popularity now all over the world among those designing buildings, house and office interiors, gardens and parks. Feng shui literally means 'Wind Water' – two forces of nature that flow easily across, above and within the landscape. By making sure that objects and structures are correctly aligned and placed, one to the other, it is felt that the energies of the landscape or building can flow in harmony and that people will feel happier working or living there.

We all know how uncomfortable we can feel in any space which is cluttered or which inhibits our movement. A room full of too much furniture, a door or window that cannot be easily reached: it can all feel rather frustrating and cramped at times! All things need to have their energies flowing freely. This means harmony. Without the free flow of energy there is only ever stagnation. So too with our own bodies! Tai chi practice is a way of getting rid of the restrictions, the tightness and the tensions that may be interfering with our movements and therefore also with the actions of the joints, muscles, tendons and, ultimately, the vital internal organs of the body itself.

Whatever way you look at it, tai chi has got to be good news, and in the next chapter we will look at how to begin working on the form and getting in touch with these internal energies through the tai chi movements themselves.

# 10 THINGS TO REMEMBER

1  Tai chi means 'Supreme Ultimate'. It does not mean Supreme Energy. Ch'i or qi (pronounced 'chee') is how we translate the Chinese character that means energy.

2  The famous Yin/Yang symbol, the circle divided into dark and light, is called the Tai Chi T'u.

3  Exercises in China for cultivating energy and health appear to date back to at least 2700 BC.

4  The tai chi form is a set sequence of movements, like a choreographed dance.

5  The philosophical concept called 'the Tai Chi' is first mentioned in the Chinese classic the I Ching – parts of which can be dated back confidently to at least the eighth century BC.

6  The earliest Tai Chi Ch'uan forms appear to date from around the thirteenth century.

7  The style of tai chi in this book stems from the Yang style, named after the family who taught it.

8  The Short Yang Form was put together by Cheng Man-ch'ing in the first half of the twentieth century.

9  The health benefits of tai chi include improved fitness, better circulation and a gradual strengthening of the immune system.

10  Vital energy, or ch'i, flows around the body through a system of channels called the jing lou.

# 2

# Gently does it

In this chapter you will learn:
- *to establish an appropriate speed and rhythm for tai chi*
- *to establish a regular plan of practice*
- *to prepare for your tai chi with special warm-up exercises.*

There is hardly anything in life that cannot benefit from being done slowly. This is certainly true of tai chi – the movements are celebrated for their graceful, gentle quality, like a floating cloud or running stream. In other words, just about as slowly as a person ever gets to be.

During the early days of training, however, most students want to perform the movements fairly rapidly and there are two reasons for this. Firstly, human beings are impatient creatures. The more hectic and stressful the lifestyle, the more difficult it is to slow down and do anything in a relaxed way.

Secondly, most of us tend to move in a rather unbalanced, haphazard fashion most of the time. When walking, for instance – and no matter how well co-ordinated and confident we might feel – we tend rather to 'fall' into each step instead of placing the feet in a controlled way. This is natural enough for anyone wanting to get from A to B quickly, but it's not what we're looking for in tai chi. Those who spend a little time practising the form, however, soon learn to control their movements and direct them precisely. This in turn draws the body and mind into a state of focused relaxation and harmony.

Of course it isn't easy at first. Patience and self-discipline need to be cultivated, qualities that you will develop through regular practice and which will set a pattern for attaining many other kinds of self-control, helping you to focus your mind, cultivate detachment and achieve results more easily through enhanced levels of concentration.

As well as developing balance and physical stability, or what is called 'rooting', the slowness of the tai chi movements also concentrates and generates the vital energy of the body, bathing all the organs in life-giving ch'i. The slow pace also serves to work thoroughly many of the muscles of the body (in tai chi, particularly the legs) and therefore helps to maintain a healthy circulation.

## Insight

Tai chi is an excellent way of helping us to stay fit and well, and also a useful means of assisting recovery from illness. It is not a cure for disease, however. At times of illness, always seek professional medical advice. It is also recommended that you check with your doctor before embarking on any new exercise regime such as tai chi – just to make sure that it is suitable for you.

## How fast? How slow?

So exactly how slowly should we be moving in tai chi? It may come as a surprise to those just starting out, but there are no hard and fast rules for this. The answer is different for each person and depends on how thoroughly you are able to relax and also, later on, upon the natural rhythm of your breathing. This, in particular, should never be forced.

These days, the Short Yang form described in Chapters 4 and 5 normally takes around eight minutes to perform, though it can be done faster if you wish – and it certainly can, and often is, done more slowly. It could be argued that there has recently been a marked trend, especially here in the West, to slow the whole thing down. When Western folk first see tai chi, their immediate observation is 'Oh, look – how slow it all is!' As a consequence, when they take it up they turn it into something even slower! In particular, this tendency grew apace during the 1960s, when – mistakenly – it was considered really 'cool' to do tai chi in a kind of trance-like mood.

Well, there is nothing wrong with feeling calm during your tai chi. You *should* feel calm. But you should also be alert and aware, and not moving so slowly that you become tense and impatient with yourself. Cheng Man-ch'ing – who, after all, originated the very sequence we are studying here – once wrote that he created the short form because he was unable to spend a lot of time each day performing the traditional long form. His own version, he stated, could be got through in just four minutes! That suited him.

Viewed in this light, our modern eight-minute sequence might seem rather self-indulgent. But the fact of the matter is, providing your limbs are relaxed and you feel the ch'i flowing, it doesn't matter a jot how fast or how slowly you do it. The main thing is that you do it – and enjoy the experience.

### Insight

Some eastern philosophies, such as Buddhism and Taoism, teach that matter arises out of ch'i, not the other way around. An interesting thought.

## Breathing made visible

The first thing we do when we come into this world is breathe. And when we cease to be, so also do we cease to breathe. We can do without food for weeks, without liquids for days, but most of us would be hard pressed to do without air for more than a few minutes, and it is little wonder that people the world over have always thought of the breath as containing the very essence and spirit of life.

When going through the tai chi form, the breath should be evenly distributed between the contracting and the expanding movements. These movements are actually timed to the breathing: in other words, gathering in during each inhalation and projecting out with the natural exhalation that follows. This is important since the energy, both muscular and vital energy, moves better when exhaling, which is why weightlifters breathe out suddenly during the main lift and why those doing karate cry out during their punches or kicks. This serves to expel the air efficiently and move the ch'i at exactly the right moment. In tai chi we remain silent, of course, but we should still always be exhaling gently during the projecting movements of the form, e.g. with movements such as Push (see page 50) or Press (see page 49).

Naturally, then, we would want to inhale in between these projecting movements – for example, the movements such as Rollback (see page 49) or the Pull (see page 56). However, most parts of the form that feature inhalation are not provided with names. Instead, the inbreath is usually viewed as a prelude to each named movement. Therefore, an inbreath precedes the final stage of Ward Off (see page 47), Push (see page 50) and so on.

This book illustrates clearly both the Yin and the Yang phases of each movement – that is, awarding equal importance to the build-up towards each position and to the final stance – again, that part that usually has a name attached to it. This leads us to a vitally important concept that is really essential to understand, and one that simply cannot be stated often enough. (If you are one of those people who skip preliminary chapters in books of this kind, but then come back later when you realize what you are doing somehow doesn't work out right, then here is the answer you've been searching for all this time!) Always, *always* remember that the tai chi form is not just a set of poses. Of course, some people enjoy posing – and that's OK. Some people look really great propping up a bar in a disco, but that's not tai chi. There is no room for posers in this game. In other words, the bits in-between are as important as, if not more important than, the final positions. The journey, in this instance, is as interesting as, if not more so than, the destination.

In tai chi and in the practice of oriental medicine, as well, we regard life as something that partakes essentially of *movement*. Where there is movement, there is life. Where movement and vitality are absent, however, stagnation arises. Never stop. Keep moving when you do tai chi. The inbreath phase should be done slowly, gently, patiently, edging smoothly bit by bit towards the conclusion of each movement. This is where the music and the magic of tai chi are to be found. Yes, there is music in tai chi! But it's to be found inside. Internally there is harmony. And where there is harmony there has to be rhythm. The rhythm is the breath.

## Insight

Ch'i is a fundamental concept in oriental philosophy and medical theory. Literally translated, it means something like 'air' or 'breath' – something, therefore, that is all around us but also within us at the same time. The breath is the medium through which we connect with the world and with all other living things. For this reason it is often venerated in spiritual disciplines the world over (latin *spiro/spira* = wind, breath of life, spirit, divinity).

### FINDING YOUR RHYTHM

Try this brief experiment and with a quick bit of arithmetic, you should be able to settle on a rhythm and a pace that are right for you.

Firstly, take a moment to relax; walk around a bit and see how slowly you can breathe without feeling agitated or short of wind. How often – ten times a minute? Twelve times a minute? There are precisely 80 cycles of breathing in the form shown in this book so if you do an eight-minute form, this works out at ten breaths per minute, or one typical tai chi movement every five to six seconds. If this feels too slow for you right now, don't worry. Speed it up! A faster, seven-minute form lets you take about 12 breaths a minute, or one cycle every four to five seconds.

Whatever pace you settle on, try to keep in synchronization with the breathing instructions accompanying the illustrations and to breathe naturally and gently at a calm, regular pace all the way through. Above all, *don't force it*! Find your own speed and don't take the above guidelines so literally that you have to use your stopwatch. There is no such thing as a tai chi inspector who is going to pop out of the bushes and upbraid you for doing your form in 5 minutes instead of 15. Do what comes naturally and you'll be fine. And never, never extend your breathing into a pattern that feels uncomfortable.

I once had a student who wanted to learn tai chi. When I asked him whether he did any kind of exercise already, he replied, 'No, but I always go out into the garden every morning and do about ten minutes of deep breathing.'

'Fine,' I answered. 'You are already half-way towards doing tai chi! All you need now is to add some body movement, shaped around the breathing, and you're there!'

Tai chi is *breathing made visible*. The breath is the source and the destination of all your tai chi studies. This is why it is sometimes referred to as a 'moving meditation' – since all forms of meditation require a quietening of the mind through regular, rhythmic breathing. A useful and pleasing metaphor is to think of the inbreaths and outbreaths as solar and lunar respectively. Tai Yang is actually a Chinese term for the Sun (the Great Light), while Tai Yin is the Moon (the Great Dark). You will encounter these solar and lunar principles more and more as you progress with your tai chi studies. Most worthwhile things in life have a mystical dimension and tai chi is certainly no exception. It is largely through the contemplation and realization of the harmony between Yang and Yin that such experiences can be attained.

> *There is an inward centre in ourselves where truth abides in fullness.*
>
> Robert Browning

# Practice

For practice it is best to have a routine of some kind, i.e. the same time every day if you can. The most favourable times are considered to be early in the morning or in the evening, but any time will do, providing you can spend at least ten minutes each session. In China and other Eastern countries, people from all walks of life are to be found every morning in the parks and open spaces, working on their exercises, including tai chi. It is part of their routine and sets them up for the rigours of their day ahead. Indeed, most teachers of tai chi will tell you that it is essential to practise every day and preferably a couple of times every day if you can. But for someone just starting out you can reduce this to once daily.

Don't feel that you have to be up at the crack of dawn for this. That's fine for some but if you lead a complex life, working an eight-hour day, commuting, cooking meals, putting the children to bed and doing housework each evening as well, you are probably entitled not to get up at the crack of dawn. Does that mean that you cannot benefit from tai chi? Of course not! Simply find a convenient space in your daily routine; be happy with the situation and try to stick with it.

Being properly prepared for practice is always a good idea and the wearing of loose, comfortable clothing and sensible footwear is essential. Make sure you are reasonably calm and collected before you approach your tai chi sessions. Never rush into the movements with haste or with reluctance – that would only be a waste of time. Likewise, never do tai chi when you have just eaten or if you are angry or upset over anything. If necessary, sit quietly for a moment and put the mind at rest before beginning. You owe that to yourself.

You should also make sure you have a peaceful location; either a quiet, uncluttered room where you will not be disturbed or, best of all, outdoors. If necessary, make it clear to your family that you will be setting aside 10 or 15 minutes for yourself each day. This is a time *just for you* and should not involve others in any sense. Children and pets can be particularly unco-operative when it comes to anyone doing tai chi in their midst. There is no need to be mysterious or secretive about your tai chi studies. Just explain your intentions and what is required and that way your desire for privacy will usually be respected. Finally, don't forget to switch the phone off!

---

## Getting started

Now, I know you are just itching to get started on learning tai chi, and on practising the form. That's understandable. After all that's what tai chi is mostly about, doing the form. 'Show me the form!' students demand, eager to begin at the top. If only it were that easy! But the body has to be coaxed into the right kind of movements and shapes for tai chi. And the best way to achieve this is to do some suitable warm-up routines to begin with. That is why the next few pages are really important to assimilate, especially if you are a complete beginner. And in fact no matter how experienced you are, your tai chi form should always be preceded by a brief warm-up session, particularly in cold weather. That way the body gets the maximum benefit from the form. Any kind of gentle exercise will do for warming up, although there are numerous Chinese-style routines that can be used and which you will acquire in abundance should you ever attend formal classes in tai chi. What is important, however, is that you gently stretch the limbs and loosen the joints. Don't overdo this, though. Warming up should never be so lengthy as to leave you with no time or energy for anything else. Keep it simple.

Here are some suggestions. It is not necessary to do them all each time. Just select a few, vary them and use what feels right. Always bear in mind, however, that those exercises that feel the most difficult for you are often just the ones you need the most! Areas of stiffness often indicate places where energy is not flowing smoothly, and tai chi is all about removing these blockages.

With all of these exercises, keep the limbs soft, that is, with the knees bent and the shoulders and elbows relaxed, never locked tight.

1 *Stand with feet shoulder-width apart, bend the knees a little, relax the shoulders and slowly allow your arms to swing back and forth together at your side, raising both heels as you rock forward, and both sets of toes as you rock backward. Only a little raising of toes and heels. Don't overdo it! The movement comes from the centre of the body rather than the feet. Do this for a while and then pick up an imaginary ball between your hands and throw it up into the air. Relax the neck muscles as you do this and allow the spine to stretch back gently. Then return to your rocking (see Figure 2.1). Relax your arms completely and try to keep your centre of gravity low by keeping the knees bent.*

*Figure 2.1 Rocking exercise.*

2  *Spread the feet a little way apart and then twist the body from side to side, moving from the waist and allowing your arms to flop around as you turn: very loose, like a rag doll. As you twist to the side, raise the opposite heel slightly. Again, the movements originate from the centre of the body, from the waist. Always aim to keep the knees apart, as if seated upon a nice plump horse; do not let the knees drift in towards each other as you turn. Let the arms 'lengthen'. Relax the spine, chest, neck and shoulders (see Figure 2.2).*

3  *With your feet again shoulder-width apart, extend the arms in front of you and simply rotate the wrists slowly, several times in each direction. The forearms should remain still as you do this. Only the wrists move. Squeeze your hands into fists, open them up, fingers wide apart, and then shake – shake the whole hand loosely and allow the shaking to extend right up the arms so that the wrists, elbows and even perhaps the shoulders start to loosen also.*

*Figure 2.2 Twisting exercise.*

4  *Rotate the ankles in a similar fashion (one at a time, of course). The knee and the lower leg should remain still as you do this. Only the ankle moves. Stretch out and curl the toes and then shake or kick – again allowing the sensation to extend upwards, in this case to the knees and maybe even the hips if you can.*

5  *Rotate the neck from side to side – gently please – gradually easing away any tightness you might feel. Make sure your hands are not screwed up into fists as you do this. Remember, the nerves and blood vessels of the arm originate in the neck and shoulders, so relax them. Relax the arms and fingers. You can even bend the knees a little too.*

6  *Placing the feet as wide apart as you can, squat down on one foot, getting a progressive stretch along the inside of one leg*

Figure 2.3 Leg stretches.

*(see Figure 2.3). Then change sides and stretch along the other leg. (Don't lean on your thigh when you do these – just stretch gently.) Experiment with different ways in which you can use this kind of movement to stretch different parts of the leg. In tai chi we are constantly trying to cultivate a low-slung stance, with a low centre of gravity. The more flexible the tendons and muscles of the legs the better in this respect.*

## Insight

It is not all that important what warm-up exercises you choose – as long as you feel comfortable with them. Never force yourself into any kind of routine that causes you to feel breathless or tired – or anything that you might find painful. You should always check with your doctor before starting out on any new kind of exercise routine to make sure it is appropriate for you, especially if you are elderly or frail or have any special health needs – i.e. if you are taking medication or during pregnancy.

7 *Circle the arms up and slowly around, loosening the shoulders. Rotate them both together or alternately, like swimming backstroke or crawl. Shake out the arms again when you have done.*

Repeat these exercises as many times as you wish, allowing yourself to become more supple each time. Build up flexibility slowly and patiently. Wonderful! Even if you do nothing else, do these. Ideal during the day if you are stuck to an office desk. Just get up and move! You're not concerned about what anybody else thinks are you? Of course not! You will be the better for it, and it will keep you relaxed and focused when you return to your work. Even better, get everybody else doing it too, and who knows where it will all lead!

# 10 THINGS TO REMEMBER

1  *Never force your tai chi movements or make yourself in any way uncomfortable with them. Work at a natural pace, in time to the natural rhythm of your breathing.*

2  *Always check with your doctor before embarking on any new exercise regime, including these warm-ups, to make sure it is suitable for you.*

3  *Each movement in the tai chi form has a name.*

4  *The outbreath usually accompanies the projecting, pushing kind of movements.*

5  *The inbreath usually accompanies any retreating or gathering-in kind of movements.*

6  *Try to practise regularly, at least once a day. Twice a day if possible.*

7  *Wear loose and comfortable clothing for practice.*

8  *Work in a peaceful, uncluttered environment with plenty of fresh air: preferably outdoors.*

9  *Go through a brief warm-up routine before you start your tai chi, using the examples in this chapter.*

10  *Try to ensure you will not be disturbed. And switch off the phone!*

**The theory and function of Tai Chi principles are found everywhere.**

Cheng Man-ch'ing

# 3

Tips and suggestions

In this chapter you will learn:
- *the basic stances of tai chi*
- *the dos and don'ts of tai chi movement*
- *the importance of relaxing the whole body.*

## Dos and don'ts

The tai chi form you are about to learn comes in two parts.
The next chapter sets out the first part and if you are a complete
newcomer, you should be aiming to learn this first. Many people
are satisfied with doing just Part One – a brief, two-minute
sequence. They repeat this several times through and arguably
derive just as many benefits in terms of health as those who do the
whole form. There is no disgrace, therefore, if this is as far as you
wish to go and if you can go through it a few times every day, you
will already be making great strides towards good health and a
relaxed mind.

Even when you graduate to Part Two, always learn each movement
*thoroughly* before going on. Remember, you are putting together
a string of pearls here and each one must be added carefully before
the next. This will not only ensure that you remember what you
have learned, but that you will be able to call upon past movements
whenever they need to be repeated, as they often are, later in the
sequence. Take a day to learn each movement and after a few
months you will have the whole thing.

> **Insight**
> There are no short cuts along the way to learning tai chi.
> Proficiency can only be gained through regular practice and
> through a positive and open mental attitude.

A common question at this stage is, 'Can tai chi be combined with other forms of exercise or sport?' The answer is, quite simply, 'Yes'. Tai chi will help improve your skills in any sport or recreational activity. In my experience it blends particularly well with the gentle stretching exercises of yoga and in fact there is a whole branch of taoist (Chinese) yoga very similar to the classical Indian hatha yoga that most people are already familiar with. So you don't have to give anything up. As long as you find time for practice, you will succeed. A sensible diet, free of junk food, will speed your progress, as will the use of therapies such as massage, shiatsu or acupuncture, which help to maintain health and vitality. These can be undertaken regularly, as a matter of course, and not just in times of illness.

Before you embark on the instruction section, it would be helpful to understand a few basic principles of tai chi movement and also to become familiar with the basic stances and methods of getting around.

*You must wave the arm and let the palm move against the wind, feeling the air as if it were water.*

Cheng Man-ch'ing

## Posture

### RELAX THE SHOULDERS

Always be aware of what is happening in your shoulders and try to let them relax as much as possible. When raising the arms, for instance, try not to tense the muscles of the neck. Whenever the arms are extended out in front of you, keep them low.

This is sometimes rather a tall order for those who suffer from stress, since it is the shoulders that tend to collect tension very easily, especially mental or emotional tension. Despite our best efforts, it is very difficult to let go of tightness in the neck and shoulders, and if you feel this is the case with you, then – again – I recommend some proper massage by a qualified therapist to help you relax. Check out those shoulders of yours now. They should feel fluid and easy to move, and you should, for example, be able to roll and rotate each one independently of the other. You should also be able to turn your head freely from side to side without moving your body. It cannot be too strongly emphasized here that any tension in this area should be addressed if you are to gain the benefits of tai chi practice.

### NEVER LOCK THE ELBOWS OR KNEES

By locking, I mean straightening the arms or legs completely, so the joints are stiff. This inhibits the circulation of blood and ch'i and only serves to create tension in the whole of the body.

You should also endeavour to keep space between your arms and your sides while doing tai chi. The moment you feel your elbows touching your sides, open up more and create space. Imagine, too, that you have a small balloon placed inside each armpit. Keep the space there open as well. And don't forget those shoulders. Keep them low.

## Insight
Master Cheng Man-ch'ing once described the movements of tai chi as like swimming in air. This is interesting. The limbs should feel as if they are floating. Also, can you feel the air with your palms as they move? This encourages sensitivity and the movement of ch'i.

### KEEP A LOW CENTRE OF GRAVITY

Imagine your weight and your breath becoming concentrated in your abdomen area. Be aware of your body's centre, which in tai chi is considered to be just beneath the navel and slightly inwards towards the spine – the 'Tan Tien', as it is called. Keep your knees soft and flexible throughout and think of being close to the ground and well rooted.

A good instructor, in my view, would be one who is constantly reminding his or her students to 'sink down' – that is, to lower the body. Just *sink*! This is a good word to remember at all times. In this way, tai chi will help you to become more grounded and *earthed*, both mentally and physically. You could say it is the opposite to having your 'head in the clouds' and is why tai chi helps us stay positively focused and calm.

## *ALLOW THE SPINE TO HANG LOOSE*

At all times, imagine you are being suspended from above by – traditionally, it is said – a golden thread, attached to the top of your head. The spine 'hangs', therefore, like a plumb line, totally vertical and relaxed. To assist this process, tuck in your bottom by raising the pelvic bones and draw back the chin a little (see Figure 3.1).

*Figure 3.1 Posture.*

Make sure you do this in a relaxed fashion – no tension, please. Standing like this – let alone moving like it – is an art that has to be cultivated over time, so be patient; be mindful of it and it will eventually happen.

---

## Basic stances

Although when you see tai chi being done it can look very complicated, there are in fact very few basic stances or foot positions employed. When you step from place to place during the form you are generally finishing up in one of the following positions. It is worth familiarizing yourself with these before you start on the next, instructional chapter.

### THE WIDE 70/30 STANCE

The width between the feet in the majority of stances is approximately the distance between your shoulders from tip to tip – a measurement to be known as 'shoulder-width' from here on. It is important to remember that even if you have one foot way ahead of the other, they both remain on lines that would run back directly to beneath your shoulders. It may be helpful to think of yourself standing on tram-lines (see Figure 3.2). A rather small tram, admittedly, but the principle is sound. In this stance, you will either have 70 per cent of your weight forward in the leading leg or 70 per cent behind in the rear leg – hence the term 70/30 stance. Sometimes, as you go from one movement to the next, this ratio of weight alternates between the two legs without moving the feet. The foot diagrams accompanying each sketch in the instruction section will help you to achieve the correct distribution.

A good example of a 70/30 stance can be found on page 47, the Ward Off movement. Again on pages 48–51 with the movements Grasp Bird's Tail through to Separate Hands and Push.

*Figure 3.2 Wide stance.*

*Note*: Except when you are transferring from one position to another, the front knee never extends beyond the tip of the foot. Figure 3.3 shows the right and the wrong ways of doing this. Too far forward and you are off balance.

### THE NARROW HEEL STANCE

In this position, most of your weight settles in the back foot, allowing just the front heel to make contact with the ground. In this, and the narrow toe stance mentioned next, the front foot is more or less in a line with the back heel – the ratio of weight being around 90 per cent back foot, 10 per cent front. When moving into a narrow stance it is helpful, and indeed recommended, to turn in the back foot a little at the very start, by pivoting on the heel.

*Figure 3.3 Knee over toes.*

This is not, incidentally, strictly the way Cheng Man-ch'ing taught it but is rather more in keeping with the traditional Yang style that preceded his own. This way is good for us, however, since it assists in relieving any tension felt in the knee when maintaining a narrow stance for any length of time.

A good example of a typical narrow heel stance can be found on pages 54–55 with the movement called Play Guitar.

### THE NARROW TOE STANCE

This is identical to the previous posture, only it is the toes of the leading foot that just lightly make contact with the ground. Again, the ratio is around 90/10 – and again, the back foot is adjusted before the movement to ensure that the back knee remains free of tension.

A good example of a narrow toe stance can be located on page 57 with the movement called Crane Spreads Its Wings. You can see from the foot diagram how little weight is actually in the toes (10 per cent) – just enough to be comfortable. If your balance

is particularly poor, however, you can always make this more –
around 25 per cent – until you feel more confident.

## Getting about

### ALWAYS SINK INTO THE SUBSTANTIAL LEG BEFORE STEPPING

As the tai chi steps are always slow, it is important to feel well
balanced in what is called the 'substantial' leg – the one that bears
your weight. So before stepping, bend the knee and always sink your
weight into the substantial leg, and only slowly raise the other 'empty'
foot, testing your balance all the while. That way you will be able to
lift the 'empty' foot and place it down wherever you want, gently and
under control. You should never lunge or stumble into a movement.

### STEP FORWARD HEEL FIRST; STEP BACK TOES FIRST

This is self-explanatory. Most of your steps are forward ones, in
fact, but when you do them, make sure it is your heel and not any
other part of your foot that first makes contact with the ground.
That way the knee will bend easily and naturally, permitting you
to flatten the rest of the foot onto the ground slowly. Conversely, if
you need to step backwards or put the foot down behind, do so by
making contact with the toes first.

### MOVE FROM THE CENTRE

Often in tai chi it looks as if the arms are very active, but in fact
it is the legs, the waist and the body that are doing most of the

work. This is highly characteristic of most tai chi technique. The movement begins from the centre, the Tan Tien mentioned on page 32. Be aware of this place and allow it to guide your movements like a beam of light. And keep those arms and shoulders relaxed!

It is sometimes helpful to think of the waist as a wheel – that is a wheel placed horizontally. The axis, in this sense, is the spine. As you become more confident with the tai chi movements in the next chapters, you will notice how much the waist and the centre of the body direct the movements of the limbs, hands and feet; the waist turning this way, then that, as you step and progress through the sequence.

This is not an easy concept to grasp at first when students are just starting out on learning the movements, as they tend to focus avidly on what the hands are supposed to be doing. The more confident you become with each movement, however, the more obvious it becomes that the centre of the body is the origin of just about everything in tai chi. This centre then ultimately becomes a mental space as well as a physical one: a place of inner strength and calm.

### ADJUST THE BACK FOOT AFTER STEPPING

Following most forward steps into a wide 70/30 stance, you will feel the need to pivot slightly on your back heel to find a comfortable position and to take any tension out of your knee.

Note: If you end up moving on your back toes instead of your back heel, and your back hip feels all locked up and tense, then you have most probably not stepped into a wide enough stance. Remember the tram-lines: shoulder-width apart.

## Insight
In tai chi, always strive to keep the waist flexible, so that it can turn freely and direct the movements of the arms as if from the centre of the body. Think of the Earth turning on its axis – the axis here is, of course, the spine.

Figure 3.4 Knee drifting inside substantial foot.

## KEEP THE KNEE OVER THE SUBSTANTIAL FOOT

Try not to let your knee drift inside the substantial foot (Figure 3.4 shows the right and the wrong way of doing this). If it keeps wanting to do this, you may possibly have an energy imbalance in the acu-channels that run on the inside or outside of the leg. Shiatsu or massage treatment is recommended to alleviate this.

> *The feet, legs and waist must act together simultaneously*
>
> Tai chi classics

## USE YOUR IMAGINATION

Always endeavour to project mental energy into the actions. When a hand extends outwards, for example, let the energy go with it – *think* it outwards. Also, tai chi is often best learned with the aid of imagery, some of which may sound rather bizarre at first. Stroking the pony's nose or holding a ball or throwing your fist – it may all seem a bit strange but you will find this sort of thing helpful during the early stages of learning. As you become more proficient you will, of course, be able to discard the images altogether and enjoy the beauty of the movements themselves.

### CONTINUOUS MOVEMENT

Remember, although the form is made up of separate pieces, it should be executed as one continuous, flowing sequence. Do not stop at any point. Let the hands and arms 'float' gently from one movement into the next, without pause.

Likewise try to perceive how the weight can be kept constantly moving, very gradually from one side to the next, from one foot to the other and back again. Weight distribution, hand positioning – everything always in motion, always changing and evolving from one movement into the next.

## Insight

The word 'relaxation' in tai chi has a slightly different meaning to that used here in the West. Relaxation in this context is not about putting your feet up with a nice cup of tea at the end of the day. It is rather about being upright but soft, with the feeling of all of the tendons and blood vessels of the body being free and uncongested. Relaxation means an absence of tension and negativity in our thoughts, as well. You can be relaxed in the tai chi sense and perfectly alert too.

### DIRECTIONS IN THE FOOT DIAGRAMS

At the start of the form, you face what is called 'south' – the favourite and most auspicious direction in Chinese popular culture. East is therefore on your left-hand side, west on your right. It is not necessary, of course, to line up with the actual compass direction of south, but simply decide on a point of reference before you start and call it 'south'. These imaginary cardinal points are very helpful for the purposes of conveying information from teacher to student – as will become obvious as you start to learn.

## Summary

To help you, here once again are the main points from this chapter. Keep referring to these, and keep repeating them to yourself every day while you are studying the movements. These are principles that have been handed down by tai chi practitioners through the ages. If you are handy with chisel and hammer, I suggest you carve them in stone. At the very least write them on a piece of paper and stick them on the fridge door. They are vital, *essential* to doing tai chi properly and not just going through a set of poses. (Remember, no posing!)

▶ *Relax, relax, relax the shoulders.*
▶ *Never lock the elbows or knees.*
▶ *Sink! Keep the stance low.*
▶ *Allow the spine to hang loose.*
▶ *Move from the centre.*
▶ *Keep moving at all times.*

That's it! All rather a lot to take in, especially as you are probably raring to go and get on with learning the form itself. However, you will benefit from referring back to these pages from time to time, especially if things aren't quite working out the way you expected. If you feel uncomfortable at any time, check the points above to find out why. And now you really are ready to begin.

> *The hands sweep upwards and downwards in a diagonal motion, resembling the flying pattern of a bird winging low over the banks of a river.*
>
> Da Liu, referring to Diagonal (or Slant) Flying

# 10 THINGS TO REMEMBER

1 *Relax the shoulders when you do tai chi.*

2 *Keep the elbows and knees flexible, never locked tight.*

3 *Keep a low centre of gravity, knees bent.*

4 *Try to become aware of your vital energy centre, the Tan Tien, located just beneath the navel.*

5 *The wide stance occurs frequently in the form. Make sure you understand it. Shoulder width between the feet, please, regardless of the length between your front and back foot.*

6 *The narrow stance can occur with either the front toes or the front heel in light contact with the ground. Make sure you understand that most of your weight is in the rear foot at such times.*

7 *Never bend the knee too far forward. As you look down, your front knee should not appear to extend beyond your toes.*

8 *Always sink your weight into what is called the 'substantial' leg before stepping out with the other.*

9 *Move from the centre of your body, using the rotational qualities of the waist to create the movements.*

10 *Practise continuous movement. No posing!*

# 4

# The form – part one

In this chapter you will learn:
- *to explore the first part of the tai chi form in detail*
- *to co-ordinate the movements with breathing*
- *to develop spatial awareness and balance.*

> *He who pursues Tao will decrease every day. He will*
> *decrease and continue to decrease, 'til he comes to*
> *non-action. By non-action everything can be done.*
>
> Tao Te Ching

# Step-by-step instructions

## OPENING

1   *Stand facing south, feet together, toes pointing*
    *out and the heels not quite touching. Take*
    *a moment to experience how the body feels.*
    *Tuck in the base of the spine and relax the*
    *shoulders and fingers. Make space under your*
    *arms, as if you have a small balloon under*
    *each armpit. Breathe in gently and begin.*

Note: Make sure your spine is vertical, as if
suspended from above, as illustrated on page 32.

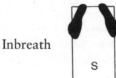

Inbreath

2   *Sink onto the right foot. Raise the left foot and place it down*
    *to the east, shoulder width from your right, the toes pointing*
    *south. Adjust your right foot so that it also*
    *points south. The feet are parallel therefore*
    *and the weight evenly distributed. The foot*
    *diagram here shows the new rectangle on*
    *which you should be standing (solid line) as*
    *well as the location of the previous rectangle*
    *(dotted line). This technique will be adopted*
    *occasionally in these pages to enable you to*
    *see major changes in position more clearly.*

50%

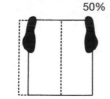

Outbreath

3 With wrists relaxed and fingers pointing
slightly downwards, allow your arms to
rise to about chest height, the forearms
parallel with the ground. Let the arms
'float' upwards – though only as far as you
can comfortably go. The shoulders should
remain still when the arms rise – one of the
ways in which tai chi teaches us to relax
and, in time, to eliminate tension from that
area altogether. The neck and shoulders
are, of course, a common place for tension
and pain to gather. Keep them relaxed!

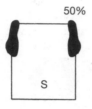

50%

S

Inbreath

4 As you breathe out, very slowly raise
and straighten your fingers so that the
tips are pointing south. Think, also, of
the wrists dropping as well as the fingers
straightening. Do this without tension.
Monitor the stiffness or otherwise of your
finger joints during this exercise. How
slowly can you move them without them
trembling or tightening up? The more
relaxed you can make your hands, the
better will be the blood supply to the joints.

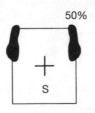

50%

S

Outbreath

5 *Draw the elbows back. Try to keep your arms away from your sides. Look at the illustration closely. See how much space there is between the elbows and the sides. Be aware, also, of the space behind, between your shoulder blades. Make sure that, in drawing the elbows back, you do not create tension in this place. Bring the elbows back only as far as is comfortable.*

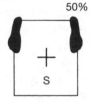

50%

Inbreath

6 *Lower your arms slowly to your sides and let your weight sink. Try to imagine roots going down into the ground from your feet. Relax the shoulders, relax the fingers and let the knees bend a little too. Try to feel a connection with the ground beneath you, but at the same time continue to imagine your body suspended – traditionally described as a 'golden thread' attached to the top of the head and going right up into the sky.*

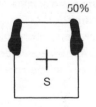

50%

Outbreath

## TURN RIGHT

1 *Sink onto the left foot and turn your waist
slowly to the west by pivoting on your right
heel. Do not lift the right heel – this is not
a step, just a turn. Simultaneously, raise
the right arm to a near vertical position
but with the wrist loose, palm down. The
left hand, meanwhile, rises as well – palm
up – to 'cup' the right elbow. The term
'cupping the elbow' should not be taken too
literally. There is plenty of space between
your upturned palm and the elbow, and the
palm is also not directly beneath it. Think
of holding a large ball and try to get the
movements of the waist and the arms to
flow smoothly together.*

90%

Inbreath

2 *Allow the right foot to go flat down and
shift your weight onto it, so that the knee
goes just over the tip of your toes as you
look down. Your right hand is at about chin
height, your eyes looking over it towards
an imaginary distant horizon. Try to feel
the ball, the ch'i connection, between your
palms. Keep the back straight.*

Note: At first, as you learn this movement,
you will need to concentrate on the hands
and feet separately, but it does not take
long before the whole thing starts to flow.
Keep trying, until all of the body feels
co-ordinated.

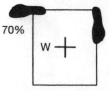

70%

W

Outbreath

## WARD OFF LEFT

1 *Here we meet with the first step into a wide
70/30 stance. Sink onto your right foot and raise
your left heel, preparing to step southwards
with your left leg. Uncurl the right hand
slightly, to show your palm to the south before
you go. Try to retain the feeling of the palms
being in communication with one another. Even
though you have let go of the ball now, imagine
it is somehow still attracted to your hands.*

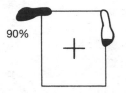

90%  Inbreath

2 *Step out south with your left heel and
bend the knee. Simultaneously, raise the
left arm into a horizontal position in
front of your chest, palm in, and drop
your right arm to your side. The surfaces
of the two palms seem figuratively to
'stroke' each other at a distance as they
go, one rising, one falling. If you have
made a proper job of this, your head, hips
and shoulders should all be facing south,
nicely squared up. If this is not the case,
and if you feel uncomfortably twisted,
refer to Chapter 3 for help and try again.*

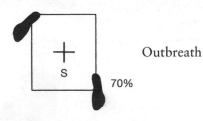

S  Outbreath

70%

## GRASP BIRD'S TAIL

1 *Sink onto your left foot and raise your right foot. At the same time allow your centre to turn slightly to your left and get your right hand to swoop around with it to 'pick up a ball' – about the size of a large beach ball – with the left hand on top, right hand underneath.*

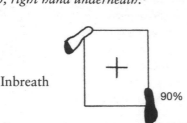

Inbreath                                90%

2 *Turn your waist and step to the west with your right heel. Bend the right knee and bring 70 per cent of your weight forward. Carry the ball with you, only imagine it getting smaller, so that your right hand finishes up at the level of your chest, the arm slanting upwards somewhat and a little out to the side, the fingers of your left hand, meanwhile, pointing towards your right palm. Finally, adjust the left foot to a comfortable position by pivoting on the heel. Your head, hips and shoulders face due west – right knee over right toes. Do not overstretch. Keep the arms in a rounded, embracing kind of aspect* Outbreath *rather than thrusting them too far ahead.*

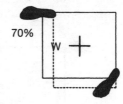

70%

## ROLLBACK AND PRESS

1 *The name of this movement is very descriptive. What happens is that you roll your hands, so that for a moment your left palm is looking up, your right looking down. Then, without moving your feet or raising your toes, you shift your weight back onto your left leg. At the same time, allow the left hand to 'cup' the right elbow – a little like you did earlier with Turn Right, but this time with the right fingers pointing upwards, palm facing south. During this movement, your centre turns very slightly to your right.*

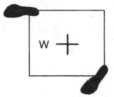

Inbreath

70%

2 *Without moving your feet, turn the waist counter-clockwise, towards the south. Open up the left shoulder and circle back with your left hand, palm up. At the same time, fold your right forearm down to a near horizontal position across your centre, palm down. Try to get a feeling for the hands moving together, even though they are quite a distance from each other, moving round with your centre.*

Inbreath finishes

90%

3   As you start to exhale, bring the
    weight forward once again into
    your right foot. Draw your left
    hand forwards and around to your
    middle as the waist itself rotates back
    towards the west. Then bring your
    palms together at about chest height
    in front of you, the heels of the palms
    themselves just lightly making contact.
    You are looking at the palm of your
    right hand and the back of your left
    hand, therefore, hips and shoulders
    facing west, right knee over right toes.

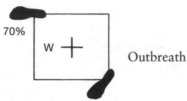

70%

W +

Outbreath

## SEPARATE HANDS AND PUSH

1   Again, the name given to this movement
    is very descriptive. What you do is simply
    separate your hands in a little swimming
    motion in front of your chest, palms down,
    and then sit back once again onto your rear
    leg. Do it slowly, trailing your right thumb
    across beneath your left palm as you separate
    the hands, and then try to imagine the lung
    energies in your chest as you breathe in.
    Keep your elbows away from your sides to
    encourage the breathing process.

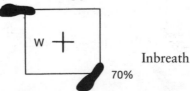

W +

Inbreath

70%

**2** *Bring the weight forward once again, right knee over right toes, and turn the palms out to create the effect of pushing forward at chest height. Don't feel that you need to thrust your arms forward to do this. You only need to turn the palms out and extend the arms a tiny bit, the rest being achieved by the forward movement of your body, created essentially from the bending of the right knee. Make sure you do not lean forward.*

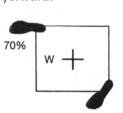

70%

w

Outbreath

## SINGLE WHIP

**1** *One of the more intricate movements of the tai chi form now follows. Firstly, sit back once again on the rear leg and turn your palms down. If you keep your arms where they are they will appear to lengthen out as a consequence of shifting your weight back, as shown in the illustration. Do not lock the elbows. The arms are straight but not rigid. And of course keep the knees relaxed, too.*

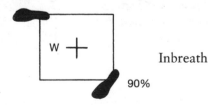

w

Inbreath

90%

**2** With most of your weight in the left foot, turn your waist counter-clockwise and pivot slowly on your right heel as you go. Your arms will naturally follow, the result being that your fingers will tend to point south-east and your feet will become slightly pigeon-toed. This may feel a little uncomfortable at first. The insides of your feet might want to curl off the ground or your knees might 'cave in'. However, because you are going to step way around to the east in a moment (see page 54), it is a good idea to get that right foot as far around as you can now, in readiness.

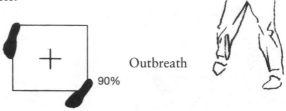

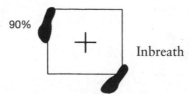

Outbreath

90%

**3** Next, transfer most of your weight back across into your right foot and allow your waist to turn again, this time slightly clockwise. Draw your right elbow across your chest and form what is called a Crane's Beak with your right hand. This is created by dropping the wrist and bunching in the fingers against the thumb – most commonly the index finger and thumb connect, as if holding a pinch of salt. The wrist relaxes into a hook shape. Also, while all this is happening, your left hand swoops down to your right hip, palm up. Imagine holding a large balloon. The fingers of the right hand hold the neck of the balloon, while the left hand supports it from underneath.

90%

Inbreath

**4** *Next, pivot on your left toes, while simultaneously projecting your Crane's Beak outwards to the south-west. The right arm goes almost straight, but make sure you do not go all the way; not so straight that the arm becomes stiff. Remember, always keep the elbows and knees soft; never lock them.*

*Note*: Although the right arm extends outwards, much of the movement is created by rotating the waist counter-clockwise. This, in turn, is guided or complemented by pivoting on the left toes. All parts of the body are connected in tai chi.

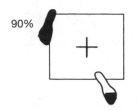

90%

Outbreath

**5** *Sink into the right foot and raise the left foot entirely now. You are about to step around to the east and it might help you if you try drawing in your left toes towards your right heel beforehand. Start to raise the left hand and keep looking at your left palm as you begin to lift it up in front of your chest. There is a big step coming up next, so make sure you are properly balanced in your right leg before committing yourself. Remember, you have lots of time – as long as it takes.*

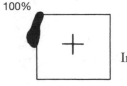

100%

Inbreath

**6** *Now take that step around. Direct the movement from your left hip – around and slightly forward so that you can place the heel down on the far corner of a new rectangle, facing east. Keep looking at your left palm, then spiral it out and around so that the left elbow finishes in a line roughly above the left knee, the fingers pressing out to the east.*
*Your hips and shoulders should also be facing roughly east, left knee over left toes. The feet are shoulder width once again – remember the tram-lines?*

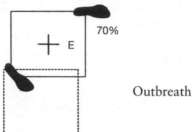

70%

Outbreath

### PLAY GUITAR

**1** *We now encounter the first narrow stance of the form. Remember, for narrow stances it is a good idea to adjust whatever foot is going to become the rear, weighted foot before you step, as clearly it would be impossible to do so once your weight is on it. So make a small adjustment now by pivoting on your left heel – not too far, but just enough to take the pressure off your knee. Then raise your right heel and pivot a little on the toes, ready to move the foot. Open your arms a little, like a bird about to flap its wings – all the while, the body is turning south and the weight transferring into your left leg.*

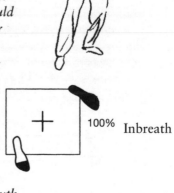

100% Inbreath

54

**2** *Draw across your right heel and place it in a narrow stance, toes pointing south and raised. The arms, meanwhile, drift in to your centre to form the typical Play Guitar shape – that is, in this case, with the right arm extended out ahead of you at about chest height, palm facing east, and the left arm a little nearer to you, the palm 'looking' at the inside of your right forearm. Keep the hands open, as if you are holding something in front of you. In other words, try to sense the ch'i between your arms.*

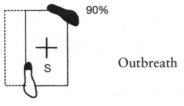

90%

Outbreath

## PULL AND STEP WITH SHOULDER

1 *Draw your right foot in closer to your left,
the toes only in contact with the ground. At
the same time lower the arms, so that your
right arm hangs almost vertically at the centre.
Still try to imagine there is a ch'i connection
between your arms and hands so that they
move together purposefully. This is a very
Yin stance and is about as close as the feet
ever get to each other in the tai chi form.*

100%

Inbreath

2 *Step out wide with your right heel, placing the
foot down, toes pointing south. Bend the right
knee and adjust your back foot a little further
towards the south-east if you wish. You'll notice
that the right arm tends to remain roughly in
the same position as with the Pull, but the body
twists slightly to lead with the outer aspect of
the right shoulder – a bit like barging down a
door. The left hand, meanwhile, rises a little to
about the height of your lower ribs, palm facing
slightly forward and down. Although this is a
wide stance, the hips and shoulders turn away
from the direction of the leading foot and finish
up facing south-east.*

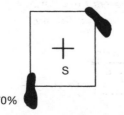

S

70%

Outbreath

## CRANE SPREADS ITS WINGS

1 *This is another narrow stance and so again it is helpful to adjust what is to become the back, weighted foot first. This time it is the right foot which is going to take the strain, so turn in the foot now. Next, rotate your centre to face the east and draw across the empty left foot to place it down in a narrow toe stance. At the same time raise your right arm, like a great wing, palm looking forward and slightly upwards, as if saluting.*

Inbreath

90%

2 *Lower your right arm, leading with the little finger side of the hand down to about hip height. Simultaneously, commence a vertical clockwise circle with your lower, left hand so that it rises and sweeps around in front of your centre. The whole thing resembles the graceful flapping of gigantic wings, like a great bird drying itself in the sunshine, head, hips and shoulders still all facing east. And that's it! It might seem like an odd place to finish but this movement, perhaps more than any other, has few apparent boundaries between itself and the one that follows.*

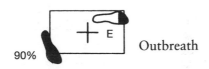

90%

Outbreath

## BRUSH LEFT KNEE AND PUSH

1  *Turn your waist clockwise, almost due south, and simultaneously circle back with your right hand at about chest height. This is a continuation of the wide circling movements of Crane. In a sense you still have wings. The palm should be facing upwards during the initial stages of this movement, rather like holding a custard pie in readiness. That might sound a bit peculiar, but it really is an accurate way of describing the orientation of the palm.*

90%    Inbreath

2  *Now, you are going to take a step forward with the left foot. It is already forward of your right foot anyway, so almost all you need to do is step sideways. The clockwise circle made with your left hand, which you commenced at the end of Crane Spreads Its Wings, continues so that the hand seems to figuratively 'brush' over the left knee toward the north, at a distance of at least six or seven inches (15 to 18 cm) between your hand and your thigh. And it is precisely as this 'brushing' of the knee occurs that you take the step with your left heel. Then the right hand comes forward, past your ear, finally to push out eastwards at about chest height.*

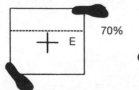

70%

Outbreath

58

## PLAY GUITAR (LEFT SIDE)

1 *Bring all your weight into the left foot and*
*allow the back foot to follow through –*
*leaving the ground and travelling forward*
*a short way. This is the first time one of*
*your feet has actually been off the ground*
*for any length of time – only for a second*
*or so, but it is a good test of how well your*
*sense of balance is progressing. Try turning*
*out the right toes a little as you do this,*
*which is good for the hip joint and ankle.*

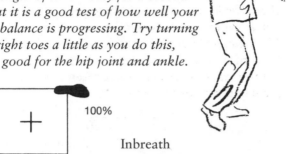

100%

Inbreath

2 *You are now going to repeat Play Guitar,*
*but on the other side, so that it is now going*
*to be the left heel touching the ground and*
*the left arm extended further from your body*
*rather than the right. Sit back and place*
*the right foot down behind, with a gentle*
*rocking back of the body westwards. Then*
*draw across your left foot into a narrow*
*heel stance, toes still pointing east, and make*
*the Play Guitar shape with your arms – left*
*arm leading, and with the palm of your*
*right hand 'looking' at the inside of your left*
*forearm.*

E Outbreath

90%

## BRUSH LEFT KNEE AND PUSH

Next in the sequence we find our first exact repetition of a movement – something you have already learned. Here, you need to repeat the section entitled Brush Knee and Push, so refer back to page 58, positions 1 and 2 for this and then simply add it to your sequence, going through it in exactly the same way as before, only of course you will begin from a left *heel* stance rather than the left *toe* stance that constituted Crane Spreads Its Wings. Don't forget to turn the waist southwards as you circle back with the palm; then step wide, 'brush' the left knee and push out with the right palm, just as before, head, hips and shoulders all facing east, left knee over left toes. Here it is again, illustrated on a smaller scale. If in any doubt, refer also to the composite illustration on pages 198–203 where the entire form is illustrated in miniature.

*Pay attention to the waist at all times.*

Tai Chi Classics

## STEP FORWARD, PARRY AND PUNCH

1   We are now embarking on a forward stepping sequence, heading
    eastwards. We do this with a 1–2–3 step; three
    movements of the feet which some students find
    helpful to count aloud while they are learning.
    Begin by shifting your weight back and turning out
    the left toes. Lower both arms to the left side and
    form a loose fist with your right hand. Then put the
    left foot flat and count aloud the number 1 at this
    point, (if it helps).

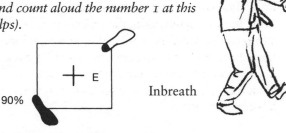

90%          Inbreath

2   With your weight in your left foot, take a step
    forward with your right and place it down at quite an angle,
    almost south. Bend the right knee and bring
    your weight forward, too. At the same time
    'throw' the fist over to your right hip, palm
    side up in readiness for the 'punch'. Count
    aloud the number 2 if it helps.

Note: It is often tempting to speed things up at
this stage. Don't. Instead, keep in touch with your
breathing and allow the movements to remain
smooth and gentle. Try to keep a low centre of
gravity as you walk: cat-like.

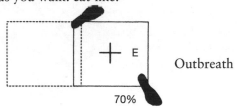

70%          Outbreath

3  Next, raise your left foot and begin to step forward straight to the east. Keep the left hand relaxed and keep the fist in readiness at your right hip. Try drawing in the left toes a little towards the right heel before stepping. Take your time during this; don't get carried away with the idea of the 'punch' you are about to deliver. Remember, the tai chi form is always done in a spirit of calm and relaxation.

Note: The left hand is not idle during all of this. Keep the palm open and soft, but allow it to follow your right fist a little, around towards the centre.

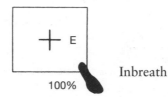

Inbreath

4  Now place the left heel down and bend the left knee, the foot facing directly east. Count aloud the number 3 if you like. At the same time, parry with your left arm or, in other words, raise the forearm to a near-vertical position in front of your body, allowing it to swing out slightly left of centre, as if deflecting an oncoming force. Then, project the fist slowly forward towards the east, finishing at about the height of the solar plexus – no higher. This is your 'punch', but do it very slowly for the duration of one whole outbreath.

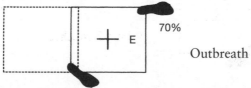

Outbreath

## RELEASE ARM AND PUSH

1 *This next movement is a little intricate
but highly beneficial for the joints of the
wrists and elbows. With a slight counter-
clockwise turning of the waist, slide the
fingers of your left hand (palm down
at first) underneath your right forearm.
Keep a little space between your hand
and forearm – no contact – and keep
those shoulders open and relaxed!*

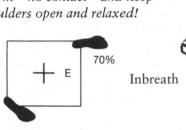

Inbreath

2 *Open the fist and turn palms up. Then,
shifting your weight back into the right
foot, draw your right arm back also,
across on top of your left forearm. The
waist turns a little clockwise as you do
this. Finally, rotate the palms inwards
and then out. Keep both feet flat on the
ground and make sure your spine remains
vertical. Do not lean back! Relax the
wrists as you rotate the hands, always
making sure the hands or the forearms
do not touch each other. Take your time,
rotating very slowly, very smoothly.*

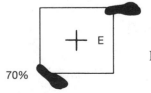

Inbreath finishes

3  Rotate the palms slowly to face outwards. Bring your weight forward once again by bending the left knee and push forward with both hands. This double-handed push is very similar to the one you did earlier (see page 50), but this time you have your left leg forward, of course, and you are facing the east. Again, your push should be no higher than the level of your chest. Keep the shoulders relaxed and the spine straight, without leaning forward.

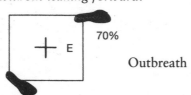

70%

Outbreath

### TURN AND CLOSE PART ONE

1  Sit back once again onto the rear foot, but this time a fraction further so that you can raise your left toes a little. Everything remains facing east at this stage – the palms still turned out, though slightly more relaxed than when they were pushing. This is a Yin, retreating movement, so let your hands reflect that quality by softening slightly and relaxing at the wrists. The aspect of the hands is, I think, a little like somebody warming their hands at the fireside.

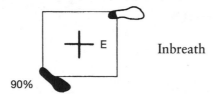

Inbreath

90%

**2** *Now, pivot on your left heel to get the toes facing south. Let your centre turn towards the south also. Once you are there, you should be starting to breathe out. Up until now the hands have remained more or less in the push position, but now they are starting to separate and move outwards from each other, initially in a wide arc but in a moment this is going to become a full circle.*

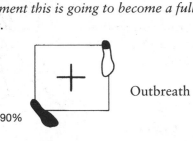

Outbreath

90%

**3** *Bring all your weight into the left leg as the hands continue to circle outwards and downwards to your sides. The hands are actually in the process of making a large circle in front of you, the right hand moving out and down to the west, clockwise, and the left hand moving out and down to the east, counter-clockwise. You should be getting to the end of your outbreath now.*

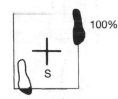

100%

Outbreath finishes

S

4   Once you feel you are properly balanced in
    your left foot, draw back the right foot to
    place it alongside, with the toes also facing
    south. The hands have reached their lowest
    point, at your sides, but with the next inbreath
    they start to rise again up through your centre,
    palms in, until they cross, left wrist resting
    upon the right, at about the height of your
    chin. The weight becomes evenly distributed
    again here at the close of Part One, and
    you should be finding a state of equilibrium
    between the two feet.

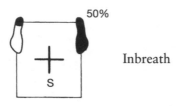

Inbreath

5   All that remains to conclude Part One is to lower your
    arms gently down through your centre to rest at your sides,
    separating naturally as they fall. Breathe
    out, sink down, relax the knees and allow
    the shoulders and fingers to relax also. If
    this is as far as you wish to go – i.e. just
    Part One – then take a few deep breaths to
    finish, experiencing how the body feels for
    a moment before moving away.

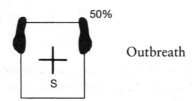

Outbreath

*Note*: If and when you proceed to Part Two, you will need to make a slight alteration to the ending of this movement. This, however, does not concern you at this stage and it will be described at the start of the next chapter.

*Reproach no man with imperfections, taught our master;*
*do you not see that he is taking the greatest trouble to make*
*progress – be it ever so little.*

Selvarajan Yesudian

# 10 THINGS TO REMEMBER

1  *Try to commit yourself to learning one whole movement each day, adding a new one each time. After a couple of weeks you will be able to go all the way through Part One of the form. Great!*

2  *Don't worry if you can't co-ordinate your movements to the breathing suggestions that accompany the illustrations. You will be flat out at first just learning where to put your feet and hands. Once you feel comfortable with each movement, however, try timing it to your natural rhythm of breathing, in and out – and see how good that feels!*

3  *Be patient. Just a little each day.*

4  *Make sure you are ready for your practice session – no full stomach, no alcohol and no anger.*

5  *Be kind to yourself. You are not stupid just because it might seem impossible to co-ordinate your hands and feet sometimes. It will all come naturally if you keep practising.*

6  *Never force your breathing into any pattern that seems uncomfortable.*

7  *Try to breathe from the 'centre' – so that the abdominal area expands very slightly as you breathe in, then relaxes back naturally as you breathe out.*

8  *Keep your arms relaxed at all times, as if floating, but stay alert!*

9  *Keep your movements flowing always one into the other, like a floating cloud or running stream, always moving. No posing!*

10  *You will naturally want to go through the movements fairly rapidly at first, but as your balance improves, try to slow down, to extend the whole of Part One so that it takes anything up to two minutes from beginning to end.*

# 5

## The form – part two

In this chapter you will learn:
- *to explore the second part of the tai chi form in detail*
- *to develop movements to the side and rear*
- *how to further relax the body through movement.*

> *Hold fast to it and you can keep it; let go and it will stray. For its comings and goings it has no time nor tide; none knows where it will bide.*

Confucius

## Step-by-step instructions

### CARRY TIGER TO MOUNTAIN

1 *From your crossed hands position at the end of Part One (top of page 66), sink onto the left leg. Then, rather than lowering your arms down to your sides to finish, as you did before, drop them down to your left side, the back of your left hand brushing, at a distance, the back of your right as you separate the hands at*

waist height. Raise the right heel and
pivot a little on the toes, allowing the
waist to commence its turn clockwise,
in readiness for a big step around to the
north-west. Then slowly raise the left
hand, palm up, to shoulder height.

90%

Inbreath

2  Step around with your right foot to place it down, heel first,
towards the north-west. At the same time, 'brush' the right knee
with your right palm and bring the left hand around above it.
Bring your weight into the right leg by bending the knee and
finally turn your right palm up, as if supporting
a large ball, the left hand on top, head, hips and
shoulders all facing north-west.

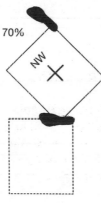

70%

NW

Outbreath

## DIAGONAL ROLLBACK AND PRESS, DIAGONAL SEPARATE HANDS AND PUSH, DIAGONAL SINGLE WHIP

If you think of the tai chi form as a piece of music, then what comes next could be termed 'The Chorus' – that is, a sequence of movements that you have already learned in Part One and which you will find repeated three more times here in Part Two. The Chorus normally consists of the movements Grasp Bird's Tail through to Single Whip – already shown on pages 48–54 – although here, just in this particular instance, we do actually omit Grasp Bird's Tail (think of the Carry Tiger to Mountain as a replacement for it) and begin the whole sequence with Rollback and Press, which is what comes next.

You can slip into Rollback quite easily from the previous position by simply sitting back onto your rear leg, raising the right arm and 'cupping' the elbow with your left hand – everything the same as the Rollback and Press in Part One (see page 49) only facing north-west now instead of west. Continue with Separate Hands and Push, still on the diagonal, and finally the Single Whip. The whole diagonal sequence is illustrated here in miniature, but if in any doubt about how to do these movements, refer to pages 48–54 for instructions. The composite illustration on pages 198–203 will also show you how these movements fit into the context of the whole tai chi form.

At the conclusion of your Diagonal Single Whip you will, of course, be facing south-east instead of east. The foot diagram given here indicates where you should be. Head, hips and shoulders are facing south-east, left knee over left toes.

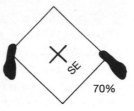

70%

### FIST UNDER ELBOW

1  *You are now going to get yourself back onto the east/west axis with some neat footwork. In all, there are just three*

*movements of the feet and it might help you to count them out loud, just as I suggested earlier with Step Forward, Parry and Punch.*

*Following the Diagonal Single Whip, sit back onto your right leg and open up the hands in a relaxed fashion. Pivot on your empty left heel and point your left toes to the east. Let the foot go flat on the ground and count the number 1 out loud.*

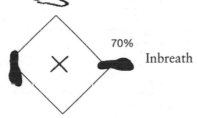

70%  Inbreath

2 Next, *with all your weight now in the left foot, slowly draw up your right foot alongside it, with the toes pointing outwards. If it helps, count aloud the number 2 as your weight flows into the right side. At the same time your arms drop and then circle round to your left side, covering your centre. Your inbreath is coming to a conclusion now.*

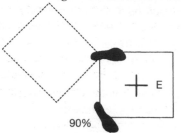

Inbreath finishes

90%

3 *Bring all your weight into your right foot and slide forward and inwards with your left foot to form a narrow heel stance to the east, counting aloud the number 3. Simultaneously, project your left arm forward, almost 'threading' it through the palm of your right hand. Finally, make the right hand into a loose fist that settles just beneath and slightly to the inside of your left elbow, abdomen height. By this time your head, hips and shoulders should all be facing east. Let your eyes settle upon an imaginary distant horizon, looking over the tips of your left fingers, and make sure your right wrist is relaxed.*

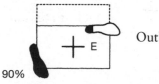

Outbreath

90%

## REPULSE MONKEY (RIGHT SIDE)

1   With your weight still in the back leg, let go of your fist and turn
up the left palm. There is a little story attached to this sequence
that assists in memorizing the actions. Imagine you are face to
face with a monkey (the monkey is in fact a much-respected
deity in parts of the Orient and

is a creature credited with much
wisdom as well as playfulness). You
are going to offer him some food
in the palm of your left hand. This
is the 'purpose' of turning the left
palm up. At the same time circle
your right palm back, rather like
you did at the beginning stages of
Brush Knee and Push.

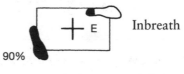

Inbreath

90%

2   Raise your left foot and draw it back. You are actually in the
process of stepping backwards here as
the monkey advances to take the food. The
right palm, in the meantime, has rotated
and is beginning to face forward. As the
foot continues to go back, allow the left
hand to drop, very slowly towards your
left hip, keeping the palm open and relaxed
and the elbow out, away from your ribs.

Inbreath finishes

100%

**3** Place the left foot down behind you, making contact with the toes first. Withdraw your left hand entirely now, down to the level of your waist, just as the monkey is coming to grab the food. The right palm meanwhile has just passed your ear and has advanced forward to push the monkey's nose away. The left leg stepping back and the right palm pushing forward all take place at the same time and are, therefore, completely co-ordinated. Finally, adjust your right foot by pivoting on your right heel so that the toes face east. Though most of your weight is in the back leg, both feet are actually flat on the ground.

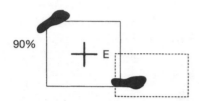

90%

E

Outbreath

## REPULSE MONKEY (LEFT SIDE)

**1** You are now going to repeat the whole Repulse Monkey routine once again, but this time starting with the right foot and the right palm forward, so that you will eventually step back onto your right foot. Begin by 'offering the food' by turning your right palm up. The left palm meanwhile starts its circle back, palm up, behind your left shoulder.

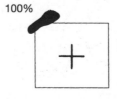

100%

Inbreath

**2** *Just like before, you step back, toes first, this time with the
right foot and at the same time withdraw your right palm
down to the level of your waist. The left palm
then circles forward to push the monkey's
nose away again, just as he is about to seize
the food. Finally, adjust the front foot by
pivoting on the heel. The left toes, head, hips
and shoulders are all facing east.*

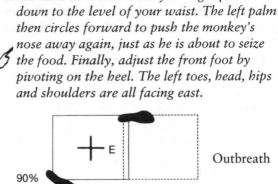

90%

Outbreath

### *REPULSE MONKEY (RIGHT SIDE)*

Continue the sequence by repeating the first Repulse Monkey (Right
Side) again, as explained in detail on pages 75–6. The only difference
is that this time your left foot starts off from a position flat on the
ground. Here it is again, illustrated on a smaller scale – stepping back
with the left foot; withdrawing the right hand; pushing the monkey's
nose with the right palm and straightening the right foot at the end by
pivoting on the heel.

## DIAGONAL FLYING

1   *With most of your weight in the left foot, turn the waist counter-clockwise and allow your right heel to follow – this relieves any strain that might result in the right knee from turning the body away from it. Form a ball, left hand on top, palm down; right hand supporting underneath, palm up. Sink well down into the left foot and prepare to raise the right.*

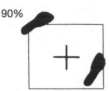

90%

Inbreath

2   *Lift your right foot from the ground, turn the waist clockwise and direct your right hip way around, so that you can put your right heel down with the toes pointing as near south-west as possible. This is another one of those big steps, like Carry Tiger to Mountain, and it is vital, therefore, as soon as the weight starts to shift into the right foot, that you adjust the rear, left, foot to a comfortable angle by pivoting on the heel. The arms, meanwhile, separate out, with the right arm 'flying' around to the south-west in a slanting-upwards aspect and the left hand sinking down to the left hip, slightly backward facing.*

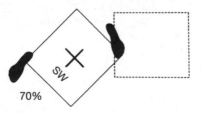

SW

Outbreath

70%

## CLOUDY HANDS (INTRODUCTION)

1  We are now embarking on a really classic set of movements –
Cloudy Hands (sometimes also called 'Wave Hands Like
Clouds'). The first thing to do is to re-align yourself with the
east/west axis and to do this you simply draw up the rear (left)

foot. It is important that it is placed down
a good distance from your right, however;
something in the order of between one and a
half to double shoulder width. At the same
time, keep your weight flowing into the right
leg and sweep your left hand round and
beneath your right hand.

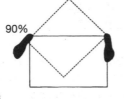

90%                                          Inbreath

2  Start to shift your weight into the left leg and change the
hands over; that is, lower the right hand down and slightly
outwards to hip level while simultaneously raising the left

hand to about shoulder level. The left
hand rises inside the right – or in other
words, closer to your body than the
right. The actions of the hands are
very soft – like describing the shapes
of billowing clouds in the air.

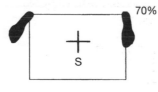

70%

S                 Outbreath

## CLOUDY HANDS (LEFT)

1  With most of your weight now in the left leg, pivot on your
   right heel so that the toes point south.
   The feet are therefore parallel. At the same
   time, draw your right palm around to face
   inwards to your centre, at about abdomen
   height. Your left palm should also be facing
   in by this stage, at about the height of your
   throat, in a line above your right hand.
   You can be commencing your inbreath at
   this point.

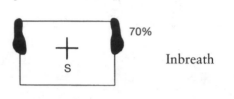

70%

Inbreath

2  Next, turn the waist counter-clockwise, bringing the arms
   around with your centre, and form a ball with the hands.
   Your weight will naturally want to concentrate in the left foot
   as you do this. Keep the knees apart, as if sitting on a horse,
   but make sure they remain flexible. Also, make sure that your
   hips (and therefore the arms, too) turn
   only as far as you naturally feel they
   want to go. If you sense the muscles
   in your waist and back knotting up
   or your knees caving in towards each
   other, then you have gone too far.
   Try to maintain a rounded appearance
   at all times.

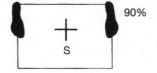

90%

Inbreath
finishes

**3** *Now empty the right foot entirely and bring it inwards towards the left, closing in to about shoulder width. At the same time change the hands over, by bringing the right hand*

*up to shoulder height and letting the left hand fall to about hip height. As with the previous change of hands (see page 79), it is the lower hand which rises inside the upper hand, or in other words the right hand rises closer to your side than the left. Think of the top hand pushing out a little to the east to make room for it.*

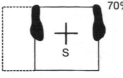

70%

Outbreath

## CLOUDY HANDS (RIGHT)

**1** *You next repeat the sequence on the other side. So rotate your waist back to face south and position your hands as before,*

*though this time with the right hand facing in at throat level, the left hand beneath it, facing in at abdomen level. Again, try to direct the movements of the arms via the waist and make sure those knees remain apart! The free turning of the waist is the key to these movements and is probably why Cloudy Hands is considered to be so beneficial in terms of aiding the digestive organs.*

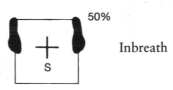

50%

Inbreath

2 Keep turning the waist clockwise as far as you can comfortably go and form a ball with the hands again, this time with the right hand on top, left hand underneath. Most of your weight will want to settle in the right leg as you go. Keep your waist and diaphragm – the large muscle under the ribs that assists in breathing – as relaxed as possible during these movements. If necessary, take time off and gently press your finger tips under and around the lower rib cage and abdomen to help loosen things. Gently please! Don't prod, just press lightly. Then return to the movement and see if it feels any different.

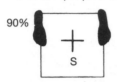

90%

Inbreath finishes

3 Empty the left foot entirely and step with it away from your right foot – i.e. eastwards – settling at about one and a half to double shoulder-width distance, the toes still continuing to point south. At the same time change hands again, this time by bringing the left hand up to shoulder height and letting the right hand fall to about hip height. And again, if it helps, think of the top hand pushing out a little to the west to make room for the lower one to rise in its place.

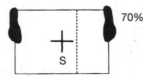

70%

Outbreath

## CLOUDY HANDS (LEFT INTO WHIP)

1   *Although Cloudy Hands Left has been illustrated before (see pages 80–81), we are going to look at it again here because at*

*the end of it there is an important variation with which we gain access to the next movement. So turn your centre to face south and position the hands as before – left hand on top, throat height, right hand underneath, abdomen height.*

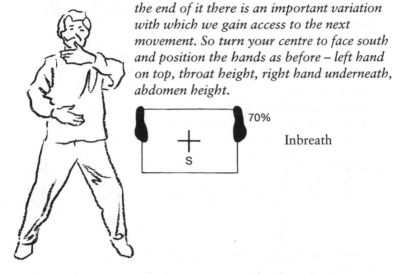

70%

Inbreath

2   *Keep turning the waist counter-clockwise, again as far as you can comfortably go. Form a ball with the hands, left hand on top. Most of your weight will want to settle in the left leg, as*

*before. Through all these movements, just let the hands 'float'. Imagine your forearms and hands have become feather-like, gently undulating through the air, or cloud-like, soft, graceful and rounded. Imagine your internal energy is holding the arms up, rather than muscle power.*

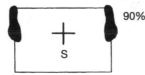

90%

Inbreath finishes

3 *Now to conclude the sequence. At this point you are, of course, in the position where you are ready to step and change once again. But this time as you change you do not step in with your right foot but forwards, just half a pace. Then, as you change, and as you draw up that right hand, you do so with it shaped into a Crane's Beak – the same hook shape that you used in the Single Whip earlier. You have, in fact, broken half-way into what is to become a Single Whip; so the left palm will want to turn up as well in readiness for the completion of the movement to the east, which is precisely what happens next.*

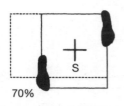

Outbreath

70%

## ISOLATED SINGLE WHIP

1 *From the previous position, which left you in the process of exiting from Cloudy Hands, you continue by emptying the left foot and raising it from the ground. Breathe in and start to be aware of the step you are going to take towards the east. Look at your left palm.*

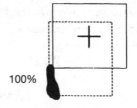

100%     Inbreath

**2** *Finish off this isolated Single Whip ('isolated' because it occurs outside the context of 'The Chorus') by placing the left heel down to the east and bringing up the left hand to point the fingers east. Make sure you have stepped into a proper 70/30 stance. Bend the left knee and adjust the right heel to*

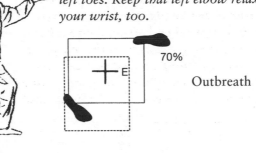

*a comfortable position, head, hips and shoulders all facing east, left knee over left toes. Keep that left elbow relaxed and your wrist, too.*

70%

Outbreath

## SNAKE CREEPS DOWN

**1** *This movement – a classical piece much beloved by painters and sculptors – is sometimes called a Squatting Single Whip because your Crane's Beak, left over from the Single Whip, remains intact throughout. To begin, you will need to create a bit more length between your feet. So slide or shuffle (depending on the kind of surface you're on) back a little with your right foot and turn on your heel to get your right toes*

*pointing back towards the south-west. Then pivot on your left heel and get your left toes pointing in, roughly to the south-east. As your inbreath finishes start to sink back and downwards, squatting onto your right foot. Keep that right arm extended.*

Inbreath

90%

**2** *Breathe out and continue sinking back. The left hand meanwhile is drawn in towards your chest, the fingers close together. Keep it going, on down through your centre, dipping in a great arc to the floor, almost scraping the ground at its lowest point and then on forward towards your left foot – by now with the palm facing south. Then, as it brushes past your left foot, not touching it, it is as though it pushes the left foot straight – the foot turning back on its heel to point the toes due east once again.*

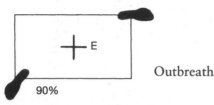

Outbreath

90%

### GOLDEN PHEASANT (RIGHT SIDE)

**1** *Now here is a test for your balance. Here you actually raise the insubstantial leg right off the ground. The whole movement emulates the proud actions of a cock bird. Firstly, however, you need to extricate yourself from Snake Creeps Down and it is surprising how many people have problems with this. Follow these simple steps.*

Bring your right foot back to its comfortable, south-east facing position. Turn out the left foot by pivoting on your left heel, then bring the weight slowly forward and bend your left knee. From here come up into the one-legged posture of Golden Pheasant.

70%

Inbreath

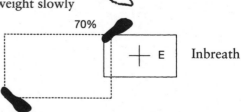

2 So, *now straighten the body and draw up the right knee and right hand, fingers pointing up. Think of a cock bird, standing on one leg. This is very much a contrast to the downward, mysterious Snake we encountered just a moment ago. Here everything is very 'up front' and showy. If at first you have trouble balancing, don't worry. Just keep your toe in contact with the ground. As long as you at least try to bring your focus of balance into the substantial leg, and as long as you can raise your right heel from the ground, you will have made a good start. Gradually, your balance will improve.*

100%

+ E    Inbreath finishes

## GOLDEN PHEASANT (LEFT SIDE)

1  *You are now about to reverse the previous posture. Start by placing your right foot down with the toes pointing south-east and then transfer all your weight into it. At the same time allow the right arm to fall naturally to your side. Do this very slowly, under control. If you feel you have to lunge or stumble down, then you are not cultivating the right degree of balance. Keep it smooth!*

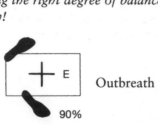

Outbreath

2  *Slowly raising the left knee and left arm, you next perform the same actions, emulating the cock bird, but this time on the other side. Try a very subtle scuffing of the ground with your toes as they come up – just like the cock bird, if you care to watch him sometime. Really try to evoke the spirit of the creature. Be part of it.*
*Also, I sometimes ask my students to think of a Swiss penknife when they practise this movement. This is because the leg and arm should be aligned in one plane, i.e. the hand, elbow, knee, shin and foot all with their leading edges facing due east.*

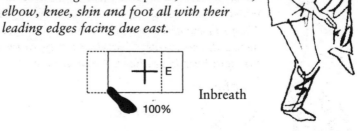

Inbreath

## PAT THE HORSE (RIGHT)

1 *Place your left foot down slightly behind you, toes first, and allow your centre to rotate naturally towards the leading foot, i.e. south-east. At the same time imagine you have a horse* 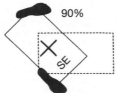 *or – more accurately, I always think – a pony there at your side. Place your right hand on his neck and hold an apple for him to eat in your left palm. This will get you more or less into the correct position – though in practice, you should eventually be aiming to make the movement more flowing, with the left palm sliding down along the right forearm somewhat as you sweep up and across with the right hand.*

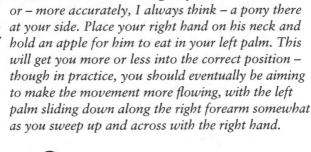

90%

Outbreath

## KICK WITH RIGHT TOES

1 *Further one-legged action here, with the first of two toe kicks. First, however, you need to gather your arms into a crossed*  *'X'-shape which will then separate out, forwards and backwards, just before you kick. To do this, turn on your right heel to go very slightly pigeon-toed. Your centre now faces north-east. Next, lower the right hand and place the right wrist underneath your left at about abdomen height. Then roll the wrists up, so that the palms face outwards (north-east). Simultaneously, draw up the right knee in readiness for your kick.*

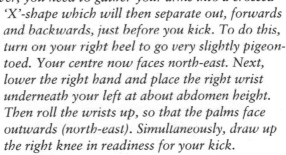

90%

Inbreath

**2** Separate the hands – the right hand going forwards, south-east, and the left hand going back behind, travelling in a great arc, finishing at shoulder height. Then straighten the rest of your leg and make a kicking motion with your right toes, out towards the south-east in a line with your right arm. The height of this kick is not important. But do draw up the knee before you kick and only bring it up as high as is realistic and comfortable for you. If you bring it up too high, you will tend to fall back as you complete the kick.

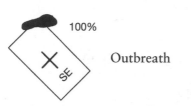

100%

Outbreath

## PAT THE HORSE (LEFT)

**1** You are now going to pat the horse again, only this time with your left hand. But first, directly following the kick and with the knee still up, you need to take an inbreath and let the shin drop into a relaxed position. Your palms tend to face in towards each other at this stage, in preparation for the next move. This pattern of breathing in directly after a kick and prior to the next Yang movement is typical of the tai chi form.

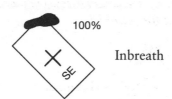

100%

Inbreath

2  Place the right heel down, again facing south-east and a little ahead of your left foot. The pony has moved around to your left side this time so, as you put the foot down, it is your left hand that you place on the pony's neck while the right hand, palm up, is the one that holds the apple. Again, once you have learned the basic 'nuts and bolts' of this manoeuvre, try to get the hands to flow more gracefully, with the right palm loosely sliding – at a distance – along the edge of the left forearm as it comes back and down to your centre, both hands moving in graceful, continuous arcs, the fingers relaxed.

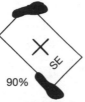

90%    Outbreath

## KICK WITH LEFT TOES

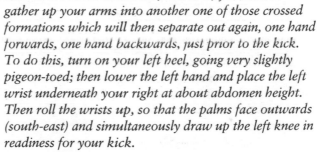

1  Step up with your left foot alongside your right and start thinking in terms of a toe kick, rather like the one you did before but this time to the north-east. First, however, you need to gather up your arms into another one of those crossed formations which will then separate out again, one hand forwards, one hand backwards, just prior to the kick. To do this, turn on your left heel, going very slightly pigeon-toed; then lower the left hand and place the left wrist underneath your right at about abdomen height. Then roll the wrists up, so that the palms face outwards (south-east) and simultaneously draw up the left knee in readiness for your kick.

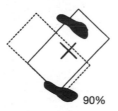

Inbreath

90%

2  *Separate the hands, with the left
   hand going forwards, north-east,
   and the right hand travelling
   back behind. Then draw up
   the rest of your leg and make a
   very slow, gentle and controlled
   kicking motion with your left
   toes out towards the north-east.*

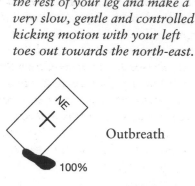

Outbreath

100%

## TURN AND KICK WITH THE SOLE

1  *This is a movement that can seem quite tricky when you first
   encounter it but it is – like most tai chi movements – 99 per
   cent practice. You are going to turn around to the west on the
   heel of your right foot whilst keeping the left
   foot entirely off the ground. That successfully
   completed, you finish by kicking out to the
   west with the left foot. Here's how.*

   *After the previous position, do not put the left
   foot down at all. Instead, just lower the shin
   into a vertical position. Drop the arms also,
   the left arm vertical through the middle of the
   body, the right just outside your right thigh.
   Then using the momentum of your left leg
   and right arm, turn counter-clockwise on your
   right heel so that the right toes face north-west.*

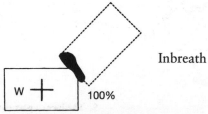

Inbreath

W  100%

2 Now gather up the hands in that by now familiar 'X' shape. Sources differ as to which wrist crosses which at this stage but I prefer to allow the right wrist to cross naturally over the left

during the course of the turn. Then raise the arms so that the palms turn out northwards. Separate the hands again – left hand westward, right hand back behind you – and then kick, as slowly as you can, with the sole of the left foot out to the west. Don't rush into this. Make sure you have turned successfully and have settled down in your right leg first. For an easier alternative to this turn, see page 138).

Outbreath

## BRUSH LEFT KNEE AND PUSH

1 We have encountered this movement before, in Part One. However, it is illustrated again here since the lead-in to it is

slightly different – for one thing, the left foot is above the ground. After the kick, drop the shin, keeping the thigh horizontal. Take an inbreath, then bring back the left arm above your knee – the appearance here being, for a moment, not unlike another Golden Pheasant. The right hand, however, is behind you, not at your side; and it turns, palm up, in readiness to push forward to the west.

Inbreath

**2** *Commence your exhalation and place the heel down, under control, ahead of your right foot and shoulder width from it. Bend the left knee to bring the weight forward as you push out with the right palm at about chest height to the west. At the same time the left hand will brush the left knee – see page 58 for a view of how this looks from the other side.*

Note: It is important not to stumble or fall into this movement. Always take that inbreath and prepare (Yin) before placing the left foot down slowly and deliberately completing the movement (Yang).

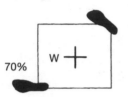

70%    W      Outbreath

## BRUSH RIGHT KNEE AND PUSH

**1** *Sit back, turn out the left toes by pivoting on the heel. Relax the right hand by turning the palm down somewhat and turn the left palm upwards, so that the hands form a kind of diagonal ball. Breathe in and start to turn your centre counter-clockwise. Let the left hand circle back, still with the palm up. This is, as you have probably guessed, going to be a mirror image of the previous movement. So prepare to step forward with the right foot.*

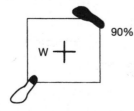

90%    W      Inbreath

**2** Step straight ahead with the right heel to the west and brush the right knee with the right palm, i.e. travelling in a northerly direction. Bring your left hand forward past your ear and then push out with the palm to the west, chest height, as you bend the right knee and bring your weight forward, head, hips and shoulders all facing west, right knee over right toes.

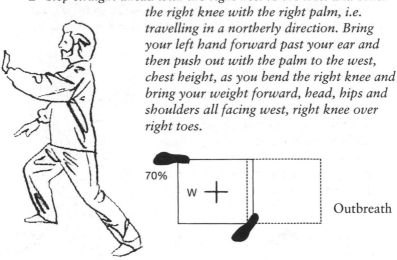

Outbreath

## BRUSH LEFT KNEE AND PUNCH LOW

**1** For the next movement, you are going to take another step forward, employing the same style of footwork – that is, turning out what is to become the back foot before stepping forward and so on. This is very similar to Brush Left Knee and Push, except that you do not push out with the right hand at the end but instead very slowly punch low with your right fist.

Begin, then, by sitting back once again and turning out the right toes by pivoting on the heel. Make a loose fist with your right hand and circle it out to your right side.

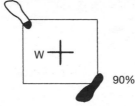

Inbreath

**2** *Place your left foot forward, pointing west and, if you like, drawing in the left toes towards the right foot a little first. At the same time, brush your left knee with your left palm and bring your weight forward by bending your left knee. Allow your body weight to sink down at this point, really low. As this occurs, spiral your right fist down diagonally to about knee height in a slow punching action which finishes with the thumb side of your fist uppermost.*

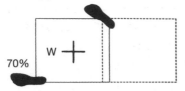

70%

Outbreath

### GRASP BIRD'S TAIL

**1** *We are now about to step into our third Chorus, this time beginning with Grasp Bird's Tail. The lead-in to it is slightly different from what we have met with before. We do start, however, with that by now familiar preparation of sitting back momentarily and turning out what is to become the back foot – i.e. pivoting on the left heel to get the toes out – and then bringing all of the weight into it. Allow the waist to follow, turning slightly counter-clockwise, and then pick up a ball, swooping under with the right hand to support the ball from beneath.*

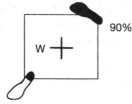

90%

Inbreath

2 *Now step forward with the right heel and bend the knee. At the same time, raise the right hand up to the level of your chest, the arm slanting upwards slightly, and position your left hand so that the fingers are pointing towards the right palm, adjusting the left foot to a comfortable position by pivoting on the heel afterwards. This turning in of the back foot by*

*pivoting on the heel is something you should always aim for when you complete a forward step into a wide stance, even if only a tiny bit. The ease or otherwise with which you can do this often depends on how well you have set up the step – i.e. how far you originally turned out the back toes before stepping.*

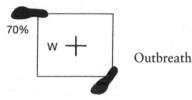

70%

Outbreath

## ROLLBACK AND PRESS, SEPARATE HANDS AND PUSH, SINGLE WHIP

Continuing with your Chorus, repeat once again the familiar sequence already learned, Rollback and Press through to Single Whip. Again, refer to pages 49–54 if in any doubt about how to do these. The movements are illustrated here on a smaller scale, and you can, of course, also refer to the composite illustration on pages 198–203 if in any doubt about how everything fits together into the overall sequence of the form.

The conclusion of the Single Whip will take you into a wide 70/30 stance, facing east, of course (see overleaf). And it is from here that you will take up our instructions once again.

## FOUR CORNERS (FIRST)

1  *Four Corners is a lengthy sequence composed of four separate movements, all similar but performed in different directions. Throughout, we will be using diagonals so each movement finishes facing a 'corner'. To begin the first corner, sit back on your right leg and pivot on your left heel, to go slightly pigeon-toed. Allow your left hand to drop and drift to your centre, palm facing in and slightly upward.*

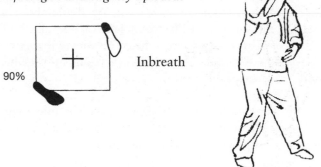

90%   Inbreath

**2** *Relax the right elbow and let go of the Crane's Beak in your right hand. Bring your weight into the left foot and take a short step with the right, placing it down heel first, toes pointing west. Allow your centre to turn naturally towards the south-west as you do this. By now the left hand is almost 'cupping' the right elbow.*

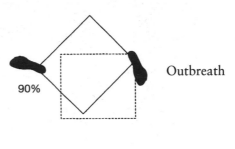

90%

Outbreath

**3** *Raise the left foot and prepare to step out towards the south-west.*

Note: Before doing this, do make sure you sink strongly into your substantial leg. This will give you stability: a much-needed advantage when performing the movements that are to follow.

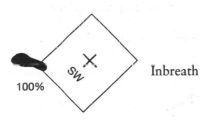

100%

SW

Inbreath

4  Place the left foot down heel first, to the south-west, and
as you bend the knee, spiral out with the hands so that the
left hand rises up to about head height, while the right hand
'pushes' slightly upwards and forwards at about chest height.
The right hand is central, in front of your
chest, while the left hand is somewhat off
centre. Allow your waist to turn naturally
towards your leading leg as the weight goes
forward, head, hips and shoulders all facing
south-west, left knee over left toes.

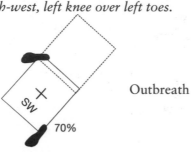

Outbreath

70%

## FOUR CORNERS (SECOND)

1  For the second corner we have to execute a
large, three-quarters turn, clockwise, around to
the south-east. To begin, transfer your weight
to the rear leg; sit back and relax. Draw in your
arms and turn the hands inwards. There are
many variations on how the hands are placed at
this point, but in the illustration my left palm is
'looking' at my left shoulder, with my right palm
in the centre, tummy height, palm up – almost
cupping the left elbow. At this point, with most
of your weight in that rear leg, pivot on your
left heel to get your left toes as far around
to the north as is comfortable.

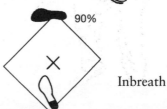

90%

Inbreath

**2** *Now transfer your weight into your left foot, sink into it and then pivot on the toes of your right foot, so that it too points*

*in a northerly direction. This movement, and the others like it in the Four Corners sequence, is excellent for the ankles. It may take you some time to loosen up sufficiently to get these turns smooth, but it is well worth the effort. Don't forget those warm-up exercises on page 25 to get the ankle joints loose before you start.*

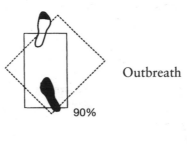

Outbreath

90%

**3** *With your weight now entirely in the left foot, start to think in terms of stepping towards the south-east by turning your eyes*

*in that direction. Raise the right foot and turn the right hip out, ready to step with your right heel. Your palms at this stage are starting to think about spiralling outward.*

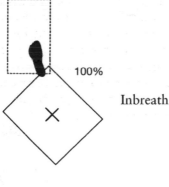

100%

Inbreath

**4** *Place the right foot down to the south-east, heel first, and bring your weight forward by bending the knee. Adjust the rear foot as soon as possible by pivoting on the heel, so that your back knee feels comfortable. At the same time spiral out with your hands, so that the right hand rises up to head height while the left hand 'pushes' slightly upwards and forwards at about chest height. The left hand is central, in front of your chest, while the right hand is somewhat off centre. Allow your waist to turn naturally towards your leading leg as the weight goes forward, head, hips and shoulders all facing south-east, right knee over right toes.*

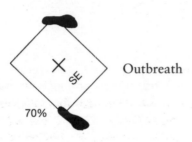

Outbreath

70%

## FOUR CORNERS (THIRD)

1  *The stepping routine for the third corner is somewhat less complex. First of all, sit back onto the rear foot and relax the hands, letting them turn slightly inwards. The left hand begins to 'cup' the right elbow while the right hand 'looks' towards the left shoulder. Begin to raise the right foot and look towards the north-east.*

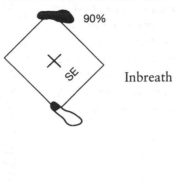

90%

SE

Inbreath

2  *Place the right foot down in front of your left foot. This might feel as if the right foot has stepped across the left, but in fact it is merely in front of it. Don't compress the groin area too much. Once done, slowly bring most of your weight into the right foot. This is a movement that helps work the inner aspect of the leg, especially if you keep your right foot pointed out. It is also beneficial for the hip joint. But don't strain, and make sure the feet are not too close together.*

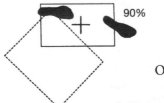

90%

Outbreath

**3** *With the next inhalation, raise the left foot and prepare to step with it towards the north-east. Sink entirely onto your right foot to do this.*

*Note*: Although the arms and elbows are fairly close in to your body at this point, do make sure – as always – that they are not touching the body. Keep a rounded aspect to the arms, even here, and allow the breath and the ch'i to move freely.

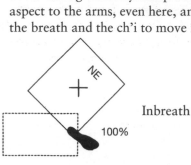

Inbreath

100%

**4** *Continue by stepping out to the north-east with your left foot, heel first. Bring your weight forward and make any necessary adjustment to the right heel. At the same time spiral out with the hands, lifting the left palm to about head height while pushing out and slightly upwards from the centre with your right palm at about chest height. The right hand is central, in front of your chest, while the left hand is somewhat off centre. Allow your waist to turn naturally towards your leading leg as the weight goes forward. Head, hips and shoulders all facing north-east, left knee over left toes.*

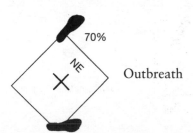

70%

Outbreath

## FOUR CORNERS (FOURTH)

1 For your fourth and final corner, you have to take the long
way around again for another three-quarters
turn, clockwise, to finish north-west. So once
again, begin by sitting back onto your rear leg and
relaxing the arms. Again, the hands turn inwards
slightly as the right hand begins to 'cup' the left
elbow, left palm looking in towards the right
shoulder. Transfer your weight into your rear leg,
then pivot on your left heel to get your left toes as
far around to the south as is comfortable.

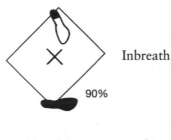

Inbreath

90%

2 Transfer your weight into your left foot, sink into it and then
pivot on the toes of your right foot so that it too points in a
southerly direction.

Note: Movements such as you find here in Four
Corners really encourage us to let go of tension
in the lower abdomen and groin area, due to
the constant opening up and directing of the
hips, a place where energy sometimes becomes
congested through emotional or deep-seated
psychological difficulties.

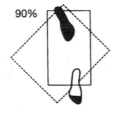

90%

Outbreath

3  Breathe in and sink entirely into your left
   foot. Start to think in terms of stepping
   towards the north-west now, by turning
   your eyes in that direction. Raise the right
   foot and turn the right hip out, ready to
   step. Always test your balance before raising
   the foot – you have plenty of time with this
   manoeuvre.

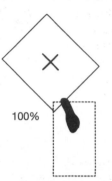

100%   Inbreath

4  Now place the right foot down to the north-west, heel first,
   and bring your weight forward. Adjust the rear foot as soon as
   possible. At the same time, spiral out with your hands, lifting
   the right palm up to head height and pushing slightly forwards
   and upwards from the centre with the left palm, at about chest
   height. The left hand is central, in front
   of your chest, while the right hand is
   somewhat off centre. Allow your waist to
   turn naturally towards your leading leg
   as the weight goes forward. Head, hips
   and shoulders all face north-west, right
   knee over right toes. And that concludes
   the Four Corners sequence.

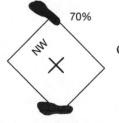

70%

NW

Outbreath

## WARD OFF LEFT

After your fourth and final corner you simply need to step southward
once again. This is achieved with a repetition of a movement you
learned in Part One (see page 47) – Ward Off. It is illustrated
again here on a smaller scale. The only difference is that you are

approaching it from a slightly different
direction this time, from the north-west
rather than simply west, but it doesn't
matter. Just relax the arms, sit back
onto your left leg and pivot a little on
your right heel to begin. Then shift
your weight entirely into your right leg
and step south. The rest is the same as
described on page 47.

## GRASP BIRD'S TAIL, ROLLBACK AND PRESS, SEPARATE HANDS AND PUSH, SINGLE WHIP

After Ward Off Left, you continue with another Chorus, the final
one. So you have a Chorus either side of the Four Corners sequence
(like bookends). Still exactly the same as described on pages 48–54,
and illustrated here once more on a smaller scale.

At the conclusion of these movements, you should be in a wide 70/30 stance, facing east, ready to continue with what comes next.

### SNAKE CREEPS DOWN

After your final Chorus, you continue by simply repeating Snake Creeps down once again.

Refer to pages 85–86 for detailed instructions and to remind yourself of just how this movement goes. Squat down with your outbreath, without straining or feeling tense. Then at the conclusion of the movement, let go of the Crane's Beak, turn out the left toes and come up with your next natural inhalation, preparing for the next movement.

## STEP FORWARD TO SEVEN STARS

1  With the left foot turned out to provide a broad base, raise
   the right foot and prepare to step forward into a narrow toe
   stance towards the east. Your hands are
   drawn up in front of you and your right
   hand is just beginning to form itself into a
   loose fist.

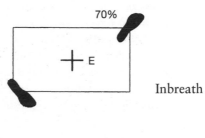

70%

+E

Inbreath

2  Make loose fists now with both hands and complete your
   narrow toe stance with the right foot. As you go, allow the
   wrists to cross, left wrist resting on top of the right, and rotate
   them so that the knuckle side of the hands are turned towards
   you. This rolling motion of the wrists feels
   particularly good, as it accompanies the upward
   and forward movement of the body. It is as if
   your entire body energy is being focused in that
   small rotation at the end.

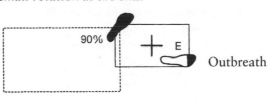

90%

+E

Outbreath

## STEP BACK TO RIDE THE TIGER

1   *Step back with your right toes. Then bring all your weight into the right foot and settle down. While this is happening, your hands separate and the right hand, after dropping a little, spirals out around in a wide arc to the side of the head in a movement that looks, just for an instant, a little like Crane Spreads Its Wings. The left hand, meanwhile, lowers diagonally to a position just left of centre, hip height. As the weight sinks into the right foot, straighten the left foot by raising it very slightly to settle back down into a narrow toe stance, facing due east. All this is accomplished with the inhalation.*

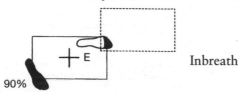

Inbreath

2   *Keep that right hand moving, swooping back down in a wide diagonal arc towards your left hip where the left hand just rises slightly in response to meet it. Turn your waist slightly counter-clockwise as you do this and really let that right hand soar, so that as it comes across and down, you should be able to see the back of the hand. The result is a really good, free twist to the joints of the arm.*

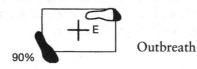

Outbreath

## SWEEP THE LOTUS AND CRESCENT KICK

1  *Here, you are going to turn the body right around through
   360°, with the left leg sweeping half of the way round off the
   ground. Prepare for this movement by sinking strongly into
   the right foot, then raise the left foot and straighten the leg
   somewhat. Next sweep the left foot around, south through to
   west, close to the ground and using the momentum of your
   arms and waist as the whole body turns counter-clockwise*

*on the ball of your right foot. This
inevitably has to be done fairly quickly,
especially when you are learning, but it
is surprising how graceful you can make
it in time. Touch down to the west with
the heel of your right foot.*

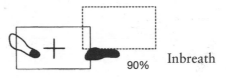

90%    Inbreath

2  *To complete the next 180°, use a combination of pivoting on
   heels and toes. Sources differ as to precisely how this should
   be achieved. Some people use left heel and right toes, others*

*the complete reverse! The best thing is to do
whatever seems comfortable to you. Providing
you have executed the first half of the circle
smoothly, with a graceful sweeping action of
the left foot close to the ground, the rest is not
so critical. Eventually, you will be back facing
east, the arms still parallel to the ground and
the right foot ahead of your left. Sink onto the
rear leg and prepare for a kick.*

100%

Inbreath finishes

3   *Allow the arms to drift a little to the right of centre and then
    set up your kick by sinking totally into the left foot. This is
    an unusual style of kick. Were you actually to be making
    contact with anything, it would be the outer edge of your
    right foot that would do so. This is because the hip directs the
    leg outwards in a great arc. But first,
    as with all kicks, you need to bring
    up the knee. Then the rest of the leg
    extends as you sweep out with it to
    the right. As this occurs, your arms
    return to the centre, travelling in the
    opposite direction.*

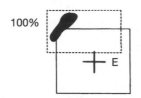

100%                             Outbreath

## SINK DOWN AND BRUSH KNEE

1   *This is not a classical tai chi movement as such and is sadly
    often rushed. I consider it to be important, however, since it
    encourages relaxation following what is a
    particularly dynamic movement. Firstly,
    drop the shin and relax the wrists. This
    should be accompanied by an inhalation,
    the foot remaining in the air. If you feel
    you may have lost your 'root' temporarily
    during the Crescent Kick, this is an
    excellent opportunity to re-establish it.*

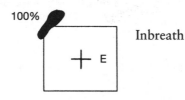

100%                             Inbreath

**2** *With the next exhalation, place the right foot down with the toes pointing outwards. Allow the arms to brush the right knee a little as you do this and bring most of your weight forward by bending the right knee. Let your centre follow, slightly clockwise, as you do this. Relax the shoulders. Try to imagine an energy connection between your palms and the ground. Sink, sink, sink. Find your roots.*

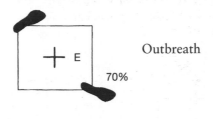

Outbreath

70%

## BEND THE BOW AND SHOOT THE TIGER

**1** *Imagine a long staff or bow which you clasp with your hands. In other words make two loose fists quite low down over your right thigh. Then, with the knuckles of the right hand turned inwards, bring the right fist up in a graceful arc to about head height and centred, as if thrusting one end of the bow into the ground.*

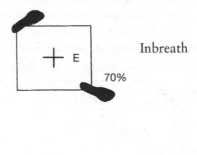

Inbreath

70%

**2** The right hand then comes back a little, closer to your head, while the left fist separates outwards and forwards at about abdomen height. The weight comes forward entirely after this, so that the back foot actually leaves the ground momentarily as the waist turns to accommodate the arm movements. Bring

the foot through, alongside your right foot if you wish, but don't overdo it. This is a movement that can easily lead to a lopsided appearance or to raised or tense shoulders. It is important, therefore, to monitor your actions closely to make sure the shoulders do not come up – especially the right side. Keep them level.

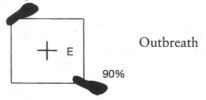

Outbreath

90%

## STEP FORWARD, PARRY AND PUNCH

**1** We have met with this sequence before, at the very end of Part One. We use it again here to close the whole form – the only

difference being that in Part One the whole thing began from a Brush Knee and Push position with the left leg forward whereas here, of course, we begin with the right leg forward. From the previous movement, it is assumed that you have already put back that left foot firmly on the ground. As this occurs, lower the arms and let go of the left fist. Simultaneously, spiral down to the left hip with your right fist and allow your weight to flow into the left foot.

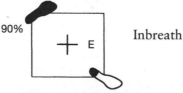

90%

Inbreath

**2** Lift the right foot and turn out the toes so that as you put it back down again, more or less in the same spot, it will point out at a good wide angle, nearly south in fact. Bend the right knee and bring your weight forward. At the same time 'throw'

the fist over to your right hip, palm side up in readiness to punch. The waist will naturally want to turn slightly clockwise as you do this. Keep the left hand low and relaxed but – as before – if you feel it wants to follow the right palm, more to the centre of your body, then let it.

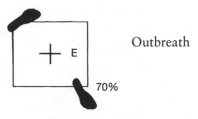

Outbreath

70%

**3** Raise your left foot and begin to step forward. Keep the left hand relaxed and the fist in readiness at your right hip. As you

go, try drawing in the left toes a little towards the right heel before stepping out to the east. As with the previous Step Forward, Parry and Punch sequence concluding Part One, it is useful to get those right toes out at a generous angle. That way you will be able to pivot on the heel and your centre will be able to 'rotate' into the movement that follows.

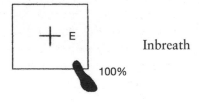

Inbreath

100%

4  Now place the left heel down and bend the left knee, the
   foot facing directly east. Just as this occurs, or perhaps just
   a fraction before, you 'parry' with your left arm or, in other
   words, raise the forearm to a near vertical
   position as if deflecting an oncoming
   force. Then punch very slowly towards
   the east. This is now precisely the same
   as the previous parry and punch and if in
   any doubt, refer back to the instructions
   accompanying position 4, page 62.
   Remember that half-turn of the fist that
   goes with the punch.

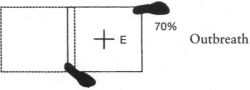

70%    Outbreath

### RELEASE ARM AND PUSH

Still repeating movements that you learned in Part One, continue
with Release Arm and Push, as described in detail on pages 63–64.

### TURN AND CLOSE THE FORM

After Release Arm and Push, you simply turn back to the south
and close the whole form – just as you finished Part One.
This concluding sequence is illustrated here again for your
convenience.

5. The form – part two    117

If you have done everything correctly, your feet should finish up in more or less the same place from which you started, emphasizing the cyclic nature of the tai chi form. Here, at the finish, take a moment just to relax, keeping your shoulder-width stance. Experience how the body feels. Imagine your feet putting roots down, way into the ground, and try to keep in touch still with the feeling of being suspended from above, with the spine straight and yet perfectly relaxed. Take a few deep breaths into the abdomen.

*Winning has to do with nothing other than feeling good about yourself.*

E. M. Hass

# 10 THINGS TO REMEMBER

1 *When you work, try to keep a fairly open aspect to the fingers and thumbs of each hand – no tension, please!*

2 *Try to experience how the weight changes gradually from side to side: never static.*

3 *Be aware of how almost all of your arm movements are directed from the waist. Try, sometimes, to move the arms only by moving the body rather than extending the arms extravagantly. You will be surprised at just how far the hands move if you use your waist.*

4 *Although some of the movements are relatively expansive and 'martial' compared to Part One, don't get carried away! Keep calm throughout, especially with those kicks and punches. Maintain your equilibrium.*

5 *Think of the kicks as slightly more elaborate kinds of toe or heel stances. There is no disgrace if you can only lift the foot a little from the ground. In terms of health, the load-bearing benefits for the bones and joints are the same whether you raise your foot a half inch (1 cm) or whether you kick the ceiling.*

6 *Be aware of how your eyes change focus as you move. With the exhalation, the eyes tend to look outward, as if towards a distant horizon. With the inhalation, they look more inward. This helps to direct the energy and circulate it more freely.*

7 *After a few weeks of regular practice, people might start to comment on changes they see in you. You are calmer, better balanced, in better shape and less prone to minor health complaints. Be modest in your achievements.*

8 *Keep the posture upright and the breathing low in the abdomen. But don't force it! Just relax those shoulders and eventually it will all come naturally.*

9   *Bend those knees! Tell yourself over and over again to sink, sink down as you go.*

10  *Congratulate yourself every once in a while. These are genuine achievements that are yours alone. You can keep that feel-good factor simply by practising regularly. It's up to you. You're in charge.*

# 6

······································································

# In depth

In this chapter you will learn:
- *further tips and pointers to each of the movements*
- *more about the naming and origins of the movements*
- *how to gain fluency with the entire sequence.*

## Additional notes on the movements

### OPENING

The even distribution of weight here between the two feet rarely
occurs in the form. It is not considered a strong position. You'll
find it at the beginning and again at the end.

The opening sequence is, of course, a relatively simple kind of
movement but it contains many important principles. For example,
keeping the shoulders relaxed as you raise your arms is vital.
Think, too, of the way the breathing is reflected in the upward and
downward, forward and backward movements of the arms and
hands: Yang and Yin right here at the very start. Also, here at the
beginning you encounter the typical pattern of stepping – that is,
shifting your weight to what is to become the 'substantial' leg, then
stepping out with the empty foot and finally adjusting the other
foot to complete the movement (positions 1 and 2). This pattern of
*Empty, Step and Adjust* is the basis of almost every movement you
will encounter in this or any other tai chi form.

Master Cheng Man-ch'ing compared this position to the primordial state, the great tai chi itself before it separates into Yang and Yin polarities. It is very much a moment of stillness and contemplation therefore, a time for making sure we feel calm and centred before we begin.

Those who work long hours at a keyboard will be aware of the significance of the relatively simple arm and wrist movements that occur here, because tense hands and fingers tend to tremble when we attempt to move them slowly. The more you do this, the better it will become.

### TURN RIGHT

If you can get your right toes 90° from your left heel, as shown in the foot diagram, great! But don't worry if you can't. Some people may feel their left knee tensing up if they go all the way and to keep on doing this would simply be counter-productive. As with all these movements, particularly during the early days when your body is accustoming itself to their demands, a little at a time is best.

Right here at this early stage of the form, do check that your right knee is properly aligned over your foot – not drifting inwards. (See Figure 3.4 on page 38.)

### WARD OFF LEFT

Sometimes also referred to by teachers of Yang-style tai chi as Grasp Sparrow's Tail Ward Off Left, this is a strong position. Great tai chi masters use it to demonstrate the essence of being rooted – with several hapless students lined up and pushing with all their might against the master's arm, unable to budge him at all. Surprisingly, most of us, with a little practice, can achieve something similar, albeit on a considerably more modest scale. Try it with just one partner pushing against your arm. Experiment by moving your feet until you feel the pressure being transferred away and into the ground.

Again, make sure your leading leg, i.e. the left leg in this instance, has its knee over the foot, not drifting inside. Imagine the left knee *spiralling* counter-clockwise – and the right knee also, spiralling a little at the same time, though in this case, the other way – clockwise. Sink down! Drop your centre of gravity, until your position becomes firmer.

Incidentally, the hand movements here are a good example of what is sometimes called 'palming'. This is when the palms appear to stroke each other, one stroking downwards, the other upwards, though at a distance, of course. During the execution of this movement, the left forearm rises roughly horizontal as its palm strokes upwards, the right forearm roughly vertical as its palm strokes down. Build up the distance between the palms, and practise until it feels natural.

### GRASP BIRD'S TAIL

We are at this point immersed in a whole set of movements which traditionally have the prefix of Grasp Bird's Tail or sometimes Grasp Sparrow's Tail. This one, for instance, is Grasp Bird's Tail Ward Off Right, while the previous movement and also those of Rollback and Press which follow are all similarly prefixed with the Bird's Tail title – all of which can be decidedly confusing. Therefore, I usually reserve the term Grasp Bird's Tail for this one movement only, since to me it most typifies the action of somebody holding a real bird. If you ever get the opportunity to observe someone who races pigeons, you will see something similar as they hold and inspect the bird's tail and wings.

Imagine how delicately you would hold the bird, so no tension please in the hands. Also make sure your arms are not too high. The hands should not be in front of your face, but rather, at the very most, only as high as neck level. Keep the elbows away from your sides.

### ROLLBACK

This is one of the few Yin movements actually to have a name. Like all Yin parts of the form, Rollback is only the duration of an inbreath, but don't rush it. It is a beautiful movement to perform, with a great feeling of energy returning inwards. Allow the hands to roll gently, the left palm almost sliding down the right forearm, all the while the weight shifting slowly backwards.

Because Rollback is essentially the Yin aspect of the next movement (Press), it is important here to let it flow smoothly, without stopping at any stage. Just as the breath keeps on changing, so too should your movements, Rollback into Press, always in motion. Make sure, also, that the angle at the elbow is not too acute. Always allow the ch'i to flow. Circulation is vital, and should never be inhibited by tightly folded joints.

### PRESS

Although when you see this movement being performed it looks as if the hands and arms are doing a lot of work, in fact they do not move all that much. Most of the movement is created by the turning of the waist, firstly towards the south, then back to the west again. Relax the arms and just let them follow the movements of the body.

Perhaps the most common error beginners make here is to actually press the hands together too hard at the end of this movement. Rather, just the lightest contact is all that is required, at chest level – not too high – and with the elbows well spread out from your sides. What all this translates into more than anything else is *relax those shoulders*!

Regarding the movement of the left hand as it circles back, don't take the instructions for 'palm up' too literally. Some people do not do it this way at all. As long as the wrist is relaxed, it's OK.

### SEPARATE HANDS AND PUSH

A common error at the start of this movement is to lean too far back, as if recoiling from something in shock. It can look quite comical. Make sure you are not doing this. Use a mirror if necessary and check that the spine remains vertical, like a plumb line suspended from above.

*Note*: Everything from Grasp Bird's Tail through to Push is done with both feet planted firmly on the ground. Try to resist any temptation to raise the right toes as you shift your weight back. It is surprising how many students find this difficult and short of actually nailing one's boots to the floor, the only way to eliminate this is through continuous practice and self-observation – and also perhaps trying to loosen and massage your knees and ankles regularly to eliminate tension in those places.

As with all pushes in tai chi, most of the forward movement comes from the legs. The arms and hands do not actually thrust forward to any great extent. In other words, allow your whole body to participate in the push, from the soles of the feet upwards.

### SINGLE WHIP

Regarding the pigeon-toed stance used during the early parts of this movement, there are many reasons why you should persevere with this. It encourages the rooting of the feet and teaches you to keep the knees apart when the weight moves from side to side. So keep trying until it starts to feel good.

Regarding positions 2 and 3 on page 52 the right forearm moves back across horizontally, the elbow pointing west. In contrast, however, the left hand should swoop down in a graceful arc to your right hip. For this, it may help to imagine a barrow full of sand – scoop up the sand. Then, as the hand lifts and spirals out to the east to complete the movement (positions 5 and 6 on pages 53–54), you are permitting the sand to trickle slowly from your hand. As this occurs, the feeling can be one of release, like setting free a coiled-up spring – a very expansive, Yang type of movement. Enjoy it.

At the very end, the shape formed by the left arm and hand should be a relaxed one. In profile it looks a bit like the spout of an old-fashioned teapot. No tension in the wrist, elbows or fingers, please. Let the arms 'float'.

Incidentally, if the name 'Single Whip' seems strange, it is because it derives from a somewhat more intricate version found in the earlier, traditional Yang-style of tai chi in which the movement of the right arm does resemble the rippling motion of a whip-cord. Although this whipping motion is no longer apparent in the short-form version, the name remains.

## Insight

In oriental medicine and philosophy there exists a subtle energy called the Shen, which corresponds in part to our Western concept of the spirit or consciousness. It is said to reside in the heart and is guided by our feelings every bit as much as by our physical bodies. Tai chi seeks, among other things, to strengthen the Shen.

### PLAY GUITAR

Those musicians among you who do actually play a guitar will have realized by now that this movement bears absolutely no resemblance whatsoever to the actions of playing a real guitar. Something has undoubtedly got lost in translation from the original Chinese name for this movement. There is, I believe, a Chinese instrument which, when played with a bow, would accommodate arm movements of this kind but it is certainly not a guitar.

It is important to adjust what is to become the back foot a little before you draw yourself into the final position, so as to take pressure off the knee. Then sit back and form the heel stance in comfort (see page 55). Although the arms make a rather tighter formation here than many of the tai chi movements, it is important still to make sure the elbows do not touch the sides of your body. Make sure also that your stance is not *too* narrow. If you draw an imaginary line through from your right toes to your right heel, and then extend this line back along the ground towards your rear foot, it should just clip the outside of your left heel. If it looks as if it is heading for the inside of the foot instead, you are too narrow. Open up!

## PULL AND STEP WITH SHOULDER

A common error at the end of this movement is that as the body rotates counter-clockwise, it tends to lean forward as well. The result is a rather uncomfortable, twisted-up appearance that will impede the flow of ch'i. Again, always think of the plumb line and keep that spine straight! If you imagine the knees spiralling here, the right knee clockwise, left knee counter-clockwise, it will also help you avoid twisting yourself into an uncomfortable and, therefore, unstable position. Try to maintain a subtle energy connection between the left palm and the right forearm during this movement, just as would have existed in the previous, Play Guitar, position. Incidentally, although the body is turned to the south-east at the end of this movement, the eyes continue to look south. This provides an opportunity to exercise the eye muscles as well as everything else. Nothing is wasted in tai chi.

## CRANE SPREADS ITS WINGS

The crane has always been an important and much-celebrated creature in oriental culture and mythology, combining two great qualities that people from all ages have always admired – strength and gracefulness. The execution of this movement – a favourite among many who practise tai chi – is often a visible indication as to how far the student has managed to integrate these two often opposing qualities in his or her life.

In addition to the many colourful metaphors that are employed in describing this wonderful movement, such as great wings circling in the air, and so on, we can add one more here. Think of the right hand as shielding the eyes from the sun as it rises up to the side of the head. This helps you get a feeling for the placement of the hand – though take care not to raise it too high, as this would only create tension in the right shoulder.

(The 'sun' in this instance is certainly not overhead or particularly high in the sky.)

*Note*: Although at the beginning of this movement the left hand appears not to be doing much, do not on that account let it hang lifeless at your side. Your hands and your feet are never entirely empty in tai chi. Always bear in mind the Tai Chi T'u symbol and the tiny seed of Yang that you find deep within the Yin, ready to transform itself into something greater.

### Insight

In the arts of the East, the crane is a favourite subject for those specialising in the tradition of paper folding – origami. It is called 'the bird of happiness' – perhaps because it dances during courtship and seems always to pursue the joy of movement. One more reason why we should seek to emulate the Crane in all of our tai chi studies.

### *BRUSH LEFT KNEE AND PUSH*

Featured here, and in the previous position, you will find a lot of wonderfully fluid, rotational movements of the arms, with several different things happening all at once. One of my teachers once likened it to a children's game in which you are urged to try patting your head and rubbing your stomach all at the same time. It requires great co-ordination. But then this is precisely one of the things you are seeking to develop with your tai chi, so stick with it. Incidentally, you can turn to page 93, where the same movement is repeated facing west, to see how this looks from the other side. Note how the left hand remains hovering somewhat over the left thigh. Don't let it fall away behind you.

Remember, too, that you need to step wide into the final position here from the relatively narrow crane stance. In fact, because the left foot is already ahead of the right, you don't really need to step forward at all, *just wide*. This is a particularly useful tip if you are practising in an area of limited space.

## STEP FORWARD, PARRY AND PUNCH

The tai chi fist is soft, loosely held, not tightly clenched. There is
no anger in this kind of fist and it does not punch. Rather, it is a
demonstration of will and self-confidence. Ideally, the thumb
and the first joint of the index finger should be in contact.
Those who do yoga will recognize this – *a mudra* – as a means
of concentrating energy.

During the forward stepping sequence (see pages 61–62) it is
acceptable to keep the left arm low and relaxed. I believe this is the
way Cheng Man-ch'ing taught the movement during his later years.
However, if you feel it wants to follow the right hand somewhat,
across to the centre of your body for instance, then let it do so.
Some people move it in a great arc from behind the left side over to
the centre (as in the traditional long form), but this is not necessary
in the context of the kind of tai chi being demonstrated here.

With the punch itself, your fist makes one half-turn as it goes, so
that whereas it started off with the palm side up, it turns in
mid-flight so that by the end you have the thumb edge facing
upwards. Finally, if you can, do pivot a little on the heel of the
right foot so that the whole body 'twists' into the movement as
your weight carries the punch forward.

## RELEASE ARM AND PUSH

The naming of movements in the tai chi form is a complex
area to delve into because the names themselves come from so
many different sources. Some reflect images of the natural world,
mimicking the actions of animals or other creatures. Others are
based on traditional martial arts techniques. The term 'Release
Arm' comes from the martial application of extracting oneself
from a hold (if someone is grabbing your wrist, for example).
For us, using tai chi for relaxation purposes, it is enough simply
to be aware of this, and to make use of the wonderful rotational
movements of the wrists and hands to help free off those tense
joints. It is intricate, yes – so try to keep everything as relaxed as

you can. Don't neglect the turning of the waist, either: at first
a little to the left, then to the right as you sit back into the
rear foot.

### TURN AND CLOSE PART ONE

This is really a pretty straightforward manoeuvre. Basically,
you need to turn to the south again and get the feet parallel, like at
the opening of the form. If you relax with it you will find that the
foot and hand movement co-ordinate easily without you having to
follow the foot diagrams too slavishly. Simply make sure you feel
balanced as you turn and that as you finally draw back the right
foot to complete the parallel stance you make contact with the toes
first. Remember the rules? – *Step forward heel first; step back toes
first.* Although there is no real step involved here, you are
still drawing the right foot backwards into the final position.
So toes first.

### CARRY TIGER TO MOUNTAIN

Also known as Embrace Tiger and Return to Mountain (which
is also the title of a famous piece of modern dance choreography,
by the way, inspired by tai chi), this movement takes us onto the
diagonal axis for the first time. The rotation of the body and the
large step around to the north-west is quite challenging when you
first encounter it. Remember to 'root' yourself firmly in the left
foot before you commit yourself – that is, bend the knee and
sink down into the left side. Then gradually raise the right foot,
draw it inwards a little towards the left, then open out the right hip
and turn into the step. Keep the shoulders aligned during all this,
don't raise one up or drop the other disproportionately low.
Keep them level, and the hips too!

By the way, sometimes you may see this movement being done
with the right palm downward at the conclusion, rather than palm
up as shown in the drawing. Both are valid. Cheng Man-ch'ing
advocated the latter – so you finish up holding a ball (or perhaps
even a Tiger – though this is not strictly recommended).

## DIAGONAL CHORUS (ROLLBACK, PRESS, SEPARATE HANDS AND PUSH, AND SINGLE WHIP)

There are two main reasons why we bother with the added complication of the diagonal axis. The first is an historic one, in deference to the Taoist world picture of nine directions – i.e. the four compass points, the four intermediate points and centre. This is set out in the *I Ching* or *Book of Changes*. Each of the points has a philosophical correlation and in one of the oldest arrangements, the north-west is the direction of 'The Mountain', of late autumn, rest and keeping still.

The second reason is wholly practical. Up to now you have been able to use your surroundings to orient yourself – using the walls of the room, maybe, to line up your feet. Now you are forced to orient yourself entirely by reference to your own centre. This increased self-awareness and the ability to sense one's own boundaries clearly is of great value.

With this first repetition of the Chorus, you add a really big chunk onto your form without having to learn very much new. However, while you are getting used to the diagonals, do please check your feet and be honest: are you still managing to retain your shoulder-width stance? Tai chi is always testing you. The moment you feel you are getting along just wonderfully and your ego starts to soar, something is thrown in your path – a challenge, of course, not an obstacle – for you to overcome. The diagonal axis is just one such challenge.

### FIST UNDER ELBOW

Don't become too carried away by the descriptive name of this movement. The fist is really a very loose one and it does not really go beneath the elbow either. To do so would be far too restrictive and artificial. Keep it as relaxed as possible. Try imagining something very fragile in your right hand even as you make your fist – like an egg or a small bird. And as always try to maintain plenty of space between the arms and the sides of the body. At the end, the feet settle into a position very similar to the Play Guitar stances. Finally, try to get some nice turns in the waist, leftwards at first, then back to centre, as you progress through these steps. Use the whole of the body.

### REPULSE MONKEY

Although the foot diagrams indicate a wide stance, you will in practice probably find yourself stepping back fairly narrow. This is all right as long as it is not so excessively narrow that you are unstable. Cheng Man-ch'ing actually advocated stepping back with the feet parallel – which is not at all easy for beginners – but why not give it a try! Also, with each step back and as the hand comes down to waist height, make sure you keep your elbow well out from your side. It's a bit like having a rolled-up blanket under your arm – really that much space between ribs and elbows. Allow yourself to breathe.

As you add these wonderfully flowing, rhythmic movements to your form you will notice a further increase in your sense of co-ordination and spatial awareness. This is because we do not really ever step backwards in normal day-to-day living. It is taking us into an area of ourselves, behind our bodies, that we are not normally aware of. For this reason alone, Repulse Monkey is a valuable experience to cultivate. It should also be performed with plenty of body movement – turn the waist each time to accommodate the generous back swing of the arm, thereby emulating the actions of a real monkey swinging through the branches. Keep your wrists relaxed at all times – again, just like the monkey. Also, allow your eyes to follow the palm each time as it circles back. The monkey will not come to seize the food if he thinks you are looking at him, so divert your gaze to the palm instead as it moves behind your shoulder. Do remember, however, that this has to be achieved without excessive movement of the head in relation to the shoulders. Just turn the waist and use the eyes. They will benefit from this gentle exercise.

## DIAGONAL FLYING

In keeping with the imagery of the monkey in our little story, here you could say you are picking up the monkey and putting him back on the tree. The right hand with its upward-facing palm does tend to have the appearance of 'offering up'. Also, the whole movement is like a spring coiling and expanding, similar in feeling to the Single Whip, i.e. progressive contraction (Yin) transforming into its opposite, expansion (Yang). A good movement for strengthening the waist and for helping to remove congestion from the abdomen and chest.

Also going by the name of 'Slant Flying' in some quarters, this movement can best be achieved by drawing the right toes in a little towards the left foot before turning the waist and stepping south-west. This little movement of the toes encourages us to really sink into the substantial foot and prepares us nicely for any big turn or step. It is a style of movement that people become very fond of the more they understand and practise the form. Generally, too, it gives a far more satisfactory feeling than simply plunging straight into a turn from a wide-apart position.

### Insight
If you find your tai chi is making you feel superior and powerful, you have probably missed the point. If it makes you feel humble and compassionate, you are getting there.

## CLOUDY HANDS

When you step inwards with the right foot (position 3, page 81) place it down *no closer* than shoulder width to your left foot. A common error here is to step in too close, so you start to wobble. The success of this manoeuvre depends largely on having sufficient width to play with initially, which means that when we draw up the left foot in position 1, page 80, we make it at a distance of at least one and a half shoulder widths from the right.

Always step just a fraction earlier prior to changing the hands. As always, the movements of the arms reflect those of the waist and centre of the body. As it turns, the hands follow, rather than the other way around. Keep in mind the phrase 'step and change – step and change' to keep the correct order. If you can manage to keep that parallel aspect of the feet, you will find that every joint in the body receives a gentle movement and internal 'massage' – the toes, ankles, knees and hips, spine, shoulders, elbows and fingers all getting worked. It does, however, require rather a lot of co-ordination and practice to perform happily and at first it may seem as if the brain is getting its fair share of arduous work as well. So here are a few tips to help you remember things.

In Cloudy Hands, always turn your waist in the direction of your higher arm. Then, just prior to changing the hands, step with the opposite leg to which you have turned. Although during the learning phase, all these movements are made in a rather precise fashion, you will eventually free up quite a bit and start to flow. To help, here are a couple of rather mixed metaphors to assist you with the actions of the hands. Think of the upper hand 'stroking' softly downwards, as if along the nose of a pony or furry creature of some kind. Meanwhile, think of the lower hand as having its fingers stuck in a pot of sticky stuff, glue or honey. Imagine the sticky strands coming up, adhering slightly to your fingers as you go.

Peculiar as all this may well sound, it encourages a certain softness in the hands and is often a great help to those wishing to deepen their understanding of the movements. For the time being, however, make sure you follow the instructions for the hands very closely.

### SNAKE CREEPS DOWN

Most Western students find this a particularly difficult manoeuvre to perform, basically because they try too hard. Unless you train and stretch yourself constantly every day you are unlikely to achieve the kind of flexibility that Chinese masters display. Do not try to sink down too far, therefore. It is not necessary to do this in order to gain the benefits from the movement. What is important is as follows:

1  *Try to retain as straight a back as possible – don't lean over just in order to get yourself down a few inches lower.*
   *The gentle bearing down of your rib cage upon your liver as you sink down is very helpful, the liver being a vital organ that performs around 500 different chemical functions for us, often simultaneously.*
2  *Do make sure you turn in your left toes a little as you sink down and then turn them straight again as your hand sweeps forward. This stimulates several important acu-points in the inside heel that are related to your kidney ch'i.*
3  *Finally, make sure your weight remains in your right foot throughout. Even as your hand sweeps forward, keep the weight back. The right knee should remain directly above the right heel to achieve this.*

### GOLDEN PHEASANT

Among the movements of the form, Golden Pheasant is unusual insofar as it has the most obvious part of the movement (lifting of the foot and raising of the hand) on the inbreath. No need to be too strict with this, however. You can, in fact, commence the exhalation at the top of this movement if you wish – in other words, just before the lowering of arm and leg.

The essence of this sequence is that of a smooth interchange and transference of weight and energy. Therefore, it is not simply a case of bringing one side down and then the other side up. Finish the first side off properly by sinking clearly into the right leg before raising the left. Also remember the Tai Chi T'u symbol and keep a little bit of energy in the less active hand. Don't let it hang lifeless while you're busy with the other side. Instead, imagine an energy connection between your lowest palm and the ground. The fingers of the raised hand, meanwhile, are close together, though not tense. Keep your eyes focused ahead; don't look down. That will help you to balance. Finally, *keep it loose* – don't crease up or hunch your shoulders and only raise the knee as far as is comfortable. Realize your limitations and be confident that, bit by bit, your balance will improve.

### PAT THE HORSE (LEFT AND RIGHT)

Despite the name of this movement, *do not pat*. This is not what is taking place. Rather, you should be stroking across gently with the palm, fingers very relaxed.

*Note*: Regarding Pat the Horse on the Left, this is not simply a mirror image of Pat the Horse on the Right. In both instances, it is your right leg which is slightly forward of the left at the finish and in both instances you turn your centre towards the leading leg, i.e. slightly clockwise as you Pat the Horse.

Don't worry if it takes you a while to get the hang of all this. Students often find this sequence the most daunting of all within the tai chi form. The demands on our co-ordination are pretty high, of course, but there is no need to be frightened of it on that score. The rewards for perseverance are, as ever, all the greater for the effort put in. It is a great feeling once you have it, so keep trying until it flows smoothly. If you seem to be getting nowhere, however, then take a lesson from nature. The horse is one of the most powerful of creatures and yet its movements are always graceful and fluent. The arms here tend to resemble the way a horse's front legs roll and strike out when raised in the air. Sometimes it really does help to watch nature and the animals named in the movements. We can learn a lot from this, often far more than from all the books and manuals and teachers rolled into one.

### KICK WITH TOES (LEFT AND RIGHT)

The separation of the hands precedes the kick; never perform these actions together, as this would simply dissipate the energy into too many limbs at once. It is also worth remembering that toe kicks are really just an extension of movements featuring narrow toe stances – like Crane Spreads Its Wings – and you should feel no less certain of your footing on one than on the other. In both cases, you are aiming for a gentle stimulation and stretch along the front aspect of the leg, thereby encouraging the flow of energy in the stomach and spleen acu-channels that are situated there. This is beneficial for many internal functions related to digestion and the assimilation and use of liquids.

## TURN AND KICK WITH SOLE

Kicks are, of course, some of the most obviously martial aspects of the tai chi form and remind us that the origins of much of what we are doing come from the great fighting arts of China in which kicks would be aimed at sensitive points on the body or limbs to immobilize an opponent. If you are studying tai chi for its health and relaxation benefits, however, it is essential not to become hasty or impulsive with these movements. We are not kicking anybody here. So forget about all those martial arts movies with people flying through the air, and just relax! These movements have enormous therapeutic value if performed correctly and especially if you do them with a sense of calm. Above all, do them *slowly*. This means attention to the following points at all times:

▶ *sink into the substantial leg as you prepare*
▶ *raise the knee gradually before you kick out with the lower part of the leg*
▶ *use your rear arm as a counterbalance to the extending leg as it kicks.*

Also, equally important, is that after each kick you commence your next inhalation before you place the foot down. And don't just topple and stumble into the next movement, either! If this is happening, it means you are not properly balanced. Keep practising until you can place the foot down slowly, at will, after the kick. Then you will know you have done it right, without losing your 'root'.

To kick with the sole or the heel of a foot, you naturally tend to point the toes upwards. This stimulates an entirely different set of acu-channels in the leg from those activated by the toe kicks. Here, as with the narrow heel stances of the form, it is the posterior aspect of the leg, the hamstrings and Achilles tendon, which get the work. Equally importantly, however, these movements tend to stimulate the kidney and bladder acu-channels of the body. This can be beneficial for all things connected to the reproductive organs, the urinary system and also the skeletal system and bone marrow.

By the way, if you are having trouble with turning into this movement, help is at hand. In the traditional long form, from which the short form was derived, a much easier way of getting around from east to west is sometimes taught. This is also particularly useful if you are elderly or are, for any reason, unsteady on your feet.

To do this, simply place your left foot down behind, to the west (after the previous movement: Kick with Left Toes), and then pivot on your right heel to get hips and shoulders facing west. Having the left foot lightly on the ground to steady you during this manoeuvre is a great help. After that, of course, you simply raise the left foot again to execute the kick itself. Not as spectacular as the version shown in the instruction section but worth remembering, especially if you are ever called upon to demonstrate your tai chi skills in public, or perhaps to that much admired loved one you so dearly want to impress. It saves the embarrassment of toppling at just the wrong moment!

## Insight
Be happy! Negative emotions such as anger or resentment tend to inhibit the flow of ch'i – to 'knot' the ch'i, as it is sometimes described. When the ch'i is unable to flow smoothly through the organs it leads to stagnation in all aspects of our lives.

### ALL BRUSH KNEE AND PUSHES

All the expansive, backward circling movements serve naturally to open up the chest area, where many of the acu-channels either

begin or end. Equally important, the vital lymph glands situated in
the chest, throat and armpits get massaged. The lymph fluid rids the
body of toxins and provides defences against disease and infection.
With the decreasing efficiency of our immune responses these days –
largely a result of atmospheric pollution and poor diet and nutrition –
exercises of this kind cannot be too highly recommended.

### BRUSH KNEE AND PUNCH LOW

As with the previous instance in which you delivered a 'punch',
here the fist does one half-turn in mid-flight. The only difference is
that here it is the knuckle side of the fist facing upwards to begin
with, whereas before it was the palm side turned up. This variation
is due to the difference in height to which the fist is to be projected
and ensures a fluid action that greatly benefits the joints of the
wrist and arm.

Try to keep your body upright as you sink into this low-slung
movement. In the Short Yang Form, we always endeavour to keep
the spine straight. For beginners, especially, this promotes greater
flexibility in the lower back and pelvis than would be the case if
one were to simply yield to the temptation of leaning forward.

### FOUR CORNERS

This elegant sequence is also sometimes called Fair Lady Works at
Shuttles, because the movements of the hands are thought to mimic
somewhat the actions of someone weaving and using a shuttle.
Whether this is entirely accurate or not is of little importance, for
the name itself does intimate the soft, delicate nature of the actions
made at the loom in which the hands alternate quite noticeably
between expanding and contracting aspects. Allow your hands to
become Yin as you turn, then Yang as you spiral out with the arms
at the end of each corner. Think, too, of a flower closing in and
opening out alternately.

Regarding *Yin and Yang hands*, this generally means palms
outward facing for Yang, and palms inward facing for Yin.

Please note, however, that outward-facing palms are not necessarily always Yang in nature, and vice versa for Yin. There are many subtle variations of hand and wrist positions that signify and promote Yang or Yin energies, but these are beyond the scope of this book.

Meanwhile here are some 'rules' that will help you to learn and remember the sequence:

1 *At the beginning of each corner, as you start to turn, simply use the lowest hand to cup the opposite elbow. It is amazing how many students make hard work of this manoeuvre by reversing the hands. Just keep the upper hand up and the lower hand low, then sit back, cup the elbow and commence your turn.*
2 *At the conclusion of each corner, the side with the leading leg always has the higher arm.*
3 *With Corners One, Two and Four, always use a combination of turning on your left heel and right toes, plus of course a large step around at the end.*

### STEP FORWARD TO SEVEN STARS

The 'seven stars' referred to here make up the constellation of Ursa Major – the Big Dipper (in the Northern hemisphere) or Great Bear. If you look at the Big Dipper on a winter's evening, you will see it with the tail end downwards. The tai chi movement described here tends to look a bit similar in profile – the leg being the tail, the arms forming the bowl shape above it.

Ursa Major is an important constellation in Chinese mythology, and perhaps one of the reasons for this is that two of its most prominent stars point directly to the Pole Star, which, as all you astronomers out there will know, is a place of stillness, around which all the other stars appear to revolve. This might also be why it has found its way into the tai chi form. Tai chi is, of course, all about inner calm, around which all our movements take place and from which, in a sense, they are also directed. *Stillness within movement* is what we are about here.

Incidentally, remember not to raise the wrists up too high at the end of this movement. In other words keep those shoulders relaxed!

### STEP BACK TO RIDE THE TIGER

At this stage of your tai chi training it is assumed that you will be able to recognize and eliminate tension if and when it occurs and here, with the raising of the right arm and the turning of the wrist joint, you must be especially vigilant. The part played by the left arm in this action should not be neglected, either. Remember the Tai Chi T'u and the energy seed always present, even in the most Yin places. Think of two friends – the right hand makes a long journey to visit the left hand, but out of courtesy the left hand makes a little trip too, just to the garden gate, to meet the other. It is this natural 'etiquette' of the tai chi movements, in which one limb is very often echoing slightly the actions of the other, that helps to ensure the Yin/Yang balance of your form.

The tiger, which crops up frequently in the names of tai chi movements, is a symbol, in part, for the ch'i. In the West we have known this as 'animal magnetism', of course. One of the images associated with this movement is of a sleeping tiger, resting on the ground. As you step back you place your right foot on his back and the left foot, very gingerly, upon his neck. When he wakes up – as it might be presumed a tiger would most likely do with somebody on its back – the idea is that your balance is so excellent with all your tai chi training that you can simply ride him, no matter how much he tries to shake you off. It is not, however, recommended that you put this into practice.

......................................................................................................

### Insight

Remember: try to practise a little outdoors if you can. In the West we are reluctant about displaying ourselves in this way, but in the East it is normal to find people exercising in the fresh air. Don't be shy! You will be astonished at how soon you will be accepted by others if you do your tai chi outside on a regular basis, particularly early in the morning when

*(Contd)*

people are either engaged in something similar – exercising or jogging and so on – or else are far too busy getting to work to notice. And if you are lucky enough to have your own garden – well, there really is no excuse.

## SWEEP THE LOTUS

Like the previous turn on one leg (see pages 91–92) this is another one of those tai chi movements best not learned too close to any precious antiques or porcelain. Don't panic with it! When some beginners first see this movement, they mistakenly believe the entire 360° turn is enacted in one go. As you have seen, this is not the case. Just concentrate initially on the first half of the turn, with the left foot above the ground. Thereafter, use both feet to complete the circle.

*Note*: It is important to make sure the forearms remain parallel to the ground during your turn. Try not to flail out too much with the hands as you go and that way you'll feel good about the movement. Sink, sink, sink and your balance will improve every time.

## CRESCENT KICK

This type of movement, where the arms and leg travel in different directions, can be beneficial for the spine, helping to relieve congestion in the acu-channels that surround it. However, if you do have a particularly bad back or are prone to disc trouble, treat this movement with caution.

*Note*: This movement is also sometimes called the Lotus Kick. The symbolism of the lotus here and in the preceding movement is rather obscure but I was once told it referred to a lotus flower on the surface of a pool. The sweeping of the lotus is therefore the removal of the flower, without presumably getting one's feet wet. This is perhaps not as peculiar as it sounds, since it encourages us to keep the foot close to the ground during the turn. Another version tells us of the lotus flower with its round petals that seem to rotate in the wind, thereby inspiring the pattern of circular movements and the swirling kick featured here.

The lotus also has a certain mystical significance, of course, and like its equivalent, the rose, in Western culture, enjoys a certain prominence in the order of things. In the case of the lotus, this derives in part from the fact that it has its roots in the mud at the bottom of the pool while its flower, resplendent above the water's surface, is something largely invisible to the roots themselves. The significance of this is worth contemplating as most of our daily lives, it could be argued, are conducted in the muddy area at the bottom of the pool. And how many of us ever think to look up?

### BEND THE BOW AND SHOOT THE TIGER

The idea of the bow here is a good one. If you imagine a flexible bow, held in your hands, it ensures the correct alignment of the two fists. Observe your hands during this sequence and make certain that they could, theoretically, always be holding a bow or rod of some kind. The bow can bend a little but it must never snap. Initially, the bow itself is picked up in a horizontal position, but then it goes near vertical as the fists separate. Whatever happens, however, always keep the hollow part of the fists aligned, clasping the bow.

---

## Test your knowledge

Here are some questions on this chapter. Just a bit of fun. See how well you do! Answers on page 208.

1  *What 'direction' should you be facing at the commencement of the Chorus. Is it: a) south, b) west or c) east?*
2  *What is the golden rule for remembering the arm placement at the end of each of the Four Corners movements? Is it: a) front foot, lower arm, b) leading leg, higher arm or c) lower arm leading leg?*

3   What is the shape in the right hand that you make when you go into Single Whip? Is it: a) monkey's tail, b) crane's beak or c) tiger's mouth?

4   What 'direction' should you finish facing at the conclusion of the Diagonal Single Whip? Is it: a) north-west, b) south-west or c) south-east?

5   What 'direction' should you be facing after the conclusion of Diagonal Flying? Is it: a) north-west, b) south-west or c) south-east?

6   What is the golden rule for remembering the direction in which to turn the waist during the Cloudy Hands sequence? Is it: a) always turn your waist towards the higher arm, b) always turn your waist towards the lower arm or c) always turn towards the side with the empty leg?

7   There is good tip to remember with Cloudy Hands and the timing of the steps to the hand movement. Is it: a) change hands and step, b) step as you change or c) step and change?

8   Regarding the two separate 'Pat the Horse' movements that occur in Part Two, which of these statements is true? a) the left foot is always forward at the conclusion of each movement, b) the right foot is always forward at the conclusion of each movement or c) the feet are parallel at the conclusion of each movement?

9   What should you endeavour to do immediately after you have completed your Crescent Kick? Should you: a) lunge forward and get you foot back on the ground as soon as possible, b) make a loud noise or c) breathe in calmly and prepare to put the foot down slowly?

10  If you go into a 70/30 stance with the left leg leading (i.e. Ward Off), what should you imagine happening to the right knee? Should it: a) spiral slightly clockwise, b) spiral slightly counter-clockwise or c) lock up tight?

Finally, for your reference, all the movements are listed in sequence on page 146. This list can be used in conjunction with the small illustrations at the back of this book. If you are confused about the repetitions (for example, the Chorus, and how it all fits together), just refer to the table on page 146.

And with that, we come to the end of the instruction section of this book. Although you have now learned the movements in a basic sense, this is actually just the beginning of your tai chi studies. In the next chapters we will explore ways in which you can deepen your understanding of the subject and enhance your experience of ch'i.

*Perseverance is one of the fundamental requirements in practising T'ai-chi Ch'uan. No results can be obtained without it.*

Yearning K. Chen

Opening
Turn Right
Ward Off
Grasp Bird's Tail
Rollback and Press
Separate Hands and Push
Single Whip
Play Guitar Right
Pull and Step with Shoulder
Crane Spreads Its Wings
Brush Left Knee and Push
Play Guitar (Left Side)
Brush Left Knee and Push
Step Forward, Parry and
  Punch
Release Arm and Push
Turn and Close Part One
Carry Tiger to Mountain
Diagonal Rollback and Press
Diagonal Separate Hands
  and Push
Diagonal Single Whip
Fist Under Elbow
Repulse Monkey
  (Right, Left, Right again)
Diagonal Flying
Cloudy Hands (Left, Right
  and Left into Whip)
Isolated Single Whip
Snake Creeps Down
Golden Pheasant (Right and
  Left)

Pat the Horse (Right)
Kick with Right Toes
Pat the Horse (Left)
Kick with Left Toes
Turn and Kick with the Sole
Brush Left Knee and Push
Brush Right Knee and Push
Brush Left Knee and Punch
  Low
Grasp Bird's Tail
Rollback and Press
Separate Hands and Push
Single Whip
Four Corners (First, Second,
  Third and Fourth)
Ward Off
Grasp Bird's Tail
Rollback and Press
Separate Hands and Push
Single Whip
Snake Creeps Down
Step Forward to Seven Stars
Step Back to Ride the Tiger
Sweep the Lotus
Crescent Kick
Sink Down and Brush Knee
Bend the Bow and Shoot the
  Tiger
Step Forward, Parry and
  Punch
Release Arm and Push
Turn and Close the Form

146

# 7

Tai chi and health

In this chapter you will learn:
- *about health and the causes of disease*
- *about the importance of proper nourishment and digestion*
- *about maintaining balance and harmony.*

Unlike traditional oriental medicine, with its well-documented network of therapeutic points and channels, the movements of tai chi have often been a source for speculation on precisely what benefits they bring in terms of health. Yet everyone involved with the subject would agree that regular practice is effective in promoting, restoring and maintaining the body's natural vitality and well-being. How precisely this happens is not always known. In this Chapter I will list those correlations that I am aware of, taken from a variety of sources, and will also include my own observations based on the teachings of Traditional Chinese Medicine (TCM).

## Circulation

Because of the emphasis on calm regular breathing and on practice in the open air, when possible, regular tai chi will inevitably assist the body's circulatory system. The extensive use of leg muscles stimulates the return flow of venous blood to the heart and lungs, while the focus on relaxed muscles in the upper body promotes an efficient supply of blood to all the major organs, to the brain and to the joints. Moreover, after an eight-minute form at a fairly low level of stance (slightly lower than that illustrated in this book) the heart rate increases gradually to a level consistent with the demands of moderate fitness training. This in turn helps to regulate blood pressure.

There are no special movements in the tai chi form that relate to the vascular system more than any other function of the body, but all heel stances and heel kicks stimulate the calf muscles, assisting circulation, and Crane Spreads Its Wings may also be helpful, since it gently stretches and brings out the heart channel in the arms. Also, the constant movement of the ankle joints throughout the form stimulates important points on the spleen, liver and kidney acu-channels, while that of the wrists and forearms stimulates the heart and pericardium channels – all of which adds to the efficiency of the circulation and the strength of the blood vessels themselves. The kidneys are also partly responsible for maintenance of correct blood pressure in terms of Western physiology so the benefits tend to dovetail nicely.

## Insight

We all need to seek advice and help from medical professionals at times, especially as we grow older. But we also hold the key to our own health through the choices that we make every day, through proper exercise and nutrition, for example. Taking responsibility for our own health is always our first line of defence, therefore. In that way, we give the doctors a helping hand and perhaps go some way towards preventing the worst ravages of time.

## Breathing

Tai chi has enormous benefits for the lungs. The continued expanding and contracting movements of the form massage and stimulate the lungs, helping them to take in life-giving oxygen and to eliminate waste gases from the blood stream. The originator of the Short Yang Form, Cheng Man-ch'ing, suffered from tuberculosis as a young man and the prognosis for his recovery was not good. Tai chi not only helped him overcome his illness, it also gave him enormous strength in later life.

With a good supply of oxygen, all the organs and systems of the body are able to function well. Oxygen helps us to maintain a suitable body weight as well, since it is essential for the burning of calories. Slimmers take note, you need to assist the process by looking after your lungs.

Parts of the form that are particularly beneficial for the lungs are: the Pushes and Ward Off movements along with Grasp Bird's Tail and Press.

---

## Lymph

The lymph is a much neglected and little understood substance. Most people are familiar with the heart and the circulation of blood in the body but the existence of an internal cleansing medium, which helps us to fight off disease and to rid the body of toxins and waste products, is generally not so well known. We usually hear about the lymph nodes – places where the lymph fluid concentrates – when they become enlarged during illness. Yet they are constantly at work for us, keeping us well.

The lymph fluid, however, does not have a pump, like the blood has the heart, to move it around the body. It relies in part on physical movement instead, exercise and so on. The gentle, expansive, non-tensile movements of tai chi are ideal in this respect. Moreover, because most of the major lymph glands are situated in the chest, throat, armpits, groin, elbows and knees, it would seem that these are expressly targeted by many of the movements found in the form: all those that open up the chest area, for instance, Repulse Monkey or Brush Knee and Push; or those that free up the groin through expansive turning movements, such as Diagonal Flying and Four Corners; and finally, all those heel kicks and narrow heel stances to stimulate the rear aspect of the knee.

> *T'ai-chi Ch'uan is closely related to Meditation. Long practice of Meditation may hinder blood circulation, but T'ai-chi Ch'uan helps to quicken it. It also helps to bring about the peace of mind and the exercise of breathing as desired by practisers of Meditation.*
>
> Yearning K. Chen

## Nerves, sensations and thought

The autonomic nervous system, that part of our body-intelligence that works independently of consciousness, is generally classified into two parts, the sympathetic and the parasympathetic. The former works mainly to prepare the body for action, increasing heartbeat, suspending digestive processes and carrying out numerous other functions of which we are not consciously aware, while the latter prepares the body for rest so that it can recover from vigorous activity.

Clearly, then, tai chi would benefit the parasympathetic enormously, while also helping us to relax and cope with stress, anxiety and insomnia. But tai chi also works on the entire central nervous system through movements that stimulate and increase flexibility in the spine such as Crane Spreads Its Wings, Golden Pheasant and Repulse Monkey. Meanwhile, the characteristically erect spine of tai chi encourages the free flow of cerebrospinal fluid, helping to relieve pressure on the intervertebral discs and spinal nerves.

### Insight

Sleep when you need to. There is lots of evidence to suggest that a lack of adequate rest or disturbed sleep patterns can result in numerous hormonal imbalances that can contribute to some of our most serious illnesses, including diabetes and heart disease. There is no disgrace in taking a 'power nap' or siesta during the day, while at night, strive for a peaceful and dark environment. That way your body becomes properly renewed and the ch'i is not wasted.

The cerebrospinal fluid itself is an amazing substance. Through research in the exciting new field of craniosacral osteopathy, a very subtle rhythm has been located – called the 'cranial rhythmic impulse' – in which not only the cerebrospinal fluid but also all the membranes enveloping every organ, muscle, nerve and blood vessel throughout the human body beat gently in synchronization. The entire body, therefore, is constantly responding to a basic tempo that originates within the central nervous system itself. Even the joints of the skull and sacrum resonate to it in a subtle way that can be detected through the fingers and palms of the experienced craniosacral practitioner.

The astonishing thing for us, in the world of tai chi, is that this rhythm, generally around 12 to 14 beats per minute, is precisely that at which the tai chi form is enacted: one cycle of Yin and Yang around every four or five seconds. Tai chi, therefore, seems to work at a level wholly in tune with our body's most basic rhythmic impulses, establishing harmony and calm throughout the entire nervous system.

But what about the conscious thought process itself? Tai chi relaxes the mind, of that there is no doubt, no matter how unlikely this may seem to beginners struggling to learn the intricacies of the form. Ultimately, however, as you achieve a certain equanimity and sense of detachment, the mind begins to function in a far more relaxed mode. This can, in fact, be measured by the frequency of electrical activity in the brain and is called the 'alpha state', in which the brain vibrates at a frequency of around 10 Hz. A similar frequency occurs just before we drop off to sleep or just as we are waking and is also achieved through the practice of meditation and yoga. The interesting thing is that during this and other highly relaxed states, there is a measurable increase in the formation of connective tissues between the brain cells, thereby enhancing our mental faculties at a very deep level.

The learning of the form not only improves our physical and mental co-ordination, it also provides us with what scientists call an 'enriched environment' – in other words, a stimulating activity to challenge our intelligence. Experiments have clearly demonstrated that an enriched environment and the repeated chemical boost we get within the brain itself from the process of problem solving also enhances the growth of connective tissue in the brain. Perhaps this is why those who regularly practise tai chi report increased mental clarity, along with better judgement and anticipation in their daily affairs.

---

## Food and how to deal with it

The constant emphasis in tai chi of turning from the centre and rotating the waist is enormously helpful for maintaining the health of the digestive system and bowels. This, together with the efficient descending of the diaphragm during inhalation, gently massages the intestines, liver and kidneys and promotes a healthy blood supply to all the abdominal organs.

Gastrointestinal disorders such as irritable bowel syndrome (IBS) or peptic and duodenal ulcers benefit from the calming effect tai chi has on the digestive system and on the autonomic nervous system that controls its activity.

Cloudy Hands is renowned for its beneficial effects on the stomach. Diagonal Flying and Play Guitar are also considered helpful, while the Single Whip and Squatting Single Whip (Snake Creeps Down) benefit the liver in particular via the gentle bearing-down pressure exerted upon it by the right rib cage. All toe stances and toe kicks stimulate the spleen and stomach acu-channels in the front of the leg and foot, aiding the digestive process and assisting with the correct assimilation of fluids into the body.

Of course, a good digestive system depends greatly on what we eat. Tai chi philosophy urges us to reflect on the Yin and Yang aspects of food so that we balance our intake with our environment and with the seasons. For instance, too many cold or raw foods (Yin) during the winter (Yin season) is bad news, as would be too many heat-producing foods (Yang) during the summer. Skipping breakfast, particularly in winter when the stomach needs warming, is also unwise in terms of TCM, as are crash diets or lengthy fasts. And of course, heavily processed or junk foods need to be avoided, being poor in natural levels of ch'i and also often containing high levels of sugar, salt and artificial flavourings and colours, all of which use up considerable energy as the body struggles to eliminate them from the system.

*If the body is healthy, it can easily assimilate the stress of modern living and even find it a creative challenge.*

Mantak Chia

## Bones

A strong skeletal system is dependent on a good blood supply to the joints and on a healthy bone marrow that, in turn, helps manufacture the precious white blood cells that fight viruses and bacterial infection. Tai chi, in fact, is legendary in its ability to enhance the quality of the bone marrow via the TCM kidney system. The ch'i is thought somehow to permeate the marrow, building up great resilience over a period of time. It was said of Cheng Man-ch'ing that his arms felt like iron bars wrapped in cotton wool. This is a rare individual, of course, but it is an indication of what changes can be wrought in exceptional circumstances.

Those who work a lot with their hands and fingers will appreciate the relaxed rotation and flexing movements of the hands in tai chi, for stiffness can easily build up in the hands. This is apparent not only in well-known diseases like arthritis and rheumatism but also with 'modern' illnesses such as carpal tunnel syndrome, brought about by continual keyboard operating. Regular practice of tai chi is also thought to combat degenerative diseases, such as osteoporosis.

## Insight

In oriental medicine there is a concept called the wei ch'i (wei qi) – which can be explained as something like 'the body's defensive energy' or 'defensive shield'. It is a special kind of energy that is concentrated in the chest and lungs and which helps to repel invading pathogens – rather like our Western concept of the immune system. Tai chi is thought to help strengthen the wei ch'i, which is perhaps why those who do tai chi on a regular basis often report an overall improvement in their health and general resistance to common ailments.

## Muscles

Tai chi won't give you big muscles. But it will tone them up wonderfully. Good muscle tone depends on exercise and on an efficient blood supply and tai chi provides both of these. The ligaments and tendons that connect the muscles to the bones are strengthened with regular practice, particularly those of the legs and abdominal region, all of which increases our flexibility and ability to resist and cope with injury and strain. Moreover, those looking for a streamlining effect will find that because the gluteus maximus and other muscles of the bottom are in constant use during the form, the bottom gradually becomes firmer, as do also the thighs and calves, after several months of practice, while the constant turning of the body can also help to trim up the waistline.

The Opening sequence of the form, because of its symmetry and equal weight distribution, is said to benefit the internal muscular system by encouraging the proper placement and alignment of the body tissue. The Opening sequence can therefore be repeated several times, very slowly, for those interested in this possibility. It then becomes a kind of ch'i kung exercise (see Chapter 9) to help cultivate balance and stillness within.

## Glands

Most, if not all, of our bodily functions rely on chemical and hormonal stimuli and it is the endocrine glands of the body that are responsible for these. There are several major glands and we need them all. The thymus gland, located in the chest, plays a significant role in maintaining the immune system, while the adrenals, in the small of the back, produce chemicals that provide stamina, reduce inflammation and regulate blood pressure. The combination of tai chi movement and breathing, along with the constant emphasis on the chest, lower back and abdominal areas, is thought to stimulate both these glands. Meanwhile, the efficient flow of blood to the brain, promoted by relaxed shoulders and neck, naturally assists the pituitary and pineal glands that are responsible for growth and for regulation of the sexual and reproductive systems.

It is known that the glands of the body – especially the thymus – thrive in a happy individual, but they function poorly in those who are depressed. Probably, therefore, tai chi's greatest contribution in terms of maintaining a healthy immune system is in the calming and positive attitude developed by those who practice the form regularly.

## Urinary and reproductive systems

As we have seen, tai chi promotes the basic kidney ch'i of the
body, which in turn greatly facilitates the efficiency of all the
reproductive organs, helping to maintain sexual vitality and
fertility. The increased mobility and blood supply to the lower
abdomen naturally also have a positive effect on the urinary
system. Crescent Kick and all twisting and opening movements,
such as Four Corners, are excellent for strengthening the internal
muscles of the urinary and reproductive systems and for clearing
congestion – recurring infections in the urinary system often
being the result of congestion and stagnation of energy.

## Sex

Bearing in mind the Yellow Emperor and his hundred wives, the
question must be asked: does tai chi make you sexier? Well,
those who are fit and healthy are usually attractive to others, for
obvious reasons – so yes, maybe tai chi does help. Moreover, tai
chi and allied Taoist practices generate considerable vital energy
that can be directed towards sexual activity, if that's what you
want – although by so doing, you can very quickly deplete your
basic levels of ch'i. Most advanced practitioners of tai chi therefore
are mindful of the Taoist teaching on sexual matters, which
urges moderation. This is particularly important for men. Males
lose much of their vital kidney ch'i through ejaculation. Women
fare much better in this respect, since the female orgasm is not
considered to be debilitating. Women do, however, tend to lose
their ch'i through menstruation and childbirth.

Regarding the controversial topic of male sexuality, therefore,
teachers and writers in the fields of oriental philosophy and
medicine have always urged the conservation of semen whenever
reasonably possible, even during sexual activity. This is thought
not only to conserve the ch'i but also, with the help of a partner,

to help generate it internally. Once again, moderation and balance are the keywords here, as in so much of life.

## Staying healthy – the big picture

So tai chi is good for us. But what about the big picture – what about all the other things that can help keep us fit and well? Tai chi is wonderful, yes, but if you smoke, drink excessively, take drugs or eat lots of junk food it does not matter how much tai chi you do – you can go through the form 50 times a day if you like, but it will make no difference. Your health will not be good.

We need to take care of ourselves in other ways in order to stay well, and even more so as the years roll by. In youth, the body can absorb all manner of abuse, especially in terms of what we eat and drink, but this is for a limited period only. And for most of us we simply cannot afford to treat our bodies badly. In particular, it is vital to nourish the body properly. Without a certain amount of care in this respect, no amount of healthy living or exercise will keep you well in the long term. Here we will take a brief look at the most important considerations to be aware of, according to the teachings of oriental medicine. See if any of these strike a chord with you and whether you can make room for them in your life.

### START THE DAY WELL

In oriental medicine the digestive system is often referred to as the 'central fire', compared to a furnace or stove that provides us with warmth and energy. In this sense, it is of little use lighting the stove half-way through the day or, as some people do, late in the evening (the first hot meal of the day for many). Of course, a really substantial breakfast is not always possible for those of us with busy lifestyles, but we should still try, and anything is infinitely better than nothing at all. If it is a hot breakfast, all the better, especially in the winter months when the cold climate in many countries makes extra demands on our supplies of natural vitality. A body which is not nourished by this means will quickly become weakened, unable to transform and transport its food and fluids efficiently, leading to an accumulation of water in the tissues, oedema, mucus, phlegm, obesity and overall lack of energy. This is why people coming off starvation diets simply pile on the weight all the more quickly. The stove has gone out, along with much of the body's natural vitality and powers of self-healing, and no amount of effort can rekindle it.

In fact, a large proportion of our meals should always be cooked. Our digestive systems are different from ruminant animals who can graze on raw vegetation. We need to break down the tough structure of food through cooking before we can digest it properly. Therefore, one of the great problems with the typical Western diet at present is the use of refrigeration. We can, if we wish, ply the body with vast quantities of cold yoghurt, ice-cream, fruit and chilled foods at any time of the day, any season of the year. Much of this is very pleasant of course, especially on a hot summer's day, but none of it is of much use to the body in its cold state. We use up as much ch'i digesting raw or cold food as we can ever possibly derive from it in terms of true nourishment. It is a wasted effort as far as the body is concerned.

Similar considerations apply to chilled liquids when taken to excess. The notion that we must consume litre upon litre of chilled water to somehow 'flush out the system' or 'cleanse the mind' is misguided because the body is perfectly able to rid itself of toxins through the normal actions of the liver and kidneys. And if your body ever needs any extra fluid, don't worry, you will know. There is that magic sensation of thirst. Unless you live in a very hot climate (where it is always wise to take on a little extra water as a matter of course), the body will let you know at just the right time when you need to drink. Trust it!

The bottom line is simple. If you want to stay fit and well, and maintain that slim athletic figure of yours (you do have a slim athletic figure don't you?) you should eat well. Eat wholesome, cooked food. Start eating it as early in the day as possible. And use that refrigerator for the excellent job it does in preserving food, not for eating and drinking from directly.

## BE PEACEFUL AT MEALTIMES

In the West, of course, we are not overly concerned with food. Apart from going to the occasional exotic dinner party, most of us tend to think of eating as a routine bodily need, to be satisfied as quickly and, for some, as cheaply as possible. For the Chinese, however, food and how it is eaten is a very important business. In China, when people meet they often ask 'have you eaten?' rather than 'how are you?' In this context, it is thought to be helpful to eat under reasonably calm and peaceful conditions. After all, mealtimes are supposed to be times of nourishment and social pleasure. We often eat in the company of our family, friends or partners, and there is a timeless association between eating and the notion of security, which begins as a baby feeding at the breast, and continues right through our adult life. Excessive noise or commotion at this time is therefore thought to interfere with the digestive process and so should be avoided as much as possible.

Interestingly, we now know that there is indeed a possible scientific correlation in this respect, and for this we need to look again at the autonomic nervous system (see page 150). The nervous system is divided into two separate parts, the sympathetic and the parasympathetic systems. The sympathetic is associated with our fight or flight instincts. It controls muscles, blood supply and the production of hormones, such as adrenaline, all processes in the body that prepare us for action. The parasympathetic part of the nervous system, on the other hand, takes over when we are more relaxed. It is associated with renewal and maintenance within the body and encourages, among other things, the digestive process. So if we go against nature, and try to get the digestive system working while at the same time exposing ourselves to stress and physical tension, it is pretty clear what can happen. Running to catch the bus while eating that hamburger will usually result in only one thing, and that is the hamburger coming back up again, and pretty quickly too! We can expect things like indigestion, nausea or irritable bowel syndrome, at the least, or more serious digestive illnesses such as ulcers or inflammatory disease, in the long term, if we continue in this way to push our nervous system in two different directions at the same time.

So, eat and be happy. Take time to relax during and after your meals, and your body will thank you for it.

> **Insight**
> Digestion is better when we are relaxed and happy.
> Enjoy your food with other people who share these
> sentiments and never argue at mealtimes.

## AVOID EXTREMES OF CLIMATE

We have already seen how tai chi is best done outdoors or in a well-ventilated space. Oxygen is the greatest of all substances. It powers all of our physiological systems and nourishes and replenishes us constantly. What could be better for our tai chi practice than a fresh, cool climate, beneath the trees early in the morning or by the sea! But as well as bestowing their favours, the elements can be unkind as well, and when the climates are extreme we should take special care. Illness can often be aggravated by extremes of climate. For instance, cold, heat, wind and damp are climates that most of us would recognize as being potentially damaging in excess, and this is especially true if the body is already weak or vulnerable. In the framework of oriental medicine, moreover, these are even perceived as being *causes* of disease!

In the far-off days when oriental medicine developed its theoretical basis, there was no knowledge of microbes or bacteria and viruses. So the cause of a disease was equated with those climatic factors that seemed to aggravate it. For example, if someone had shivers, a runny nose and an aversion to cold, the cause of the problem was simply said to be 'cold'. And cold was treated accordingly through any number of tried and tested acupuncture routines or herbal prescriptions, until it was eliminated from the body.

These principles are still used today. It's all remarkably simple. And it works!

These extremes of climate are sometimes referred to, perhaps rather dramatically, as 'the external evils'. If all this sounds rather quaint to those readers of a strictly orthodox medical persuasion, do not be deceived! They are still relevant for us today, because they can hasten the onset of illness, either through damaging the body's immunity or by aggravating already existing internal weaknesses or viral infections. Here, then, are those 'external evils', along with some of the consequences if we are exposed to any of these in excess:

- ▶ Cold: *fixed pains in joints, backache, urinary, kidney, bowel and other digestive problems. Pre-menstrual pain, infertility.*
- ▶ Wind: *respiratory diseases, headaches, stiff necks, hay fever, skin complaints and general aches and pains.*
- ▶ Summer–heat: *sun-stroke, dehydration, dizziness. In extreme cases inflammatory illnesses, severe headaches, fever and mental disorientation.*
- ▶ Damp: *oedema, swollen, aching joints and muscles, fungal infections, phlegmy conditions, overall feelings of congestion and malaise.*
- ▶ Dryness: *dry cough, dry throat, sore eyes, flaky and dry skin.*

We can take steps to avoid the worst ravages of all these through simple common sense measures, by doing the kind of things that Grandma always used to urge us to do – that is, by wrapping up in cold and windy weather and protecting vulnerable areas such as the throat, head and kidneys. We can also make sure we are not exposed to excessively hot, dry or damp conditions, and do not walk around in damp clothes or go outside with damp hair on a cold day. We can avoid draughts, and make sure we have a warm and wholesome domestic environment in which to live. In short, we have to take care of ourselves. That way we give the wonderful therapeutic value of daily tai chi practice a chance to work its magic.

## AVOID EXTREMES OF EMOTION

As well as external causes of disease, there are also several *internal* causes that we can generate perfectly well within ourselves without any assistance from outside sources at all. In fact one of the most exciting features of oriental medical theory is that it recognizes the importance of emotional factors in the onset or aggravation of disease. Certain emotions, moreover, can affect particular organs and so can have quite profound effects in terms of our internal constitution. We all know, for instance, that worry can cause stomach problems such as ulcers. You don't have to be an expert on oriental medicine to realize that. But there is more.

Here are the internal causes of illness, together with the kinds of symptoms apparent when they take a hold:

▶ **Anger:** *affects the liver and prevents the smooth flow of ch'i throughout the body. This leads to a general stagnation of energy and blood circulation. Stiff joints and muscles, shoulder and neck pain, migraine, irritable bowel syndrome and pre-menstrual tension.*
▶ **Fear:** *affects the kidneys. Urinary disease, backache, tinnitus, chronic anxiety and compulsive behaviour, impotence.*
▶ **Worry, or over-thinking:** *affects the stomach and digestive system generally. Indigestion, ulcers, lethargy, cold limbs, poor appetite, prolapse of organs, loose bowels.*
▶ **Grief or sorrow:** *affects the lungs and the respiratory systems. Sunken chest, round shoulders, weak voice. Frequent colds and flu, asthma and skin complaints such as eczema.*

▶ **Joy:** *a difficult one, this, as we tend – quite rightly – to think of joy as a positive emotion. But seeking constant excitement and stimulation can have its downside, as well, leading to injury of the heart energies of the body. Insomnia, palpitations, restlessness and hypertension can also result over time. Shock is considered to have similar consequences, with its well-documented effects on the heart, although it can also affect the kidneys.*

In other words, a balanced emotional life is necessary for maintaining health. We should try to view negative emotions as existing independently of ourselves rather than as being a part of us. In this, we can simply tell ourselves, for example, that, 'There is anger', rather than, 'I am angry!', 'There is fear', rather than 'I am anxious and afraid'. There is a big difference in these two types of statements. Tai chi, of course, encourages us to stay balanced emotionally as well as physically, and to cultivate a healthy sense of detachment, but we sometimes also need to remind ourselves that feelings and emotions are a source of disharmony if taken to excess. Stay cool and be philosophical about things! That's a survival strategy not to be ignored in our modern world that takes us so often on a roller-coaster ride of wasteful, unnecessary stimulation and emotional extremes.

It is hoped that this chapter has provided some insight into the intimate relationship between tai chi and our bodily processes. Tai chi is not like most other exercise systems where you are urged to run around endlessly, getting hot and irritable. Rather, it is about looking after your entire being, at all levels.

# 10 THINGS TO REMEMBER

1  *Tai chi is not a cure for illness. The health benefits of tai chi are more apparent in the general strengthening of the constitution rather than affecting specific areas or complaints.*

2  *Tai chi benefits the cardiovascular system through a regime of gentle, regular exercise.*

3  *Tai chi helps circulate lymphatic fluid and stimulates those areas where lymphatic tissue is most concentrated – strengthening our immunity and resistance to disease.*

4  *Tai chi's calming effect stimulates the parasympathetic nervous system, which is responsible for the process of assimilation, renewal and preparing the body for rest.*

5  *An efficient digestive system relies on our being relaxed at mealtimes and eating warm, wholesome food whenever possible.*

6  *Regular tai chi practice provides vital load-bearing exercise for the lower limbs and thereby helps combat diseases such as osteoporosis.*

7  *Making use of the waist in many of the gentle turning and twisting movements of tai chi benefits the digestive and reproductive organs by increasing blood supply and removing stagnation.*

8  *Start the day with a warm breakfast in order to 'warm the centre.'*

9  *Avoid extremes of emotion and extremes of climate – these are considered by oriental medical theory to be very real causes of disease.*

10 *Try always to eat slowly and to chew your food properly. This helps to assimilate the ch'i along with the general goodness of the food itself.*

*T'ai Chi Ch'uan brings the physical, emotional, mental, and spiritual energies into alignment once again as undivided oneness.*

Michael Page

# 8

Tai chi – the learning experience

In this chapter you will learn:
- *the answers to many common questions regarding tai chi*
- *how others have dealt with difficulties and misgivings*
- *useful tips about methods and styles of tai chi.*

Well, by now I hope you have gone some way towards learning the tai chi form, or at least the early movements. It is not an easy journey you have chosen, as you probably realize by now. Tai chi is a graphic example of nature not surrendering her secrets lightly, and also illustrates the principle that if anything in life is worthwhile it almost always involves a degree of personal sacrifice and challenge. There are obstacles to overcome in learning tai chi, and many of these are within ourselves, on the mental level every bit as much as the physical. Overcoming obstacles is what we all do in life as we grow and evolve, of course, and it is a healthy activity. Where there is movement and change, there is life and vitality at work, and once that movement and change have ceased, stagnation and decay can only take their place. Change is at the heart of the life process, therefore, and in tai chi the changes and achievements you go through become something that is entirely yours, which no one can ever take away from you. It is something genuine in a world that is often far from genuine; something very real in a universe often governed by irrational fantasy and hype.

**Insight**

> Some people are born stronger than others and are able to
> excel at tai chi and reach their goal faster and more easily. In
> all cases, however, it is not the destination that is important,
> but the journey – the Tao or 'way'.

This chapter draws on the many observations that fellow students
have made and which I have noted in the course of my years of
involvement with tai chi. Here you will also find letters from people
studying tai chi, and their experiences – and there are also some
accounts written by students who have, themselves, even gone on
to teach the subject to others. There are frequently asked questions
(FAQs) and answers as well – the kind of things that, if you are not
able to attend a tai chi class yourself, you would probably be longing
to ask someone by now. In short, if you have any concerns or
misgivings at all about your progress – and we all have these at one
time or another – don't worry! The chances are you will find at least
a friendly echo, if not always a definitive answer, to them right here.

## Questions in class

**Q**
Why does the tiger crop up so often in tai chi. Like Carry Tiger to
the Mountain – or Bend the Bow and Shoot the Tiger. Why the
tiger – why carry him and shoot him so much?

**A**
Yes, the poor old tiger does get treated rather badly, doesn't
he! Actually, the tiger image occurs even more frequently in the
traditional long forms of Yang tai chi from which the short
form is derived. This is, of course, a creature of great strength,
and in oriental philosophy is associated with the Yin principle of
nature, which has great depth and hidden power. Just think of
it as a symbol of ch'i – you carry the ch'i to the mountain

(itself a symbol of being rooted and of something permanent and strong), or you project, or shoot the ch'i. There is a technique of sudden ch'i projection used in the martial arts called Fa Ching – and it can feel like being shot, if you are at the receiving end. Very powerful, just like the tiger when it strikes.

> *I not only desire my country to be strong, I would also like to share the benefits of Tai Chi Chuan with all mankind.*
>
> Cheng Man-ch'ing

Q
What sort of clothes should I wear for tai chi?

A
This is a question often asked by the more fashion conscious among us. In actual fact, it really doesn't matter a jot what you wear. There are no special uniforms or anything like that in tai chi. Perhaps in some of the more formal schools you might come across coloured belts or badges for grading, like in the martial arts, but mostly tai chi is an uncompetitive activity. As long as your clothing is of a loose, natural fibre, like cotton or wool for instance – so there's no static electricity flying about – and as long as you don't tie yourself up with lots of tight belts or corsets or things that might restrict your breathing, it's OK. As for footwear, it is best not to have too high a heel. And of course if you do your tai chi outdoors, your shoes should be waterproof as well. A lot of people use kung fu slippers for tai chi – which usually come from China and often have rope soles. These are very comfortable, but are not waterproof, so really not much use outdoors on a wet morning. Remember it is important to keep yourself warm and dry when you practice.

Q
I do a lot of keep fit, and exercise, but tai chi seems different because a lot of the movements are only done on one side. It's not symmetrical at all. Why is this?

**A**

Well, you can, if you want to, do the form on the other side, too. That is, you can do a Turn to the Left after the Opening, instead of a Turn to the Right – then a Ward Off to the Right instead of to the left, and so on all the way through. Some people like to do this, to be consistent, side to side. Also if you do some of the partner-work of tai chi, things like Push Hands which you find in martial arts practice, for instance, you will do a lot of these movements, or something very similar to them, on both sides, over and over again. But the form is, as you rightly say, asymmetrical – for instance the Single Whip. It's only ever done with the right arm extended in a Crane's Beak, never the left. But, there again, if you know your anatomy you will also realize that the body is not symmetrical anyway. The liver is behind the lower right rib cage, for example, while the spleen and pancreas tend to be placed left of centre in the abdomen. One of our kidneys is higher on one side than the other – and, of course, the heart is located a little towards the left side, too – making the structure of the lungs different one side to the other as a consequence. So the tai chi form is, in a clever way, I like to think, designed to take all this into account, which is why, most of the time – and especially when you are just starting out – it is done just the one way around.

**Q**

At what time of the day is it best to do tai chi?

**A**

I would say the best times are early in the morning or in the evening – in other words just after sunrise or just before sunset when the forces of Yang and Yin are more or less evenly balanced. In fact it never feels quite right to me doing tai chi in the middle of the day, especially if the sun is beating down. Too Yang!

Of course sunrise in the summer months can be around 4 a.m., or earlier! – and I for one have to confess that I don't see too many sunrises at that time of the year. Also it might not always be possible in the winter months for people who work away from home to get back or out in the park, or whatever, in time to practise before the sun sets. So really the best rule of thumb here is that any time is better than no time at all. Never use the weather or the time of day as an excuse for not doing your tai chi. Just do the best you can. Try to get a balance of Yang and Yin, a good feel to where you are, and that's fine.

Q
Is it true that if you don't do tai chi as a martial art, you aren't doing it right?

A
Certainly not! Tai chi is a martial art, of course – that's why many of the movements have a strong, dynamic aspect to them. Punches and kicks are not in there by accident. But there is more to tai chi than fighting. Tai chi as we know it probably came into being around the eleventh or twelfth century, but its underlying basis is much older than that. The philosophy of Taoism and even earlier exercise systems such as ch'i kung all had a big input into the development of the martial arts in China. Tai chi blended these ideas and systems with boxing and wrestling techniques. That is why tai chi is such a perfect blend of soft and hard, Yin and Yang – and is also why your tai chi will always be better for a degree of understanding of the martial aspects. A lot of people get the wrong idea about tai chi. It's not about waltzing around, waving your arms in some kind of mystical trance. It's about being rooted, with your feet on the ground, properly balanced and aware of your surroundings. Knowing something of the martial applications of the movements helps sometimes to develop these characteristics. That's what people are driving at when they say you might not be doing it right. But no, in answer to your question, you don't have to be a fighter to do tai chi properly. If that was the case, a good majority of all those people doing tai chi in the world today would be out of the running. And I certainly wouldn't be here taking this class with you.

**Q**

I am 65 years old and have arthritis. Recently I had a hip replacement, too. Would tai chi be suitable for me? I'm also a bit worried that I might hold the rest of the class up. You all look so fit and well!

**A**

Well – I'm glad you think we all look fit and well! Actually, tai chi is suitable for just about anybody. You just need to work within your capabilities and be patient. In time, and with regular practice, your arthritis might even start to moderate and you will then be able to do even more. And don't worry about holding up the class. Most tai chi classes have people of mixed abilities, and we are no exception here. Nobody is competing with anybody else. That is the spirit of tai chi when done in a group. The way to judge if a class is going to be suitable for you is to listen for laughter. If there is lots of laughter going on in class, then it's OK – and you don't need to worry about anything except studying and enjoying yourself.

## Insight

There are some misconceptions regarding ch'i (qi) – as if it is some kind of commodity that can be bought or sold, and that having lots of it somehow makes for a 'better' person. In fact ch'i is something we all of us have anyway. It's what keeps us alive and it circulates in our bodies every moment of every day. As with food or water, there is only so much that we need or can tolerate. Practitioners of oriental medicine consider that having an excess of ch'i can be just as much a cause of disharmony and illness as having a deficiency.

**Q**

Why don't you do tai chi to music? I think that would be really great.

**A**

It may well be – if you happen to view your tai chi as some kind of dance. But the question then arises, what kind of music is suitable?

What you think might be really great music might not appeal to others in the class. Not only that, but essentially tai chi is an internal sensation, with its rhythm centred around the breath. The breath is at the core of tai chi movement, and your breathing rhythm might not match that of the music being played. Music very rarely has a constant rhythm, especially for ten minutes at a time. It is an interference in tai chi, really, and a distraction that does not work at all well. You can try it at home, of course, and you might enjoy the experience. But dancing to music is not what tai chi is about.

Q
Can I do tai chi alongside other exercises, like yoga and swimming?

A
Sure. Tai chi can be combined with all sports and exercises, and particularly well, I think, with yoga. A perfect blend of active and passive, tai chi and yoga. The only thing to remember about tai chi and vigorous exercises such as running or swimming is that you should be relatively relaxed and calm when you approach your tai chi practice. As long as you approach your tai chi in this way, it is perfectly OK to blend it with just about anything.

## Letters and correspondence

Sometimes, in the past, folks have told us a little about themselves in their letters, and this can be interesting, as well as quite inspirational at times. Letters have come from some extraordinary places and from some extraordinary people too – from Buddhist monks in Wales to Catholic nuns in Ireland, from people in overseas service, or those serving time in prison. Everywhere, it seems, people are doing their tai chi! Those learning tai chi with the help of books or video material are often among the more elderly in our community, and they bring their own special needs and observations to the fore when they write in. I am including a few extracts here as they might strike a chord with readers of this book, and also because many of the difficulties raised in these letters will have been shared by us all at various times.

### FROM JS, MIDDLESBROUGH

*... being 68 and my wife 62 we feel that this form of fitness training would enable us to obtain a better way to spend our remaining years in this life. I first noticed this art practised in China in 1951 when I was sent overseas by the Royal Navy for 3 years. I used to watch people of all ages and in all forms of employment doing tai chi – on banks, in parks and after alighting from public transport even, everywhere that people went. I did not speak Chinese but I used to sit and watch these crowds of people doing these beautiful movements thinking that it was only for Chinese and Malayans to do. When I came home in 1954, I told my future wife about this beautiful practice of the art, but I did not find out its name. Just recently my wife and I went to our local library and we saw your book on the subject. I recognized what it was at once because who could ever forget the sight of all these Chinese people putting down their baskets or cases and just doing tai chi in any public place that they happened to be!*

This is a lovely letter and well illustrates how, even as a spectator, and even over a period of many years, the experience of tai chi can endure in the mind. It also shows how, until only quite recently, things like tai chi (or yoga, or meditation, or whatever) were thought to be exclusively for people from the East. Now we all know we can have a go, and can benefit from learning these techniques, no matter how imperfectly. And if, like the author of this letter, you can share your learning experience with somebody else, all the better, because you can each bring your own strengths and observations into the process. This letter shows courage and optimism, because it makes it clear that it's never too late to start!

## Insight
He who knows he has enough is rich. *Tao Te Ching*

## FROM FR, ISRAEL

*I am a retired person, aged 75 and I am all too aware of the necessity for physical exercise in order to maintain a reasonable quality of life. ... I am learning tai chi by myself using your book and video cassettes. So far I managed to go through the whole form, and I am more or less satisfied with my performance, except for the kicks. I simply don't have the strength and balance required to execute them. Could you advise me how to overcome this difficulty?*

Doing the kicks in tai chi often presents a problem for the elderly. And it is no accident that they do not occur in the form until around the half-way mark, a time where most people, if they are learning in the sequence given, have been doing some kind of tai chi for a good few weeks, if not months already. Also, early in the form there are several movements that are very similar to kicks. If you think about the narrow toe stances such as Crane Spreads Its Wings, or the narrow heel stances, such as Play Guitar, these movements encourage us to place much of our weight on one leg, the other foot having either its toes or heel in only very light contact with the ground. It's all a bit like learning to ride a bike as a child – with the stabilizers on. Remember that? Once your balance improved, you took the stabilizers off, and away you went! The toe and heel stances are like the stabilizers; they prepare us for the kicks. In time, with daily practice, your balance will improve and the kicks will then seem easier. Also, and this is most important, don't feel you have to kick too high! A shallow kick, to knee height is quite sufficient since all we are trying to achieve here is to cultivate balance and to give the legs the beneficial load-bearing exercise they need to help maintain healthy bones. Think of your kicks as slightly more elaborate toe or heel stances, therefore. Sink into the back leg. Raise the front knee just a little and then extend the toes or heel outwards. Not too far. Not too high. That's enough.

Don't be too hard on yourself! There is no limit to the degree of sophistication that you can aim for in the world of tai chi – and no end to the amount of time and money you can spend in the process of striving for excellence. Try always to know what your aims and ambitions are, therefore, and be realistic. There is no disgrace in knowing only a little. There is no disadvantage to approaching the subject in a spirit of humility and moderation.

*FROM PL, LYMINGTON*

*I had been to tai chi classes for a number of years, with several different teachers ... but eventually gave up doing the form because I found it led to knee problems, which at my age (now 70) it wasn't possible to ignore. But I couldn't work out what I was doing wrong, and two different teachers weren't able to help. However, I did keep up with some Taoist exercises. So I started using your book rather gingerly, but I find it both so clear and so detailed in the explanation of the movements that I have had no knee problems – and as I've been doing the 'Snake Creeps Down' and kicks now for a while without running into difficulties I feel I've passed the real hurdle! As I really enjoy tai chi, I'm very grateful.*

This is a nice letter – always good to receive, of course, if you are a writer. I have included it here, however, because it shows how important it is to listen to what your body tells you. If you experience any pain with tai chi, and it does not go away with practice, the chances are there is something wrong, or something you are doing which isn't suitable, or needs to be done differently. One of the most common problems people encounter in the early stages of tai chi is discomfort in the knees due to placing too much strain on the one knee joint at a time. This occurs with movements such as Play Guitar, Crane Spreads Its Wings or, of course, the kicks. If you look closely at the foot diagrams in this book, however, you will see that you are encouraged to always place the rear, weight-bearing foot at a comfortable angle to the leading foot, usually around 45° or so. Also, what sometimes happens is that students going through the form, and having placed their feet correctly into a movement, often forget to adjust what is to become the rear foot of the next movement before going on. The result of this is that once they do complete the next movement they are left stranded in an uncomfortable stance in which the rear foot could be as much as 90° angled from the front one. This puts quite a lot of pressure on the rear knee and, when repeated daily, can be too much for some. In a busy class situation, a teacher might not always be able to spot this, either. This is where books of this kind are so useful.

## Insight

Don't feel discouraged if your teacher is reluctant to pass on his or her entire lifetime of experience to you in a single lesson. He or she has probably had a thousand students just like you quizzing them for their knowledge, only to see them give up and abandon their tai chi studies a few days later at the slightest distraction. You have to demonstrate your sincerity if you would expect others to share their hard-fought knowledge. Prove it with humility and then be very patient.

A student repays his teacher badly if he or she remains always a student. One of the best things, for me, about having taught tai chi to others over the years has been to see people go on to eventually teach others themselves. There has been a strong tradition in tai chi, one with links to the original concepts of how traditional knowledge was transmitted in eastern cultures, that you should never presume to teach until you have undergone years of rigorous training and had the full blessing of a master. This has its merits, of course, but it does little to promote this wonderful art to the majority of people, and as tai chi becomes increasingly popular and widespread, there would simply never be enough teachers to go around if we were to adhere to all this too strictly!

There is, however, a lively counter-tradition to this idea in modern China that can be best seen in the field of oriental medicine. Some decades ago it was realized that in order to bring health to the people, many more doctors were needed than were available at the time. What were subsequently called barefoot doctors then entered upon the scene, not academically brilliant, but capable individuals trained in the bare essentials of healing, either through herbs or acupuncture. Despite their humble state and limited knowledge, barefoot practitioners were sent out to the villages and rural communities to do their work – and this has largely been a successful policy in primary health care in China. Many of us now teaching tai chi, and passing on the little we know to those who perhaps know a little less, are what could be called barefoot tai chi teachers. To illustrate this new trend in practice, which is going on all over the world, here is a brief note from a friend and former student who has gone on (I don't know whether barefoot or not) to teach what he knows to others.

### FROM IH, KENT

*My involvement in tai chi began nine years ago through an interest in Buddhism. Learning the form was good but it seemed then that the discussion of Taoism, Buddhism and things 'New Age' in the pub afterwards was equally significant. Time passed and my interest had reached a plateau when a friend at work, unable to find a tai chi group, was happy to share my knowledge. Suddenly I found myself with a group of six or eight 'students'. This new role forced me to examine and improve my form, and I have learned together with my friends. It seems that tai chi has once again been the catalyst that develops the individual and brings people together.*

So there you are! What I hope all these quotes have shown you more than anything is that there is an infinite variety of experiences at large within the world of tai chi – that there is much more to it than simply learning the movements and going through the form daily. There are the many connections tai chi makes beyond the physical realm; connections to ideas, to philosophy, to sharing experiences with others. In the next chapter we will be exploring these connections a little further.

# 10 THINGS TO REMEMBER

1  *People's experiences of tai chi are wide and varied. And all experiences are valid.*

2  *We should not worry about what to wear for tai chi. Just make sure you keep warm and dry and that you can move freely.*

3  *The best times for doing tai chi are probably morning and evening – a balanced time for Yang and Yin.*

4  *It's OK to do tai chi for health and relaxation purposes. You aren't necessarily doing it 'wrong' if the martial heritage doesn't interest you.*

5  *Tai chi when practised for health is not competitive. Don't worry if you have physical frailties or limitations. A good tai chi class focusing on health will welcome all comers.*

6  *The only rhythm you should pay attention to in tai chi is the natural rhythm of your own breathing. Tai chi to music might be pleasant enough at times, but remember the rhythms will vary and, ultimately, it becomes a distraction.*

7  *It's OK to do tai chi in conjunction with other exercise programmes.*

8  *It's great to be able to share the learning experience with someone close. Quicker, too.*

9  *No matter how frail or unwell you might be, you can gain something from taking up tai chi. There is space for everyone in tai chi, East and West, young and old, strong and not-so-strong.*

10  *Don't be bashful about showing others a little tai chi. Passing on the little we know to others who might just happen to know a little less is the way most great ideas are transmitted. As long as this is done in a spirit of humility, explaining to others your own limitations, it's fine.*

# 9

........................................................................

# Body, mind and spirit

In this chapter you will learn:
- *more about the nature of ch'i*
- *about the philosophy of Taoism*
- *about related topics such as ch'i kung and meditation.*

## Finding a teacher

I hope this book has inspired you to go out and join a tai chi class or to find a teacher. Perhaps you are already attending evening classes or a formal school for tai chi, in which case it is pretty likely you are doing something similar to what is laid out in these pages. Yang-style tai chi is very popular at the present time, but there are, of course, many variations of style and of emphasis even here. Some instructors, for example, teach tai chi wholly for its martial aspects and in so doing may fail to balance this with a transmission of the vital qualities of relaxation, calm and humility, all central to the Taoist tradition. Others might teach it entirely for its beauty and gracefulness and as a consequence may fail to generate real energy or any measure of strength in their pupils. These are the two extremes and, thankfully, you won't encounter them too often.

Look for balance, therefore, in this area as much as in any other. Also don't be anxious about asking your would-be teacher what precisely he or she intends to teach. You have every right to this information, especially if you are going to part with hard-earned cash. A good tai chi teacher will always be prepared to answer your questions and will not try to make you look small or hold you back from reaching the same level, in time, as they have reached themselves. A good teacher is also usually broad-minded and cheerful. The moment you encounter anybody who needs to justify their own standards by denigrating the work of others, you should proceed only with great caution. Those who have truly found the Tao in their lives realize the richness and depth of tai chi and will never put their own preferences and individual specialities over and above any body else's.

And now for the transmission of a great secret. Often pupils search the world over for the magic 'touch of the master' or just the right word at the right time that will transform their lives. Often they wait for decades for the one vital crumb of information that will take them to the heights of enlightenment and skill in their chosen art – tai chi or anything else. Yet so often they are disappointed and the reason is very simple. They have overlooked the one really important principle that is at the very heart of excellence, a principle that can be described in just one simple word: practice.

Just keep doing it – don't give up! Certainly you will need an instructor at various times, especially during the early days. Most students go through several until they find the right one. But unless you are priming yourself to become a super-human fighting machine, the basic techniques of tai chi – despite what many will tell you – are straightforward and easy to learn. Then it is mostly a matter of getting on with it and adhering to daily practice and study. That is the great secret – and it is all there, quite literally in your own hands.

> *Overcoming others requires force.*
> *Overcoming the self needs strength.*
> *He who knows he has enough is rich.*

Tao Te Ching

# Between heaven and earth

By this stage, the two great polarities of Yang and Yin will feel more real for you, as you know where to find them in your tai chi movements and in your breathing also. But Yang and Yin do not stop there and the following table may help to broaden this concept a little, for the contemplation and realization of these forces through the tai chi is ultimately a celebration of all nature and of our place within it (see Figure 9.1).

| | |
|---|---|
| Positive | Negative |
| Light | Dark |
| Day | Night |
| Summer | Winter |
| Spring | Autumn |
| Dry | Moist |
| Warm | Cool |
| Expansion | Contraction |
| Forward | Reverse |
| Active | Meditative |
| Spirit | Matter |
| Firm | Yielding |
| Analytical | Intuitive |
| Fiery | Watery |
| Surface | Depth |
| Conscious | Unconscious |
| Extroverted | Introverted |
| Forthright | Reserved |
| From above | From below |
| Dispersal | Renewal |

*Figure 9.1 The qualities of yang and yin.*

Helpful and interesting as such tables of correspondences are, you will probably have realized by now that everything in this respect is relative. A candle is Yang compared with a glow-worm, but Yin compared with the brilliance of the sun. And when we explore these relationships further we can see in more depth the way Yang and Yin react to each other in practice. As well as being in opposition to one another, Yang and Yin can, at any one time, also be:

▶ **Interdependent:** *that is, each relying on and supporting the other. Without an action (Yang), for instance, there* *can be no reaction (Yin). Often, too, it is only by reference to a point of stillness (Yin) that we are ever conscious of motion (Yang).*

▶ **Inter-consuming:** *Yang and Yin draw upon each other. Too much water (Yin) puts out fire (Yang). Think about the way the body uses nutrients, too. The food we eat nourishes (Yin) by providing energy (Yang). But at the same time we use energy (Yang) in order to digest the nutrients (Yin). This is an important aspect to bear in mind for all those trying to lose weight. All sensible diets urge us to eat selectively, never to starve ourselves. That way we use up plenty of energy with digestion and the body does not need to store excess nutrients as fat.*

▶ **Inter-transforming:** *Too much heat (Yang) will cause things to evaporate, leaving empty space (Yin). Intense cold can also burn, of course. So opposites can also transform one into the other at their extremes. Refer again to the Tai Chi T'u diagram (Figure 9.1) to see how the rotational, changeable quality of the symbol accommodates these actions. The seeds of Yang and Yin within the two halves show clearly the potential for change and transformation.*

Interesting stuff. What is even more remarkable is that men and women were already contemplating and acting upon these principles thousands of years ago, for instance, in the field of practical medicine and philosophy, simply through their observations of nature and the environment in which they lived. The earliest written reference to Yin and Yang can, in fact, be found in the *I Ching*, the *Book of Changes*, parts of which, if you recall, can be traced with confidence to at least the eighth century BC, by which stage the concept was clearly already at a high level of sophistication, intimating a still greater antiquity. The people of these times understood the opposition and the interdependence of all things. They had no problem with contradictions or relative values, either. It was all part of the richness and mystery of life.

Nowhere, perhaps, has this subtle relativity been expressed with more skill and insight than in the Taoist arts. Here, the relative strengths and inter-relationships of the Yang and the Yin can be discerned constantly – in the empty spaces, for example, that so many drawings and paintings contain, contrasting with but somehow also supporting the more tangible contents of the picture. In Taoist poetry, also renowned for its brevity, it is often what is left unsaid that creates the meaning to the verses, rather than the words themselves.

In your tai chi work, too, this concept can be a rich source of inventiveness and spontaneity. Try doing a very Yin form sometimes or a very quick and forceful Yang one. Or contemplate the Yang within a Yin form – only very slightly Yang. The breath can also be revisited in this respect. The inhalation can be Yin if you are doing the tai chi form in the usual way, but Yang if you are engaged in some forms of passive meditation or pure contemplation of the movement of internal energy.

> **When the breath wanders, the mind is unsteady, but when the breath is still, so is the mind still.**
>
> Pradīpikā

## Ch'i kung

Closely allied to tai chi practice, and certainly pre-dating it by many centuries, is the widespread practice of ch'i kung, the circulation and cultivation of ch'i through breathing and concentration. It is an amazingly complex area and if it is true that there are several, if not dozens, of different styles and variations within the world of tai chi, then in the closely related sphere of ch'i kung there are probably hundreds!

Ch'i kung is usually, though not always, done standing and body movement is kept to a minimum. One of the most basic styles, especially suitable for those beginning tai chi, is shown in Figure 9.2. The feet are parallel, just a little more than shoulder width apart, the arms extended out in front of the chest as though embracing a large tree. The straight spine, the gently tucked in sacrum, the rounded aspect of the arms will all be familiar.

You can think of it as tai chi without movement. Try it for a few minutes, perhaps at the beginning or at the end of your tai chi form. Keep the knees apart, 'spiralled out' like sitting on a horse. Sink down and think of your roots, the body itself suspended from above by that golden thread – upright between heaven and earth, between Yang and Yin, spirit and matter, the centre of its own universe.

*Figure 9.2 Chi Kung posture.*

Breathe deeply into the abdomen and be aware of the Tan Tien. Think of Yang energy and light as you breathe in and imagine a tiny golden ember smouldering away there. Every time you inhale, you fan it so it glows brighter. Then, as you breathe out, let the energy it produces spread throughout your entire body. Keep the breath deep, long and even. Let it, and the movement of energy in the Tan Tien, fill your consciousness entirely.

Later, try concentrating the feeling of energy into the spine, from where it rises to the shoulders, then down the arms. Let it connect down through the legs, to meet with the earth ch'i beneath your feet, or at a place on the sole of each foot called – very aptly – the 'Bubbling Spring'. Eventually, try letting it climb all the way up to the top of the head and then down the front again, via the forehead, throat, chest and abdomen, and returning to the Tan Tien – a circle of energy that transmits life-giving ch'i to all the organs of the body in endless cycles of generation (Yang) and storage (Yin).

If at this stage you place the tip of your tongue lightly against the roof of your mouth – as if saying the letter 'L' – it will greatly facilitate the flow of ch'i. This 'circuit' of energy is also a good safety precaution. Ch'i naturally likes to rise and if it gets lodged in the head it can contribute to problems including high blood pressure and headaches, and so this safe technique of circling the energy back down is particularly valuable.

The ch'i kung position should be held for a reasonable length of time, say at least two minutes at first, building up to as long as you wish later on. Up to 15 minutes is possible with practice. A variation on this position is simply to lower the arms down to the level of the solar plexus – a welcome change, after a while, as the arms start to tire.

This has been just a very brief look at what is really a fascinating subject and a very rewarding area of study.

## The five elements: pathways between body and mind

Any overview of tai chi philosophy would not be complete without a look at the five elements. The elements, as such, are not unique to China, of course. Every great culture has classified the natural forces of their environment into four or five universal categories. The Greeks, the American Indians, the brilliant artists and humanists of the European Renaissance, they all had their elemental forces. The Taoists recognize five elements: Fire, Earth, Metal, Water and Wood.

The term 'element' in the scientific sense usually means a particular atomic configuration these days and this can lead those of a purely orthodox persuasion to look down their noses somewhat at what they see as a primitive attempt to classify matter into its respective parts. But nothing could be further from the truth. The classical elements of antiquity go far beyond a mere preoccupation with matter. They are, in fact, a means of contemplating and understanding aspects of the whole environment – earth, sky, water, spirit, fire and energy, life and death, great and powerful forces to which the people of those times felt themselves both mentally and physically united, a kind of attachment to which those of us practising tai chi should also aspire, perhaps.

Consequently, and because of their pleasingly abstract quality, the elements have always been applicable to the field of medicine – and, indeed, still are – furnishing the practitioner of oriental medicine with an invaluable guide through the otherwise impenetrable complexity of the human body and the world around it. Fire, Earth, Metal, Water and Wood are all to be found in an energetic sense within the various organs and systems of the human body. Moreover, each element has a Yang and a Yin aspect. There are Fire organs, such as the heart, or Water organs, such as the kidneys, as the following brief tour through the elements will show (see Figure 9.3).

| *Wood* | *Fire* | *Earth* | *Metal* | *Water* |
|---|---|---|---|---|
| Spring | Summer | Late summer | Autumn | Winter |
| Germination | Growth | Ripening | Harvest | Storage |
| East | South | Centre | West | North |
| Wind | Heat | Dampness | Dryness | Cold |
| Green | Red | Yellow | White | Black/blue |
| Liver | Heart | Spleen | Lungs | Kidneys |
| Eyes | Tongue | Mouth | Nose | Ears |
| Anger | Elation | Pensiveness | Grief | Fear |
| Shouting | Laughing | Singing | Weeping | Groaning |
| Forest | Heath | Fields | Clouds | Rivers/sea |
| Life | Sunshine | Soil | Minerals | Rainfall |
| Creativity | Inspiration | Common sense | Melancholy | Contemplation |

*Figure 9.3 Attributes of the five elements.*

When the elements are working together, we are healthy; the body and mind act as a meaningful and dynamic whole. If, however, one element or organ becomes weak or overactive, the others will tend to compensate, which is all right for a while, but if the imbalance continues, illness will arise.

We can now refer back to the health considerations we looked at in Chapter 7 and see how the elements help us to link together lots of otherwise seemingly disconnected ideas about our own bodies, our emotions and the environment in which we have to function. For instance, we saw how grief damages the lungs and the respiratory system generally (see page 162). We also saw how dryness affects the respiratory system (see page 160). All this can be seen in Figure 9.3, where we note that under the element Metal we have the colour white, the nose and the season of autumn listed together. Autumn is, of course, a time when leaves and plants dry up, wither and die. The weeping tone of voice is also related to Metal and of course when we grieve, or if we have any form of respiratory problem, our voice tends to assume a weepy, breathless quality as well. On a brighter note, if we explore the element of Fire, we can see how joy affects the heart, makes it leap and rejoice at times, and that the season most associated with these tendencies is summer. This is arguably the most joyful period of the year, and the warm vibrant colours we associate with fun and excitement, such as red or gold are predominant in the natural world at this time. All this relates to the Fire element. These connections are fascinating to explore, and give us a great insight into how the human body and mind work together and how these, in turn, echo what takes place around us in the environment.

For those of you trained in Western physiology, it is helpful to understand that in oriental medicine the organs are described by their function throughout the whole body rather than by their mere physical structure or anatomical location. Each one, moreover, will borrow from and lend energy to neighbouring elements or organs, each affecting the other in endless cycles of creativity and dissolution. The cycles of interchange are described neatly by arranging the elements on a five-pointed star, enclosed by a circle. The generative or creative cycle is ranged around the circle, while the controlling or destructive cycle is shown by the internal star (see Figure 9.4).

It is easy to imagine how the Taoists first perceived these cycles in the natural world around them. Take time yourself to contemplate how they work out in any area of experience you care to apply them to. Let's work through an example, a small journey of a kind, and see where it takes us. The element of Wood is all about

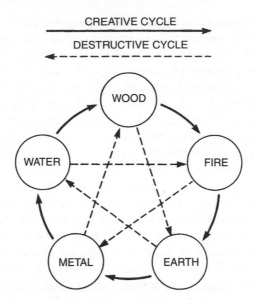

Figure 9.4 *Creative and destructive cycles and the five-element star.*

expansion, growth, the colour green and the season of spring. Things begin to grow and blossom at this time of the year, just as a human being begins its journey as a child and grows into puberty. This, in time, transforms itself into the next element in the creative cycle, Fire, which corresponds to summer, to maturity and adulthood. This is a time of 'getting things done', of fecundity, abundance in all things. This transition from youth into adulthood is a remarkable time, and contemplation of the elemental theme here can give us enormous insight into this process and its implications. If we find a lot of laughter taking place among people going through this transition we shouldn't be at all surprised, or disturbed either. After all, if ever there is a time for frivolity and joy, this has to be it!

No matter what age we are, however, we can always discover smaller cycles of creative energy that mature into something rewarding and inspirational, at any time. It might be painting a picture, or learning a new language. It could be any new relationship, or any process of developing our capacity for joy and laughter. This is just a small segment of a journey that, if carried through, will also lead to a time of ripening and harvest, and eventually consolidation and letting go. All things have a natural life-span, including ideas, people and places. In thinking about the cycle of the elements, and applying these to any undertaking or idea we have, we can accept change and work within it, rather than against it. This acceptance of change makes space in our lives for the next big idea, and off we go again.

Be prepared for these associations to occur in your life. They will want to make themselves known anyway, spontaneously as you continue with your tai chi journey and become more and more receptive to the currents and forces at work around and within you. Let it happen.

Think of the seasons; think of the cycles in nature and human affairs – it is a wonderful meditation in itself. Try also looking in depth at one element – say, one each week. Let it become a special part of your life for that period of time. Collect items from nature that exemplify that element – stones, shells, feathers and so on. Visit some water, the sea or a river; visit the woods; contemplate fire in all its manifestations; take up work in a garden.

Thus, through tai chi practice and its related studies we find not only a highly effective means of maintaining health through working on the physical body, but also are able to effect change on a far more powerful energetic level. It is a widely held view in oriental medicine that if the body is balanced so too will be the mind and, ultimately, the spirit. 'Spirit' is a strange word in our modern society. Many will refuse to recognize its existence and question the worth of pursuing such a vague and possibly illusory goal. The only reply to such cynicism is to continue with the tai chi – keep trying, keep working at it and eventually the answer will be found.

## Taoism

The Chinese philosophy of Taoism (pronounced 'Daoism', by the
way) has always remained something that has to be experienced
with the mind or heart, rather than the intellect. Of all belief
systems or cultural practices throughout the world, Taoism is
possibly unique in its refusal to be pinned down or classified.
The main text on Taoism, the *Tao Te Ching*, written some time
around the sixth century BC when Taoism was already an old and
venerable subject, has the clue to this elusive quality set forth in the
very opening lines:

> *The Tao that can be told is not the eternal Tao.*
> *The name that can be named is not the eternal name.*
> *The nameless is the beginning of heaven and earth.*

What the author, Lao Tse, is referring to here is the source of
existence. The Tao precedes the Tai Chi, therefore, in the great
scheme of things, the order of creation, which like the five
elements, is evident in everything around us (see Figure 9.5).

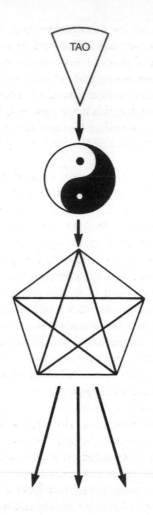

*Figure 9.5 The creation tree.*

Lao Tse as a man is as illusive as Taoism itself, and many scholars
believe the name Lao Tse, which literally means 'the old sage',
or 'teacher', refers not to a single person but to a whole group of
philosophers working together in China around the time of the
sixth century BC. This reluctance to credit an individual with the
creation of what may, to us, seem such formidable undertakings
is often applied to other great literary figures of the past, such as

Homer or Shakespeare, for example. Perhaps this is because the works in question are so magnificent and so vast that we feel it must surely be beyond the abilities of any one individual to achieve alone. Whether this is true or not is really of little importance. In Lao Tse's masterpiece, there is a common thread of original thought that is remarkably consistent and this is why the text itself has survived for centuries and been translated into all the major languages of the world. It is in fact more widely read today than ever.

According to legend, Lao Tse was keeper of the archives at the imperial court in China, an eminently important position. When he was very old and wished to retire from court he set out alone for the remote western borders of China, somewhat disillusioned with the false world of political intrigue and all the greed of the metropolis. At the border post, the man on guard asked Lao Tse to write down his philosophy before he passed through and on into the wilderness. He is then said to have composed, quite spontaneously, in some 5,000 characters of text the *Tao Te Ching* that, translated into English, is sometimes referred to as 'The Way and its Power'. That this great work should have been left as a memento of a journey is itself poignant, since the Tao or way is often likened to a journey through life which is itself a metaphor for personal evolution and change.

So what is Taoism all about, and why is it relevant to those of us studying tai chi? Well, central to the philosophy of Taoism is a rejection of formality and regulation and a celebration, instead, of innocence and spontaneity and what is termed wu wei or 'no mind'. By wu wei we do not mean stupidity or lack of thought, or selfishness and egoism, but rather a kind of almost child-like simplicity and spontaneity that allows us to respond easily and effortlessly to challenges without trying to meet them aggressively head on. This avoidance of confrontation and the notion of easy movement without effort is ideally suited to the thought process of tai chi. Although there is a strict form to be learned in tai chi (with movements that have to be executed with a high degree of proficiency) once all this has been achieved, the next and most important stage in our tai chi development is to simply 'let go', to become natural and free in what we do. In other words, once we no longer have to think consciously about what we are doing in tai chi, about what movement comes next, and how the feet should be placed, and how the breath should go and so on, once we have placed all that behind us, we start to travel into the realms of what is called 'moving meditation', another excellent way of describing wu wei.

## Insight

A vessel that is full has no space left for anything new to enter. People are the same. This is the meaning of the Taoist ideal of cultivating emptiness and of letting go of things. This is the key to evolution and change at all levels.

The lessons that this experience has for us, repeated daily, are immense. Life itself then becomes a kind of moving meditation through which we can move with freedom and spontaneity while at the same time keeping in touch with the basic ground rules of common sense that enable us to function in society and in the company of others. It is this combination, in reality so difficult to achieve, that is prized most among those engaged in the Taoist arts – be it philosophy, exercise, medicine, martial arts, calligraphy, poetry.

By doing nothing, therefore, the Taoists believed that they could, in theory, achieve anything. If this sounds odd, as much of Taoist thought does at first, then this passage from the *Tao Te Ching* might help clarify things a little:

> *The Tao abides in non-action,*
> *Yet nothing is left undone.*

Taoism is about shedding limitations, therefore. In other words, if we empty ourselves of tensions, of second-hand beliefs, political dogma and pride, there is always going to be at least some space left inside for opportunity and for new ideas and experiences to arise. And, of course, what better way of achieving this state than to practise our tai chi form regularly. With tai chi we can relax, let go! We are not 'full up' with opinions or desires then. We do not limit ourselves in any sense with what is irrelevant, but instead 'open up' and renew each day the vast potential of life that lies before us. In this way, everything becomes possible and 'nothing is left undone'.

It is this wonderful abstract, formless quality about the original Taoist teachings that can also be so liberating and appealing to the modern mind. Although it is true to say that Taoism itself has undergone many changes over the centuries, just as the Chinese culture has, and that it has passed through some relatively decadent phases in which a great deal of ceremony and superstition arose, at its core there remains a timeless and fathomless quality that can never be fully exhausted or comprehended in its entirety. It is this magical core that people today find worthy of study, and the *Tao Te Ching* is the beginning and end of all these endeavours. It is not a book which one reads and then forgets, but rather one which the student returns to and refers to over and over again during their own special journey through life.

## Insight

By developing the powers of ch'i in ourselves there can be only one worthwhile outcome: to transform ourselves and our environment into something more helpful to others – to change the world around us, in no matter how small or modest a way, into something better, something more useful, more gentle and kind.

The great Tao itself, of course, is something beyond our experience and therefore beyond our powers of description. However, every living thing has its own smaller, more personal tao – we could write it in English perhaps with a small 't' – its own path or purpose in life. The central idea of Taoism is that when we, as individuals, realize our own individual tao, it then becomes indivisible with the greater, universal Tao. Finding one's own 'way' means realizing what is essential in one's life. It might be exhilarating to realize this or it could be painful.

Whatever the outcome, the Way is begun with the integration of Yang and Yin, the realization of the Tai Chi in one's own life.

After that, one simply waits for the Tao to express itself. In this respect, the qualities that have been prized by the Taoists, such as spontaneity, non-violence, humility and detachment, can help us to overcome the ego and the endless desire for power and self-importance, so valued by our society yet which can never be really satisfied. Through these qualities a state of peace and harmony gradually arises, by which we can find the unifying principle of the Tao in the world about us as well as within our own hearts.

In this sense, once again, it is not the destination but the journey that is of importance. You can view your tai chi practice, therefore, as symbolic of the journey to find the Tao. It then becomes synonymous with the archetypal 'Quest' or search so often described in great literature or fable. It is the Grail, the heroic journey, the battle for understanding. When viewed in this light, even the martial aspect of tai chi becomes a symbol for something far greater. Thus, in the Tao are all things reconciled.

You have now come to the end of this book. It is not intended to be an exhaustive summary of the subject. A thousand books could not even begin to be that. It is a signpost, that's all, and the journey lies ahead. I cannot tell you where it will lead, for it is *your* journey, not mine or anybody else's. It is your tao and yours alone.

There is an old Chinese saying: 'If you cannot find it within yourself, where will you go for it?' Have faith in your own powers, therefore. And may all good fortune be with you.

# 10 THINGS TO REMEMBER

1  It's a good idea to find a tai chi class and get some formal instruction sometime.

2  Look for a balanced approach in your teachers – not too soft, not too hard.

3  Practice is vital. Without constant practice you will not achieve anything at all with tai chi.

4  The 'Tai Chi' mentioned in the Chinese classics is a combination of the two great forces of Yang and Yin working in harmony.

5  Tai chi is a celebration of nature and your place within it.

6  Yang and Yin are not merely opposites. They also support each other and transform themselves, one into the other. They maintain health and facilitate progress through mutual support and co operation.

7  Ch'i kung is a process in which energy is circulated around the body, guided by the breath. It can teach us a lot about what we should be feeling when we do our tai chi.

8  The five elements of oriental philosophy can be found everywhere in nature, including the human body.

9  Taoism (Daoism) is an ancient Chinese philosophy that teaches wisdom, humility and acceptance of nature's way.

10  Taoism is about shedding limitations, being at peace and finding the right path or way through life.

*Just as the path of the eagle in the air and the path of the snake are invisible, so also is the path of the sage.*

The Buddha

# Composite illustration of the sequence

The composite diagram on the following pages shows the whole form without interruption, including all the repetitions. Work along each row, right across both pages, before going on to the next row below.

Composite illustration of the sequence    203

# Taking it further

## Further reading

Cheng Man Ch'ing. (1985) *Cheng Tzu's Thirteen Treatises on T'ai Chi Ch'uan*, Berkeley: North Atlantic Books

Hass, E. M. (1981) *Staying Healthy with the Seasons*, Berkeley: Celestial Arts Press

Klein, B. (1994) *Movements of Magic*, North Hollywood: Newcastle Publishing Co.

Page, M. (1989) *The Tao of Power*, London: Green Print

Parry, R. (2008) *Prevention Better*, Charleston: Book Surge Publishing

Tse, Lao. (1989) *Tao Te Ching*, trs. Gia-Fu Feng and Jane English, New York: Vintage Books

Wing, R. L. (1987) *The Illustrated I Ching*, London: Aquarian Press

## Further sources of information

The author's website, dealing with the health and relaxation aspects of tai chi, can be found at: www.orientalexercise.wanadoo.co.uk

This site is updated regularly and, if you have enjoyed this book you may find something of interest there.

Beginners should also try their local adult education centre to see if it offers classes. Many now do. These are ideal for those just starting out and are usually excellent value for money. For those more interested in the martial arts aspects of tai chi, meanwhile, there are numerous sites available on the internet, with lots of updates on regional groups and courses. Just go to any search engine and type in 'tai chi'.

# Glossary

**Ch'i (qi)** The life force or vital energy that flows through all living things.

**ch'i kung (qi gong)** The art of circulating ch'i through breathing and movement, similar, therefore, in many ways to the kind of tai chi presented in this book.

**elements** Abstract forces that combine many different aspects of nature and life. They are used extensively in oriental medical theory and relate to the organs of the body as well as to many other diverse subjects such as the seasons and even the tastes of food.

**jing** Internal vitality associated with the adrenal glands and sexuality.

**oriental medicine** A term encompassing several ancient healing arts such as acupuncture and shiatsu that work through regulating the flow of ch'i throughout the body. Tai chi, therefore, shares many of the principles of oriental medical theory and can affect the health and well-being in a similar way.

**Shen** The vital spirit or 'mind' in oriental medical theory.

**Tai Chi T'u (double-fish diagram)** This is the famous divided circle symbol – see page 3. It represents the harmony and interchange of opposites so central to the practice of exercises such as tai chi.

**Tan Tien** Vital centre located in the lower abdomen and from which the movements of tai chi are directed.

**Taoism** The enduring philosophy of Chinese culture that emphasizes detachment and calm – ideal, therefore, for understanding the thought process underlying exercises such as tai chi.

**Yang** Abstract force of nature (opposite to Yin) that relates to many diverse experiences, such as expansion, advance, light, activity, external strength and conscious thought.

**Yin** Abstract force of nature (opposite to Yang) that relates to many diverse experiences, such as contraction, retreat, darkness, mystery, inner strength and intuition.

# Answers to 'Test your knowledge' questions

| | |
|---|---|
| 1 | Correct answer: **a** |
| 2 | Correct answer: **b** |
| 3 | Correct answer: **b** |
| 4 | Correct answer: **c** |
| 5 | Correct answer: **b** |
| 6 | Correct answer: **a** |
| 7 | Correct answer: **c** |
| 8 | Correct answer: **b** |
| 9 | Correct answer: **c** |
| 10 | Correct answer: **a** |

# Index

# Image credits